Praise for Georgia

The Secret Poet

"[O]ne of the author's best works and one of the best romances I've read recently…I was so invested in [Morgan and Zoe] I read the book in one sitting."—*Melina Bickard, Librarian, Waterloo Library (UK)*

Hopeless Romantic

"Thank you, Georgia Beers, for this unabashed paean to the pleasure of escaping into romantic comedies…If you want to have a big smile plastered on your face as you read a romance novel, do not hesitate to pick up this one!"—*The Rainbow Bookworm*

Flavor of the Month

"Beers whips up a sweet lesbian romance…brimming with mouth-watering descriptions of foodie indulgences…Both women are well-intentioned and endearing, and it's easy to root for their inevitable reconciliation. But once the couple rediscover their natural ease with one another, Beers throws a challenging emotional hurdle in their path, forcing them to fight through tragedy to earn their happy ending." —*Publishers Weekly*

One Walk in Winter

"A sweet story to pair with the holidays. There are plenty of 'moment's in this book that make the heart soar. Just what I like in a romance. Situations where sparks fly, hearts fill, and tears fall. This book shined with cute fairy trails and swoon-worthy Christmas gifts…REALLY nice and cozy if read in between Thanksgiving and Christmas. Covered in blankets. By a fire."—*Bookvark*

Fear of Falling

"Enough tension and drama for us to wonder if this can work out—and enough heat to keep the pages turning. I will definitely recommend this to others—Georgia Beers continues to go from strength to strength." —*Evan Blood, Bookseller (Angus & Robertson, Australia)*

"In *Fear of Falling* Georgia Beers doesn't take the obvious, easy way… romantic, feel-good and beautifully told."—*Kitty Kat's Book Review Blog*

The Do-Over

"You can count on Beers to give you a quality well-paced book each and every time."—*The Romantic Reader Blog*

"*The Do-Over* is a shining example of the brilliance of Georgia Beers as a contemporary romance author."—*Rainbow Reflections*

The Shape of You

"I know I always say this about Georgia Beers's books, but there is no one that writes first kisses like her. They are hot, steamy and all too much!"—*Les Rêveur*

The Shape of You "catches you right in the feels and does not let go. It is a must for every person out there who has struggled with self-esteem, questioned their judgment, and settled for a less than perfect but safe lover. If you've ever been convinced you have to trade passion for emotional safety, this book is for you."—*Writing While Distracted*

Calendar Girl

"A sweet, sweet romcom of a story…*Calendar Girl* is a nice read, which you may find yourself returning to when you want a hot-chocolate-and-warm-comfort-hug in your life."—*Best Lesbian Erotica*

Blend

"You know a book is good, first, when you don't want to put it down. Second, you know it's damn good when you're reading it and thinking, I'm totally going to read this one again. Great read and absolutely a 5-star romance."—*The Romantic Reader Blog*

"This is a lovely romantic story with relatable characters that have depth and chemistry. A charming easy story that kept me reading until the end. Very enjoyable."—*Kat Adams, Bookseller, QBD (Australia)*

Right Here, Right Now

"[A] successful and entertaining queer romance novel. The main characters are appealing, and the situations they deal with are realistic and well-managed. I would recommend this book to anyone who enjoys a good queer romance novel, and particularly one grounded in real world situations."—*Books at the End of the Alphabet*

"[A]n engaging odd-couple romance. Beers creates a romance of gentle humor that allows no-nonsense Lacey to relax and easygoing Alicia to find a trusting heart."—*RT Book Reviews*

Lambda Literary Award Winner *Fresh Tracks*

"Georgia Beers pens romances with sparks."—*Just About Write*

"[T]he focus switches each chapter to a different character, allowing for a measured pace and deep, sincere exploration of each protagonist's thoughts. Beers gives a welcome expansion to the romance genre with her clear, sympathetic writing."—*Curve magazine*

Lambda Literary Award Finalist *Finding Home*

"Georgia Beers has proven in her popular novels such as *Too Close to Touch* and *Fresh Tracks* that she has a special way of building romance with suspense that puts the reader on the edge of their seat. *Finding Home*, though more character driven than suspense, will equally keep the reader engaged at each page turn with its sweet romance."—*Lambda Literary Review*

Mine

"Beers does a fine job of capturing the essence of grief in an authentic way. *Mine* is touching, life-affirming, and sweet."—*Lesbian News Book Review*

Too Close to Touch

"This is such a well-written book. The pacing is perfect, the romance is great, the character work strong, and damn, but is the sex writing ever fantastic."—*The Lesbian Review*

"In her third novel, Georgia Beers delivers an immensely satisfying story. Beers knows how to generate sexual tension so taut it could be cut with a knife…Beers weaves a tale of yearning, love, lust, and conflict resolution. She has constructed a believable plot, with strong characters in a charming setting."—*Just About Write*

By the Author

Romances

Turning the Page

Thy Neighbor's Wife

Too Close to Touch

Fresh Tracks

Mine

Finding Home

Starting from Scratch

96 Hours

Slices of Life

Snow Globe

Olive Oil & White Bread

Zero Visibility

A Little Bit of Spice

What Matters Most

Right Here, Right Now

Blend

The Shape of You

Calendar Girl

The Do-Over

Fear of Falling

One Walk in Winter

Flavor of the Month

Hopeless Romantic

16 Steps to Forever

The Secret Poet

Cherry on Top

The Puppy Love Romances

Rescued Heart

Run to You

Dare to Stay

The Swizzle Stick Romances

Shaken or Stirred

On the Rocks

With a Twist

Cherry on Top

by

Georgia Beers

2022

CHERRY ON TOP

ISBN 13: 978-1-63679-158-6

This Trade Paperback Original Is Published By
Bold Strokes Books, Inc.
P.O. Box 249
Valley Falls, NY 12185

First Edition: August 2022

Credits
Editor: Ruth Sternglantz
Production Design: Stacia Seaman
Cover Design by Jeanine Henning

Acknowledgments

Social media fascinates me. Growing up into a person who confides in a very small group of trusted friends and family, I'm always equal parts interested and horrified when I see somebody posting about their most personal, most emotional, most private thoughts/events/life happenings on social media, people who work through their emotions online for all to see. And since hesitantly starting my own TikTok account, I've been even more fascinated by the people who post endless content, who actually make a living off that endless content. I'm also fascinated by the, for lack of a better word, debate between being online too much and not being online enough. Between those who live and die by their social media accounts and those who find them brutalizing or even dangerous. I have friends who are on their smartphones for hours and hours a day. I also have friends who have decided social media is detrimental to their mental health and avoid it for the most part. I fall somewhere in the middle, as I think a lot of us do. I know I'm much happier not being tied to my phone 24/7, but I also admit that I experience a little FOMO (fear of missing out) when I'm away too long. I worry my friends will leave me behind, and so I pick up my phone and the cycle starts all over again. Welcome to the digital age, am I right? Anyway, I wanted to explore that a little bit, and I wondered what would happen if one person from each side of that debate fell for someone on the other…

Thank you to all the usual suspects: To Rad and Sandy from Bold Strokes for being positive and professional. To Ruth Sternglantz for helping to make me look like I know how to write a book. To my fellow writers and other friends who check in on me regularly: Melissa, Carsen, Paula, Kris, Fiona, Ann, Rey. To my animals, Archie and Emmett, for being here with me for the past two years of near isolation and loving me when there were no people around. And to my readers. Thank you so much for the support over the years. I can't believe this is book #32. I don't feel old enough to have written thirty-two books, but apparently, I AM!

I hope you love it.

Chapter One

How many people have plunged to their deaths while taking selfies? The thought ran through Cherry Davis's mind just as she glanced over her shoulder at the drop-off behind her and decided maybe using the tripod was the better way to go. With a sigh, she pulled out the telescoping tripod and set up her phone on it. She posed a couple different ways and snapped some shots, then went through them until she settled on the best one.

She edited and smoothed out the flaws and then posted it on all her socials with the caption: *Walking on this lovely day in the park with my sweetie, who insisted on taking this horrible shot!* She added a wide-eyed emoji, gave it a proofread, then posted it, tagging the park and adding a bunch of hashtags for maximum views. Seriously. It was all about the hashtags. Nobody needed to know that there was no actual sweetie with her. At least for now.

Her stomach rumbled loudly as she put her tripod back into her backpack, telling her it was way past time for breakfast, so she headed to her favorite spot to eat, have some coffee, and do work, and forty-five minutes later, after having changed into her work clothes, she was sitting at her usual table by the window.

Now those *are some nice legs.*

Cherry watched—subtly, she hoped—as the waitress walked away after dropping off her yogurt parfait. Was she new? Cherry was in Sunny Side Up at least three mornings a week and had never noticed this woman before. And she *definitely* would've noticed this woman before. She watched her go, then refocused her attention on her breakfast.

The parfait was pretty. Layers of white yogurt separated by deep indigo blueberries, happy, bright raspberries, topped with walnuts and a sparkling drizzle of honey. Sliding the glass dessert-type dish closer to the window allowed it to catch the mid-April sunlight, and she took a couple photos. Picking the best one, she again used her editing app to quickly make it look even better. Then she posted it to Instagram and did the hashtag thing. She had gained seventeen new followers overnight, and when she clicked over to TikTok, she had twenty-three new ones. Excellent. Her viewership was growing every day, and that's what she needed, to be able to say good-bye to insurance forever.

There was an old-fashioned bell over the door, and it jingled happily every time somebody came or left. Some might find it annoying, and to be honest, Cherry was surprised she didn't, but she loved Sunny Side Up and everything about it. While most young business professionals were standing in line at Starbucks, frantically scoping out the tables and couches to see where they might have a shot at sitting, she had a cute little corner table all to herself, and she could see Black Cherry Lake if she craned her neck just right. Instead of the bustling of a coffee shop, she was in a more laid-back environment. Not that there wasn't bustling. There was. Of course there was. It was nine in the morning on a Wednesday, for God's sake. It was busy. Just not Starbucks-level busy.

The café was old, had been a staple along Black Cherry Lake for decades—long before Jefferson Square came along as the new hot spot in Northwood, and long before some prime sites around the lake became offices and shops and restaurants—and now it felt a little… outdated. Cherry had heard talk about the owners either selling or trying to modernize a bit, but for now, it was just fine with her. She preferred the quieter setting, the way it was situated at the end of the lake—so it still got foot traffic but was a bit off the regular beaten path.

She sipped her coffee. God, was there anything better in the morning? Hot, strong, and sweet, just the way she liked it. She'd never let that on to her followers, though. No way. They wanted her drinking trendy stuff. Lattes and macchiatos. Fraps and whips. So she'd do a post a little later at—you guessed it—Starbucks. Right now, though, she had to do her temp work.

Which wasn't really actual temp work, but that's what she called it in her head because working for the insurance agency was only temporary to her. That was the plan. She had no desire to be a claims adjuster her entire life. Hell, no. Cherry on Top, her brand, her social media handle, was going to be her primary income eventually, she was sure of it. Just wait and see.

Her phone pinged, and as if she'd read her mind, it was her boss, Amanda Crowley. Or Cruella, as Cherry preferred to call her. In her head of course. She had a streak of silver right in the center of her dark hair. Which would look super cool if she wasn't such a bitch. A quick glance at the text confirmed what Cherry already knew—she was being checked up on.

Peterson claim?

Cruella didn't believe in greetings or small talk. Right to the business at hand. Always. There were many times that Cherry would shine a spotlight on that. Text back something like, *Good morning to you too.* But not today. She had no patience for her boss today.

In progress. She sent it.

"More coffee?" The voice surprised her, and she looked up into sparkling blue eyes. They were large and framed by very dark lashes. The waitress again, and apparently, her face was just as sexy as her legs. For just a split second, Cherry thought about kissing her. No warning. Just reaching for her face, pulling her down, and kissing her senseless. She swallowed, because what the hell, brain?

"Please." She held out her cup and the waitress filled it up. "Thanks so much. It's a gorgeous day, isn't it?"

The waitress smiled, and the smile was just as beautiful as the rest of her. Straight teeth. Full lips. Smooth cheekbones. Light, wavy hair. "It really is. I love spring. It's like you get to start over again." There was a moment of held eye contact. Deliciously held eye contact, if you asked Cherry. And then the waitress asked, "Can I get you anything else?"

Your number? A date with you? You could kiss me...

She said none of those things because of course she didn't. She simply shook her head with a soft smile and watched for a second time as the beautiful waitress with the sexy legs walked away from her.

The sound of another text arriving pulled her out of fantasyland and into the present. Cruella again.

ETA?

"I will slay this claim if you'd give me five freaking minutes," she muttered, returning her attention to her laptop screen. *Soon*, she texted back, knowing the vagueness would tick Cruella off and not caring. With a last wistful glance at the waitress, she forced herself to focus on her job.

❖

Ellis hated waitressing. She hadn't been hired as a waitress at Sunny Side Up—she'd been hired to manage Sunny Side Up. And most of the time, that's what she did. She was much better with spreadsheets and invoices than she was with actual people sitting at tables and wanting stuff. But two of her waitresses called out sick that morning, and her backups didn't respond in time, so she had no choice but to shimmy into a uniform, tie an apron around her waist, and jump into the fray.

That redhead, though? Yeah, she made it bearable, because *day-um*. And she did *not* say that lightly. The color of her hair was like a mixture of everything and anything with vibrant shades of red-orange. Sunsets and autumn leaves and fire. She wasn't what her dad would've called a carrottop. Her hair was more auburn. Deeper than traditional red. It looked soft and rich, and Ellis had a moment standing there next to her table where she envisioned herself leaning forward to smell it, wondering if she'd get whiffs of strawberries or coconut or something else entirely. She had to clench her teeth to keep herself standing upright. The last time she'd been that physically affected by a woman was…yeah, never.

Not that she had the time to spend thinking about pretty girls. Waitressing was grueling. She knew that, she did, in her brain somewhere. But knowing it and experiencing it were two *way* different things. Her shift had begun at six, and her feet were already killing her. How people made a career out of being a server was beyond her, and she found herself with new respect.

"Order up." Cal's voice was like a shotgun blast from the kitchen as he slid a plate onto the little holding area under the heat lamps and smacked the small bell with his metal spatula. Sunny Side Up was nothing if not stuck in time, though Ellis would be hard pressed to name *which* time. The fifties? Seventies? Eighties, maybe? Whatever year it was, it was not this one. But Cal had been the short-order cook for longer than Ellis had been alive. He was a sweetheart of a man, no matter how hard he tried to be gruff beneath his dark mustache—sprinkled with gray and with the long sides down to his chin—and Sunny Side Up was always packed, so they were doing something right. Nobody made french toast like Cal did. Ellis could testify. She had it for breakfast at least three times a week.

"Got it," said Kitty, one of those women who'd been waitressing her entire life. Watching her fascinated Ellis. Despite being, by Ellis's estimate, well into her sixties, the woman could carry the meals of an entire table of four in one trip, plates up and down both arms, and never seem the slightest bit worried about spilling a thing. Ellis, on the other hand, preferred to make several trips if it meant not dropping a Western omelet in somebody's lap. She'd dropped things twice that morning—a mug of coffee and a small plate of toast—but both times, she'd been behind the counter, thank God, and between her and Kitty, they'd cleaned it up quick, and even laughed about it.

By the time nine thirty rolled around, things started to clear out, tables emptied, and Cal got to take a breath. Only a few customers remained. A man in an oxford and tie scrolling on his phone. A woman with short strawberry-blond hair reading a book. Ellis took a rag and spray bottle of cleaner and hit the empty tables, one of which was next to the redhead, who had slipped on a pair of black-rimmed glasses that did nothing to diminish the sexiness factor. In fact, they added to it.

"You're still here," she said to her. Good one, Captain Obvious. She internally rolled her eyes.

The redhead looked up from her laptop, and Ellis noticed her eyes were large and brown. "I am. Do you need the table?" She blinked and looked around the diner.

"Oh no. No. Not at all. You can stay there as long as you like." Smooth, Ellis was not. Exhibit A: what just happened. Her plan had been to engage in more conversation, but after that, she just felt stupid and couldn't get away fast enough. Back behind the counter, she sighed. It was probably better this way anyhow. Who had time to date? Not her. And while it was super unusual for her to be so physically attracted to somebody so fast, the redhead was clearly out of her league. Dressed in a business casual outfit of dark jeans and a green top, she looked professional and competent.

And here's me in my rust-orange uniform and dirty apron. Yeah, way, way out of her league.

Her phone was in the pocket of her uniform, and she felt it vibrate once, quickly, which meant a text. She slipped it out and took a quick look, just in case it was the residence with a question or issue.

It wasn't. It was from *The 11th Commandment.*

Are you available for an interview? Today, our offices, 3pm.

She rolled her lips in and bit down on them as she read it again, then typed out her response, telling them she'd be there. When she looked up, the redhead was smiling widely as she took a selfie. Ellis watched. She couldn't help it. Something about her was fascinating.

"She's here a couple mornings a week, you know." Kitty's voice was quiet and very close to her ear. "You stay cooped up in your office in the back, and you miss things."

Ellis flinched in surprise, turned to meet Kitty's eyes, and blurted, "She is?" before she could stop herself.

"Mm-hmm," Kitty said and turned away to make a fresh pot of coffee. "Always sits at that table. Goes between her laptop and her phone. Takes lots of pictures. Of herself. Of her food."

As manager, Ellis did spend most of her time in the back office, dealing with orders and invoices and payroll. It was rare for her to be out here on the dining room floor. She watched the redhead pack up her laptop and move toward the door where she stopped with her hand on the handle and turned back. Her eyes met Ellis's. Held. A smile. Then she pushed through and out into the day.

Yeah, maybe she needed to start coming out of the back office a bit more often…

❖

"Well, it'll bring in a little extra money." Ellis used speech-to-text to communicate with Evan, one of her besties. It was too hard to type while walking, and she was already running late to see her sister, but he'd asked her to update him as soon as she got out of the interview. "I don't love the premise of the place. Do you know what the eleventh commandment is?" She sent the text, zigzagged around a woman who'd stopped in the middle of the sidewalk, and made her way to the parking lot where her ten-year-old Honda Civic was parked. "Gotta drive," she spoke into her phone when Evan hadn't answered back.

Her tiny apartment was within walking distance to the diner, but the residence home where her sister lived was just outside the city limits. It took her about half an hour to get there if traffic wasn't crazy, and she did her best to be there at least a couple hours a day. When Evan called her halfway there, she put the phone on speaker.

"Sorry, I was in a meeting," he said. "The eleventh commandment is *Don't get caught*."

"Exactly. So this place is about catching people in lies. Celebrities. Politicians. Local businesses. Etcetera."

"So, it's an online tabloid?" Evan laughed, the sound deep and throaty.

"Kinda? But it's just writing the articles. I guess the photographers are the real investigators. They give me info and photos, and I write it up and send it off to the editor."

"Quick and dirty."

"Sounds like it. Both things. Not really my jam, but at least I'll be writing again. And the pay's not awful. It'll help with some of my sister's incidentals."

"I get that," Evan said. "You do what you gotta do."

"Will I see you later?"

"Depends on my client. He needs hand-holding like he's five." Evan's irritation was clear. He was a financial advisor, and some of his clients made him feel more like an elementary school teacher, he'd told her.

"I'll make sure Kendra eats something."

"Appreciate it."

They talked for another minute or two and then hung up, and a few minutes after that, Ellis turned her car into the long driveway for Hearts and Hands Residence Home.

It wasn't a commercial building, but a large, one-story house that had been turned into a home for residents who needed twenty-four-hour care, but not a hospital. A nicely maintained place with immaculate landscaping, they only took on five patients at a time. Three spots were short-term, for people in rehab. Two were for permanent residents. Ellis's little sister, Michaela, was one of the two.

The staff knew her by now. Michaela had been there for just over a year. Finding Hearts and Hands had been difficult, and once she had, getting her sister a bed there had been even harder, but Ellis had made a giant pain in the ass of herself until Michaela had the right home.

"Hey, Corrine," she said to the silver-haired woman behind the front desk. "Here you go. Cal says hi." She handed over a Ziploc baggie with two of Cal's buttermilk biscuits in it, Corrine's favorite.

"Oh, Ellis, you are too good to me. Thank you, sweetie."

"She good today?"

"Her usual sunny self."

With a rap of her knuckles on Corrine's desk, Ellis headed down the hall, smiling to herself. That was their conversation every time. She'd ask if Michaela was having a good day, and Corrine would say something like *Her usual sunny self* or *She's been running laps around the house* or *She knit an entire blanket this morning*. And they'd smile at each other wistfully. Because if only any of those things was actually the case.

Michaela's room was at the end of the hall in the back corner of the house. Ellis knocked softly, which she did every time, even though it wasn't like her sister was going to call out for her to come in.

"Hey, Mikey," she said softly. "How are things in your world today?" She went in, pressed a kiss to her sister's forehead, pulled a chair close to her bed, and sat. It was an honest question, one she asked often. Because Michaela was definitely in her own world, and Ellis wished she could visit there.

"So, I had to waitress today." She snorted a laugh. "Yes, you heard that right. Me. Carrying plates of food. Can you believe it? I only dropped things twice. And not *on* anybody, thank freaking God." She took a moment to just look at her sister, which she didn't do every time because it could overwhelm her. She wasn't as blond as Ellis, something she'd endlessly complained about when they were teenagers. Her hair was more of a light brown. Today, it was in a braid—she'd have to thank Shaq for that. He was the nurse who always did her hair or her nails, which were a new shade of pink. He'd bathe her, give her a pedicure, brush her hair, rub lotion on her arms. Her blue eyes, so much like Ellis's, were open as usual, and for about the millionth time, Ellis wondered what she saw. The room? The view out the window? Something in her own head? Something only she could see? Anything at all?

"I like this pink," Ellis said, stroking the back of Michaela's hand. "It's a good color for your skin tone." She reached toward the nightstand and grabbed the book that sat there. It was a well-worn copy of *The Girl on the Train*. Michaela had never been one to read romances or heartfelt drama. She liked gritty psychological thrillers. Paula Hawkins. Ruth Ware. Riley Sager. Opening the book where the bookmark was, she asked, “Ready? Where were we?”

And she began to read.

CHAPTER TWO

Okay, so tomorrow afternoon, I'll get some happy hour shots," Cherry muttered to herself as she sat in Starbucks and studied the calendar on her phone. Pretty shots of pretty drinks always garnered interest, so she made plans to stop by that cute bar near the office after work and order something fruity and fun. Pink.

She'd surpassed twenty thousand followers, not bad for somebody who had a very small built-in base as it was, but her growth seemed to have slowed. Every day she got a comment or seven asking after Alyssa. *Where's the hot gf?* Or *Haven't seen your sweetie lately*. When she went back and did the math, she got way more engagement from shots that included or mentioned her girlfriend than solo stuff. Seemed her base liked seeing a stable sapphic couple over a single girl on her own in the city. But she wasn't about to tell them that Alyssa had run off with her fitness trainer. Her male fitness trainer. Her male fitness trainer *and* his wife. This was embarrassing. Cherry wasn't left for somebody else, she was left for *two* somebody elses, and they'd all moved to Colorado together to live in some yoga retreat commune thing, and Cherry hadn't been able to tell anybody. Not a soul. She was too mortified.

Some emo dude was singing along to his acoustic guitar over the speakers in the ceiling. Cherry shook herself back to the present. She should've taken a shot of her latte before she drank any, but then she tilted her head. The print from her dark pink lip gloss on the cup made it look kinda cool, so she set it next to the bud vase in the center of the table, angled it so the light hit just right, and snapped a couple photos. Picked the best one, used her editing app to clean it up, then posted it to Snapchat, using a pink filter with hearts and tagging Starbucks. Not that she'd ever get any acknowledgment from them. They were too big. But you never knew, right? She tagged every place and every company she could, which was paying off in small ways because every now and then, she'd receive some product in the mail. Super cool. And totally the goal. She knew some of the big influencers got tons of free products and sponsorships. One of these days…

Speaking of products, she had to do a mascara post. It had been a while since she spotlighted makeup. And the last video was up to seven thousand likes and almost ten thousand views. Not too shabby.

She tossed her napkin and was headed out of Starbucks when her phone buzzed a text. Shea Gibbons—one of her roomies and her BFF and the self-proclaimed voice of reason in Cherry's life.

Bach 2nite, came her text, followed by an emoji of a rose.

Yasssss, she texted back with a grin. She didn't love the show *The Bachelor* nearly as much as Shea did, but she found it entertaining and used it as a way to spend time with her best friend. Plus, it gave her fodder for posting, and Shea was always a willing partner in crime when it came to creating videos. She had a great eye, and she was funny, two things that Cherry was always happy to use. They'd make a couple videos as they watched. *Bachelor* ones always got lots of views.

Shea was still at work, and Cherry walked from the Starbucks back to their apartment. Adam, her other roommate, was just pulling into the parking lot when she got there.

"Hey, bitch." His standard greeting. He wore khaki pants and a black polo shirt, the uniform of the pet store he worked at during the day, and his dark hair was so perfect, it looked like it had been drawn. Animated. Complete with a fun swoop to the right side of his head, which would change direction the next time he ran his hand through it.

"Your hair is stupid perfect. I hate you."

"Get in line."

Their apartment wasn't fancy at all, but it didn't suck. Three bedrooms, two full bathrooms, a decent-sized living area, galley kitchen. It was on the top floor of a three-story building that housed five other apartments.

"You working tonight?" she asked him as she dropped her keys on the small table by the door and hung her laptop bag on the coatrack.

"Ugh. Yes. Dashing. Someday, I'll have a job that pays me enough, and I won't need to work three." He headed toward his room, and Cherry knew he'd likely take a quick nap before he had to do his DoorDash shift.

She turned on the TV but kept the volume low. That was something cool about living with these two—they were all very cognizant of the others' schedules. When Adam was Dashing, he might work until after midnight. When he did his bartending gig, he'd sometimes not be home until three or four in the morning. So he needed to grab sleep where he could, and the last thing she wanted to do was have the TV too loud and keep him from catching some z's.

They'd met taking classes at Northwood University, more than ten years ago now. They'd bonded over how much school was not their thing. They'd dropped out together, met Shea at a Pride event one night when she was being an ally to her cousin, and the three of them became a bonded trio for several years. They'd only moved in together two years ago, and Cherry couldn't be happier. Would she like her own place? Sure. There was plenty of time for that. Besides, she'd be lonely without her besties—she couldn't imagine living all by herself.

She flumped onto the fairly new couch, velour or microfiber or something like that, dark blue and super soft. She really needed to do the mascara post, but she was exhausted today. Cruella had been relentless, she had five claims to look into before the end of the week, and all she wanted to do was sit and watch the latest episode of *The L Word: Generation Q*, which was sitting right there on the DVR, but she'd promised Shea she wouldn't watch without her. Then after they watched the show, they'd order a pizza and settle in for *The Bachelor* later. Her favorite kind of night.

A commercial for Motrin came on, and the model was blond and pretty, and suddenly, without warning, Cherry's thoughts went to the waitress from that morning.

What was her name? What was her deal? Where had she come from? And why couldn't Cherry get her out of her head? Her kind eyes. Warm smile. Those legs. God…those legs…There was something about her…something magnetic. Pulling her attention.

Before she could analyze it any longer, the front door opened, and Shea burst in like somebody had shoved her. That's how she entered any room. Quick, loud, a burst of energy.

"You better not have watched *The L Word* yet," she said in greeting, pointing a prematurely accusatory finger at her.

Cherry held her own finger to her lips, then pointed in the direction of Adam's room.

"He gotta drive tonight?" Shea asked, her voice considerably lower.

Cherry nodded. "And I haven't watched. I waited for you, as promised."

"Cool. Gimme five." Shea headed to her bedroom.

Cherry pulled out her phone and scanned her socials, looking at likes and reading comments. She got a very mixed bag as far as comments. Lots of praise from others in the LGBTQIA+ community. Bible verses and scripture quoting from religious fanatics. Then there were the trolls. The ones who told her she was fat or ugly or untalented. Or worse, the gross sexual things they'd like to do to her. She liked to picture them as pasty, greasy-haired twentysomethings living in their parents' basements and playing *Call of Duty* all day long, fingers stained orange with Dorito powder, completely unfamiliar with things like fresh air and sunshine. As Shea returned with two cans of Red Bull and a bag of salt and vinegar potato chips and dropped down onto the couch next to her, Cherry laughed. "This guy says I'm a *no-talent useless flesh bag* and I should stick to doing the things I was meant to do like cooking and cleaning." She made air quotes around his words.

Shea shook her head as she popped a can open. "God, people are just assholes. I don't know how that stuff doesn't bother you."

Cherry shrugged. "I checked. He's taking the time to write me shitty comments, *and* he's following me. That counts."

"Girl, you've got way thicker skin than I do. Props to you." She lifted her can in a salute.

"Please." Cherry gave a snort. Her childhood had given her that thick skin, not that she'd wish it on anybody. "You're sweet and sensitive, and that's better any day. Ready?" She held up the remote and tipped her head in question.

"Go," Shea said and ripped open the bag. As the show began, she said, "Speaking of props, I don't care that Jennifer Beals is almost the same age as my mom. I'd date her."

"Oh my God, same," Cherry said, grabbing a handful of chips. "So much same."

CHAPTER THREE

How are things?" Aunt Tracey asked her standard question as Ellis cooked an omelet. Her phone was propped up against the butter container, her aunt's smiling face taking up the screen in a FaceTime call.

"They're good. I started a new job this week." Ellis stirred the mushrooms as they sautéed in the pan.

"You left the diner?" Tracey's surprise was clear.

"No, no. I started a second job. It's writing, so in my field, sort of." Ellis grinned at the phone, trying to alleviate the concern she could see on her aunt's face, even over the small screen.

"Do you need two jobs?" Tracey's worry was quiet, the way she did everything. She and Ellis's father were siblings, and it wasn't until Ellis's dad was gone that she'd started to notice just how much he and his sister were alike. "The life insurance should be covering things, right?"

"It does." More smiling because the last thing she wanted was her aunt to be stressing from a state away. "But I like to make sure Mikey has nice things, you know? The better lotion. Nice shampoo. Comfy pajamas." She opened the egg carton as she added, "Yes, I hear myself. I know that stuff probably doesn't matter to her, but..." She shrugged, and her aunt picked up the rest of the sentence.

"It matters to you. I understand that, sweetie. I just don't want you working yourself ragged for things you don't need to work yourself ragged for. You know?"

Nodding. Because the lump in her throat wouldn't let her form words. She cracked the eggs into a bowl and whisked them with a fork, using the sound as an excuse not to speak for a moment. Just as she'd pulled herself together and poured the eggs into the pan, Tracey spoke again.

"I wish you'd come visit. Take some time. Come see me. Give yourself a break."

She asked nearly every time they spoke, which was at least once a week. And she was only in Cleveland. Not that far. A day's drive. Again, she was quiet, firm but never pushy, her light eyes so like her brother's. And Ellis gave her the same answer she always did. "I know. I will. I definitely will. Just need to figure out logistics."

"Sweetie, Michaela will be fine if you don't visit her for a few days. You know that, right?"

Would she, though?

"That's why she's where she is. So she's taken care of, and you can have a life."

It wasn't a new discussion, not by a long shot. Ellis nodded at the words—she always did. "I know." And she did know. She absolutely did.

"Okay. Well." Tracey gave up. She always did because Ellis gave her no choice. "You know I'm here, and you're welcome anytime."

"Hi, Ellie!" Her uncle's face popped onto the screen like a living, breathing photobomb, and he waved. "Come visit us soon!" And then he was gone.

"An Uncle Jamie drive-by for you." Tracey laughed. "Talk to you later, sweetie. I love you."

"Love you, too." She kissed her fingertips and blew toward the phone, something she'd done since Tracey had taught her at the age of three. Tracey caught it, pressed it to her heart, then waved, and the screen went back to Ellis's app icons.

When the omelet was perfectly golden—she sent silent thanks to Cal for teaching her exactly how long to let it sit before folding it—she slid it onto a plate and sprinkled it with the cheese she'd shredded beforehand. Then she took it to the couch where her laptop was open on the small coffee table.

She'd gotten her first assignment from *The 11th Commandment*. Some school board member who'd been touting anti-LGBTQ rhetoric had been caught spying on the boys' bathroom with a camera he'd installed. Creepy and awful and the site wanted her to write up the correlation between the two. They'd sent her police reports and statements, along with a couple video clips of board meetings so she could hear him for herself. She hated that she was now going to have to teach people that there was *zero* connection between being gay and fucking pedophilia, but she would do it, because no way was she going to write it up like they were intertwined.

For the next two and a half hours, she researched and read and listened and watched. She got about half the story written and was happy with the direction, but when the third yawn in fifteen minutes cranked her jaws open wide, she closed things down and headed to bed because her alarm was going to go off at oh-dark-thirty.

Diner work, man. It started with the roosters.

❖

Ellis had forgotten all about the redhead.

Well. No. That wasn't true.

She'd *mostly* forgotten about the redhead. *Mostly.* 'Cause she did hang out in the back of Ellis's head, to be trotted out on occasion. Like last night. In a dream. A sex dream. Yeah. Ahem.

And now, she was here. In the diner. On a normal Thursday morning in April. And Ellis couldn't help herself—she wanted to say hi. To talk to her. To ask her questions about her life and her thoughts and her dreams and *What the hell is actually happening in my head, oh my God?*

Kitty was watching Ellis with interest laced with amusement. She could feel it. Like her eyes were accusatory fingers, poking at her, saying things like, *Mm-hmm. I see you. I see you lookin' at her.* But then laughing about it. Laughing *at her* about it.

But Ellis felt brave. Why and how, she had zero clue, but she wasn't about to question it. She picked up the coffeepot and gave Kitty a questioning glance. Kitty smiled and nodded and gave her a subtle shoo motion with her fingers. Ellis crossed the diner.

"Hi," she said to the redhead. "Can I warm that up for you?"

"Yes, please," the redhead said with a smile and a sparkle in her dark eyes.

"I was thinking maybe we should engrave this chair and table with your name, since you sit here so often." Okay, not great, but not awful.

A little stilted. But the idea was cute, right? She winced internally but managed to pour coffee without spilling it anywhere, so that was a win regardless.

"You know, I like that idea." The redhead's light chuckle was adorably cute. Not girly, but kind of sweet, like the tinkling of sugar cubes falling into a cup. And God, she had gorgeously full lips.

"Well, I'd have to know what name to put on it..." Holy shit, did she really say that?

The redhead's grin grew as she arched one dark red eyebrow. "Okay, that was pretty smooth. I have to hand it to you."

She could feel her own blush climb up from her chest, cover her neck, and rise into her cheeks. And it *was* smooth, if she said so herself and thank you very much.

"And just when I thought you couldn't get cuter, you start blushing."

Holy shit, did the redhead really just say *that*?

With a clear of her throat, Ellis switched the coffeepot to her left hand and held out the right. "Ellis Conrad."

"Ellis. Unusual. I like it." The redhead put her hand in Ellis's. It was warm, the bones fine, but the grip sure and firm. "Cherry Davis." And before she could comment, Cherry Davis went on. "Yes, it's actually my name. A redhead named Cherry. I know." She rolled her pretty brown eyes. "What can I say? My dad had a sense of humor."

"Well, I like it, and I think it suits you." And somehow, it did.

"Thanks."

"So, what is it about this place?" Ellis asked. When Cherry frowned, Ellis searched for better words to express her thoughts. "I mean, why not a Starbucks or a Dunkin'? You're young and cool and hip. Seems like this place might be a little...stodgy for you."

"Hmm. I mean, first of all, I love that you think I'm cool and hip. Thanks for that. Second, don't get me wrong, I love me some Starbucks. But there's something"—she pressed her pink lips together like she was searching for the right words—"comforting about this place. Warm. Inviting. Plus"—she picked up her coffee and watched Ellis over the rim—"I like the view." And her eyes stayed on Ellis even as she sipped.

That eye contact held, and a current akin to something electric ran between them, hot and sizzling. Way beyond interesting. Ellis felt herself blush some more, and her smile grew. She had to clear her throat before she could form words but finally managed to say something along the lines of, "Well, I'm glad you're here."

"Good. Me, too."

Another beat went by before Ellis gave a small nod and took her coffeepot back behind the counter. Wow. That was…wow. At least her heart waited to pound and her armpits waited to sweat until she'd set the coffeepot back on its burner, waited until she was safely away from Cherry Davis.

"That was impressive," Kitty said as she gave an order to Cal. "I could feel the chemistry all the way over here."

"You could not," Ellis said with a soft laugh.

"Totally could. You two would make a really cute couple."

She rolled her eyes. "Okay, let's not get cray." There was a huge difference between an attraction and a relationship. A huge difference.

Obviously.

❖

Cherry would be much happier working in her office if she had a boss who wasn't such a miserable witch. Seriously, did Amanda Crowley even know how to smile? Was her face broken? Cherry had no reason to think so, and when she racked her brains to try to recall a time when maybe there had been a smile, it was a giant fail.

That being said, she still had to report in. She was allowed to work from home a couple days a week—or in her case, work from wherever—but she was expected to show her face in person every so often. Today was one of those days, and she pushed her way into the office building, took the elevator up to the fifth floor, and was just reaching for the door handle when she heard her name.

Amanda, coming out of the ladies' room.

Cherry stifled a sigh and pasted on a smile.

"I was going to give you a call," Amanda said as Cherry pulled the door open and waved for her to enter first. "Three of your claims are—"

"In your inbox," Cherry said before Amanda could finish. "I emailed them about twenty minutes ago." If she'd learned anything about her day job, it was that as long as she stayed on top of it and completed her work in a timely manner, Amanda couldn't complain about her not being in the office. She was so much happier working out in the world rather than chained to her desk, and since the company handbook said that was allowed as long as productivity was acceptable, there was nothing Amanda could do as long as Cherry performed her duties.

The wind visibly left Amanda's sails, and Cherry allowed herself to smile. "Great. Just checking." Amanda headed down the hall to her corner office while Cherry grabbed an empty cubicle. Since the claims adjusters were all in and out at various times, nobody was assigned a particular desk. You just grabbed one that wasn't currently occupied.

She logged on, checked her email, read a couple of new articles from the corporate office, scrolled on her phone through the photos she'd taken today so far, and stopped on the one of Ellis, used her finger and thumb to enlarge it. Okay, she'd taken it without Ellis knowing, while she was talking to the other waitress behind the counter, and yeah, that was a little shady, but she wasn't going to do anything with it. She just wanted to look at her again. She was *so* pretty. Average height, maybe five six. Blond hair that Cherry had only ever seen in a ponytail, and she wondered how long it actually was. What it smelled like. If it was soft. She wasn't quite sure if her eyes were green or blue—she was pretty sure they were blue—but she knew they were light and large, that her lashes and brows were darker than her hair, and that her skin looked creamy soft.

She might also have taken note of Ellis's ridiculously awesome ass as she walked away. Twice. Yeah, that ass was fire. Whoa.

With a sad little sigh, she put the photo away and scrolled through others she'd taken that morning on her way to and from the Sunny Side Up. Shots of the lake, selfies with the lake in the background, a patch of daffodils just poking their heads up through the soil along the way. She chose the selfie with the lake and posted it to Instagram, then put the flowers on Snapchat and hashtagged #nofilter and also #springhassprung. She had picked up twenty-one more followers overnight on TikTok and was thinking about her next video for that when she got a text from Amanda asking her to come into her office for a few new claims. Right after that came a reminder from her phone that the Barkathon was this weekend.

"Queers love their animals," she whispered aloud. She'd been looking forward to the Barkathon for weeks now, and there'd be tons of good stuff for posts. She had a crap ton of hashtags to use that should get her in front of lots of newbies and gain her some serious followers. Andi Harding—a super successful LGBTQIA+ influencer who had become a friend—was at over a hundred thousand followers when she'd checked this morning. Oh, to be there one day. She loved posting content, but more than that, she loved coming up with it. She loved having a setting catch her eye or thinking up a great little tale to share. She lived for it, and she wanted it to be her living in the near future.

As if she'd conjured her up just by thinking about her, a text came through from Andi.

Hey newb, free 4 lunch?

Cherry gave her schedule a quick check. She always said yes to Andi whenever possible. There was so much to learn from her. Plus, she liked her. Bonus. Andi had become a good friend.

Yes! Where?

They settled on a place and time just as another text came through, this time from Amanda.

Today, pls.

She grimaced, gathered her things together, and headed into her boss's office.

CHAPTER FOUR

I like the purple," Cherry said as she gave Andi's short hair an affectionate tug when they hugged. "I think it was pink, last time I saw you."

"It was. I went lavender this time. I might keep it for Pride month."

They stood in line at Pita, a Mediterranean restaurant they met at often. While Cherry wasn't super-fond of the cafeteria style counter and trays, the food was amazing. Once they had their lunches, they managed to snag an empty table. Before anything else was said, Andi rearranged her lunch in a more photogenic layout and took a couple shots with her phone. *Document everything* was the first thing she taught Cherry. Even if you ended up not using it, at least you didn't miss it.

"Going into the stockpile?" she asked with a grin.

"You know it." Andi put her phone aside and dunked a carrot stick into freshly made hummus. "Last time I tagged these guys, they sent me a twenty-five-dollar gift certificate." She popped the carrot into her mouth, chewed, then asked, "So, what's new? How's life?"

Cherry adored Andi. She was so cool and so much of what Cherry wanted to be. At thirty-nine, she was a few years older than her, but she gave Cherry something to shoot for. A visible goal. "It's good. My day job is annoying. No. That's a lie. My *supervisor* at my day job is annoying. Just a miserable human."

"Your posts look great. I loved your beach stuff."

She blushed a little. She could feel it. Andi was referring to her posts from two weekends ago where she'd walked the shores of Black

Cherry Lake, found rocks and shells, and generally talked about spring. "It was freaking cold," she said with a laugh.

"Yeah, Julianne pointed out how rosy your cheeks were. She said it made you look all cute." Andi's wife of four years featured prominently in a ton of her posts. She told Cherry once that she felt it was important to portray a regular married life so straight people could see that queer people weren't any different. So Andi hashtagged things like #wifelife and #datenight so they'd show up in places right alongside married straight couples.

"Thanks, Jules," Cherry said with a soft laugh, even though she'd never met the woman. "Glad freezing my ass off made me cute."

"The things we do for our art, am I right?"

Hanging out with Andi was easy, and Cherry loved that about her. Despite having a huge queer following online, she was extremely chill. Very real. Nothing phony or uptight about her. Cherry wanted to be like that, but her control-freak tendencies made it difficult. "What's up next for you?" she asked, taking a bite of her Greek salad. "Any travel?"

"I've got a trip to the Adirondacks coming up fairly soon. There's a sporting goods store there that wants me to take some shots, rent a kayak, stuff like that. Jules has to work, so she can't come with me, which is a bummer." And it was—Cherry could tell by the dejected look on Andi's face. She wondered what it was like to be that in love with somebody else. Andi seemed to shake herself and then grinned at her and lifted one shoulder. "Ah, well. What can you do, right? How about you? What's going on with you?"

"Doing the Barkathon this weekend at that animal shelter near the park."

"Junebug Farms? Cool. Your *girlfriend* gonna be there?" Andi made air quotes and gave her head a small shake. She was the one person in the world who knew there was no girlfriend now, that Alyssa was long gone, and the partner Cherry referred to often in her posts was fictitious.

"Yeah, she is." A grimace. "I know, I know."

Andi shook her head. "I've said it before, and I'll say it again—it's deception. People don't like being deceived."

"I know," Cherry said again, and she did her best to keep her irritation in check. "But my followers are much more engaged with posts that include reference to my partner." She had no idea why, but the first time she'd posted anything with Alyssa, people were all over it. What a cute couple they were. How long had they been together? Where did they meet? And once Alyssa had left and Cherry had fibbed and told a little white lie about having a new sweetheart, she felt she had no choice but to keep fibbing. Her following grew, her likes increased. She'd never given her fake girlfriend a name, never posted any kind of photo, obviously, but referred to her sweetie, her partner, her better half often.

Andi made no comment, just shook her head. Cherry knew how she felt, so there really wasn't any need for discussion.

"You got your dog from Junebug, didn't you?" she asked, desperate to change the subject.

It worked. Because coaxing Andi into talking about her dog was the second-best way—after coaxing her into talking about Julianne—to get her to light up. And light up, she did.

"Yes! They're so great there. I forgot Barkathon was this weekend. Maybe I'll go and bring Auggie. Would make for some good posts. Queers love their dogs."

Cherry smiled at the line she'd just muttered to herself earlier. "I wish I could get a dog. Maybe one day."

"Why can't you?"

"I have two roommates, and we're all on different schedules. Plus, I don't really have the time right now."

"That's really responsible of you." When she gave Andi a skeptical look, Andi added, "No, really. You're being honest with yourself, and you seem to know that a dog would need more of you than you can offer at the moment. You'll know when the time's right."

"One day," Cherry agreed. A quick glance at her phone told her she had about twenty minutes to get to her next appointment, so they wrapped up their conversation and headed outside into the cool spring air. "I'll look for you this weekend then," she said as she wrapped Andi in a hug.

"Definitely."

They said their good-byes and went in opposite directions. As Cherry slid into her car, she hopped on Instagram and called up Andi's page. Looking at her posts that included Julianne, she felt a little twinge. An unexpected one. She'd been on her own for a long time now, focused on her work and her online trajectory. Alyssa had been gone for almost two years. Dating barely made her top five things that were important to her, but every now and then, that little poke would happen. Like a little person that lived inside her was saying, *Hey, look at that. You want that, don't you?* She looked at a photo from four years ago. Andi and Julianne on their honeymoon in the Bahamas. On the beach. Sun-kissed skin. Jules in a hot pink bikini, her mass of dark curls blowing in the beach breeze. Andi in a swimsuit of boy shorts and a sports-bra-like top, her hair her natural blond. The two of them looking happier than anybody had a right to be…and there was the twinge again. And then something weird happened. Something unexpected and confusing and…perfect. Cherry's brain replaced Andi and Julianne with Cherry and Ellis the waitress from Sunny Side Up. It was them on the beach. Ellis in a bikini. Ellis smiling at her with love in her eyes that was clear to anybody who looked, her gaze on Cherry as they held hands and ran together into water so crystal-clear green-blue that it didn't even look real. She stared, tipped her head, stared some more, and warmth filled her chest because what if—

HONK!

A car horn blasted her back to the present, and she jumped in her seat, startled.

"What the hell was that?" she asked and let herself believe she was asking about the car horn and not about…the other thing.

❖

"I think I want to get a cat."

Ellis made the comment to Michaela out of the blue. No prompting. No rhyme or reason.

Or was that actually true?

No. No, it wasn't. Because the fact was, she knew exactly how her brain had gotten to that sentence. She'd had Cherry Davis in the back of her mind all day. All. Day. Which in and of itself was a new thing. Ellis didn't get hung up on people, especially people she'd just met. But Cherry Davis had staying power, apparently, and she'd made herself a little campsite in Ellis's head. Pitched a tent. Built a fire. Sat down to roast some marshmallows. And it reminded Ellis of the one word she'd been trying to avoid for quite some time now. The one she tried her best to tuck into a box and store away on a high, high shelf.

Lonely.

It wasn't something she enjoyed dealing with, her loneliness. She didn't have time for it. She had jobs, and she had Michaela, and that was more than enough to take up her days. Since their father died, she'd taken up the sole responsibility of her sister's care. And yes, his life insurance would help keep Mikey in Hearts and Hands. But Ellis was the last one left, the last member of the family to take care of Michaela and speak for her—and *to* her—and that meant she had to focus. Her own needs came a distant second.

All that being said, "I could use the company, you know?" She was polishing Michaela's toes with a deep ruby color called I'm Not Really a Waitress, which made Ellis chuckle with its nail-on-the-head accuracy. "There's a shelter just outside of town that Kitty mentioned. And I've seen their ads online. I may pop over there this weekend." She shrugged. It didn't matter that Michaela couldn't see it. She'd learned that early on, to just be herself, act like herself, make the same gestures or faces that she normally would, even though Michaela's open eyes didn't seem to see anything. And sometimes, that meant just thinking out loud. It was safe to do that here, in this room, since it was just the two of them, and the likelihood of Michaela sharing whatever Ellis told her was, well, unlikely wasn't a strong enough word. Even though in her own head, she often played Michaela's role and decided what she might say.

"I think a cat's better than a dog, considering how often you're not home." Her friend Kendra Jackson came walking into the room, clean towels in her arms, and put them on a shelf in the small closet to the left of the bed. The beads at the ends of her Fulani braids made a fun clicking sound as she moved, and she walked right up to Ellis and hugged her. "Sorry. Heard you talking."

"No worries. I thought the same thing. About the cat." She watched Kendra for a beat. She'd worked at Hearts and Hands for years now, and when Ellis had moved Michaela in, they'd hit it off. Most of the employees there were a bit older, but Kendra was only a few years older than Ellis, and they'd built a solid friendship very quickly. Kendra was married to Evan, and for whatever reason, they'd elected themselves Ellis's caretakers, having her over for dinner several times a month, texting to make sure she was eating, talking to her about her sister. Having no other family besides her sister, Ellis found herself indescribably grateful for the two of them. They were like additional siblings, and Ellis could talk to Kendra about anything.

She cleared her throat and waited for Kendra to meet her gaze before continuing. "So…there's this girl that comes into the diner." She dipped the brush, held Michaela's foot in her hand. "She's got this beautiful auburn hair. Easy to pick her out of a crowd. I noticed her last week when I had to waitress, remember that?"

"I do," Kendra said with a nod. "You said she was stupid attractive."

Easy, slow strokes with the small brush as she smiled and nodded and went on to the next toe. "I don't know what it was about her, K, but it was something because it's like I'm pulled toward her." She stopped painting and looked up into the empty air, searching for something that even *slightly* resembled a logical explanation. "Like there's some invisible string that she tugs on when she's in the diner." She refocused on her sister's toes, went back to polishing. "I introduced myself to her today." A glance up at Kendra's face. "Can you believe that? I have never in my life just introduced myself to some random girl. Not once."

"No? Well, you get extra points for today then." Kendra took a look at the whiteboard on Michaela's wall that told her when various chores and services had been performed last.

"Know what else I did? I flirted with her. *I fucking flirted*, K. You'd have been so proud of me." She shook her head with a huge grin as she recalled Cherry's face, how she looked up at her with those big dark eyes, how she'd made her blush. "And she said I was cute."

She finished polishing, then used a magazine to fan Michaela's toenails dry. And the color reminded her of Cherry's hair, which was ridiculous because they were two vastly different shades of red.

"You ask her out yet?"

"I knew you'd ask me that." She laughed and shook her head. "I mean, maybe. Maybe I will. I don't know. One step at a time, you know?" Ellis waved toward Michaela's feet with a flourish. "Ta-da! What do you think?"

"Oh, that's a good color on her. Looks nice with her skin tone."

"It's her favorite." It wasn't lost on Ellis that she spoke about Michaela's likes and dislikes in the present tense when the truth was, using the past tense was probably more accurate. The red *was* Michaela's favorite. It had been. Once upon a time. 'Cause she didn't really have a favorite anything now, did she?

Kendra heard it, too—Ellis could tell by the quick flash in her eyes—but she said nothing. "Have you eaten?" Kendra asked instead. "Why don't you come to the dining room and eat with me and Evan tonight? He's bringing sushi."

"That sounds amazing." And it did. "But I've got to get a story written tonight. I put it off, so I could come spend time with Mikey, but it's due by midnight."

For a moment, it looked like Kendra was going to argue with her, and Ellis knew from experience she wouldn't win. She'd never won any kind of debate against Kendra. She was too good. But she surprised Ellis by nodding. "Okay. But promise me you'll grab some dinner. You're getting too skinny. Don't make me fatten you up, as my mother would say."

Ellis laughed. "Are you trying to scare me with cuisine? Horrify me by telling me you're gonna make me eat your excellent cooking? Is that supposed to be a threat? 'Cause I gotta tell you, it's not."

Kendra laughed. "Yes, that was a threat!"

"You might wanna look up the word *threat*, 'cause I don't think it means what you think it means."

They laughed together for a moment and then Kendra looked at her. The way she always did. Like the big sister Ellis never had. "Seriously. You doing okay?" Her soft brown eyes held concern, and while Ellis didn't always love the way Kendra could see through her, she was endlessly grateful for her presence in her life.

She nodded. "I am. Tired, but okay." At Kendra's head tilt, she added, "Promise."

A second or two went by before Kendra nodded once, seemingly accepting the answer. "All right. Don't make me worry about you."

"Who are you kidding? You'll worry about me anyway."

"Truth." Kendra was headed for the doorway, presumably to her next patient, when she turned back and smiled at Ellis. "You should totally ask that girl out. You're too awesome not to be dating. You know?"

Ellis grinned at her, the compliment warming her from the inside. "Thanks, K."

CHAPTER FIVE

The day had started off crappy for Barkathon. Not freezing, but rainy. Then just gray and damp. April showers at their best. But the forecast called for sun later, and Cherry did her best not to let the lack of sunshine get her down. She needed to post some content. It's why she was there.

The shelter consisted of three buildings. The main headquarters housed cats and dogs that were up for adoption. Then off to the left was a huge barn where livestock were kept, horses and pigs and cows that had been surrendered or rescued and were in need of new homes. To the right was the smaller goat enclosure, always a big draw for the kids. Between the main building and the barn, there was a row of tents and tables where all the Barkathon vendors were, selling their wares, chatting up attendees, stopping to pet the dozens of dogs that people brought on leashes to walk around the property.

She wandered around, taking various shots of people, animals, booths. She'd go through it all later and decide what to use, what to stockpile for a later date, that kind of thing. She'd learned about stockpiling from Andi, because there would always be days when she either had no time to come up with content or her creativity was nowhere to be found. Those were the days to dig into her stockpile and find something to post.

Glad she'd put her hair in a ponytail so the dampness couldn't send it into frizztastic status, she held the phone in front of her and checked her look. Not too made-up, but not barefaced, she gave a nod and hit record, then slowly walked down the aisle of vendors, white tents on either side of her.

"I'm at Junebug Farms today where they're holding their annual Barkathon to raise money. Junebug is a no-kill shelter here in Northwood, and I'll show you around as we go. If you could send them some cash, even five bucks, it would go a long way to helping the animals here find their forever homes. Donation link's in my bio." She stopped recording, then went through the plan she'd laid out in her head when she'd first arrived. Then she'd put it all together later and post. She got to work, took shots in all the planned places—spots with the best lighting and the most interesting compositions. Then she took a few selfies as she wandered and used her selfie stick a couple times to make it look as if somebody else had taken the shot—her sweetie. She was just finishing up outside when somebody spoke behind her.

"Hey, you." Cherry turned toward the familiar voice to see Andi smiling and waving at her. In one hand, she had a leash with a black and brown dog who looked to be a beagle mix of some sort. With the other, she held hands with a very pretty fair-skinned woman with hair to die for that Cherry recognized from Andi's posts as her wife, Julianne.

"Hey, you," Cherry said and wrapped Andi in a hug. "I forgot you said you were coming." She turned to Andi's wife, who was smiling at her. "And you must be Julianne. I have heard *so much* about you. It's nice to finally meet you in person." She reached out a hand and Julianne shook it.

"I could say the same to you." Her eyes were kind, and her smile was soft.

"And this must be the famous Auggie," Cherry said as she squatted down. Hearing his name, Auggie's tail started to wag, and he stuck his face right in hers, then licked her chin enthusiastically. "Aw, who's a good boy? Is it you? Is it?"

They chatted for a bit, talked about the event and shots they'd taken, posts they had in mind. Cherry actually liked when they discussed their thoughts on posts when they were at the same event because then she could make sure hers weren't the same. Andi had way more followers, but they also had many in common. The last thing Cherry wanted was people thinking she copied Andi's content. It was great that Andi was so open with advice and guidance, but Cherry was her own person who did her own thing, and she wanted that to be clear to anybody who checked out her socials.

They said their good-byes, and Andi and her wife headed toward the barn while Cherry walked toward the main building. She had enough stuff to make a couple of good posts later, but she really needed a bit more. She wanted to emphasize donating to the shelter. She hated seeing so many homeless animals. With a sigh, she grabbed the handle of the main building's front door, was blasted by the marked increase in volume, and muttered, "I absolutely should not go in here—" And the rest of the sentence stuck in her throat because was she really seeing what she thought she was seeing?

Across the lobby at the front desk stood a familiar blonde with a carrier at her feet. She wore jeans that hugged her ass in a way that grabbed Cherry and wouldn't let her look away. Her hair was down, which she'd never seen before, only ponytails, and it was wavy and looked soft and did it smell like coconuts maybe? Peaches, she wondered?

"Jesus, get it together, Davis," she muttered to herself, but before she could do or think anything else, Ellis turned her way and their gazes met. And then Ellis's face blossomed into a beautiful smile, and escape was impossible, and Cherry's insides went warm and mushy and what the hell was wrong with her?

"Hey, you," Ellis said with a wave, raising her voice over the noise. "What are you doing here?"

"I was…" The words stuck in Cherry's throat as she crossed the lobby to Ellis so they could actually hear each other, and then she rearranged her face into a smile, hopefully erasing the shocked expression she was sure she'd worn. "I saw the commercial on TV and wanted to pop by. I mean, who doesn't love animals, right?" She didn't stop to think about why she'd tucked the truth away in a pocket—she just kept smiling.

"Exactly. And want to help them."

Cherry pointed to the paperwork on the counter that Ellis had clearly filled out. "And what's going on here?"

"That would be my attempt at influencing the Universe to make a cat like me." Ellis's cheeks flushed a pretty pink, her eyes blinked rapidly, and she looked down. "I'm waiting for a volunteer to take me to the visiting room."

"Have you already found a cat?"

"I did. Online first. Then I went in and saw him in his cubby. The visiting room was full, so I'm waiting until they have space for me and Nugget to meet."

"Nugget? OMG, that's too cute."

"Hey, do you…" Ellis stopped and cleared her throat, then shifted her weight from one foot to the other. "Would you wanna meet him with me?"

"I'd love to." God, she'd answered quick. Didn't even think about it. That wasn't like her. More time with Ellis? Yes, please.

What was happening?

"This place is cool," Ellis said as her gaze wandered the room. "Do you come here often?" Her eyes went a little wide as she must've realized what she said. "I meant that as an actual question, not as a pickup line."

"Oh, that's too bad," Cherry said, not stopping to wonder why she suddenly became the Queen of Flirt around Ellis, because the surprised look on Ellis's face was totally worth it. "And I actually used to volunteer here to walk the dogs when I was in high school. So, yes, I do come here often. Or I did."

"Really? That's so cool. Did you want to bring them all home?"

Cherry snorted. "No, I wanted to stay here with them." She grimaced at the words, but when she looked at Ellis, there was nothing but sympathetic understanding on her face. And before anything else could be said, they were interrupted by a tall woman with short hair whose name tag said she was Lisa.

"Hi there," Lisa said with a pretty smile, her eyes on Ellis. "You ready to meet Mr. Nugget?"

"I am," Ellis said. With a glance at Cherry, she added, "I'm suddenly nervous."

"Not unusual," Lisa said and looked to Cherry. "Would you like your friend to come with you?"

"Please."

"Absolutely. Leave the paperwork here and follow me." Lisa led them through a door with a line drawing of a cat on it, and once the door closed behind them, the volume of overall noise was cut by a lot.

"Oh, that's so much better," Cherry said. "It's loud out there."

"You should try working in the dog wing all day," Lisa said with what seemed to be an affectionate chuckle. "Barking never stops. Somebody's always got something to say."

"I bet."

Ellis was quiet as Lisa led them to a room with windows looking onto the hall.

"Have a seat and I'll go get your boy." Indicating several orange plastic chairs, Lisa closed the door, and it was just Ellis and Cherry in the room.

"I don't know why I'm so nervous," Ellis said with another grimace. "It's just a cat." And then she swallowed audibly.

"Because you might be about to change your whole life," Cherry said simply. "Makes sense to be nervous."

"Well, I…" Ellis rubbed her hands together and Cherry looked at them for the first time. They were pretty hands. Long fingers. Tapered nails. Neat. "This is gonna sound weird, but I'm really glad you're here. Thank you."

"You're welcome." Why did it seem perfectly natural to be here with Ellis, a person she didn't know well at all? It wasn't weird. Why not? It felt like she was exactly where she was supposed to be in that moment, and that was a feeling she'd heard people talk about and that she'd read about in books. But she'd never experienced it herself. Ever. In her entire life.

The door opened, cutting off any more overanalyzing, and Lisa walked in with an orange cat in her arms. His eyes were a golden yellow, and he seemed to take them in, looking from Ellis to Cherry and back.

"Why don't you have a seat," Lisa said, "and we'll see how he likes your lap."

Ellis grabbed the closest chair and dropped into it, like an eight-year-old trying to win a game of musical chairs. Cherry noticed her eyes had widened just a bit, likely with excitement. "Hi, buddy. Hey. Hi there. Come here."

Lisa handed the cat over and watched for a moment. "Okay. I'll be right out there. Take all the time you need. I'll check back in a bit."

The door closed quietly, and Cherry watched as Ellis and Nugget looked each other over. Phone in her hand, she took a quick photo, then slipped it into her pocket.

"He's so soft," Ellis said, her voice quiet with obvious wonder.

"And his eyes. Did you see them?" She spoke quietly, as if she worried about scaring him away by being too loud. "Hi, handsome." She glanced back up at Cherry, then indicated the chair next to her with her eyes. "Here, sit."

"He's beautiful," Cherry said, sitting as she was asked to, then gently nudging the chair so she was close enough that their thighs touched. It was the closest she'd ever been to Ellis, and that gave her a little thrill. Also made her antsy. And she could definitely smell her now. Apples. She smelled like apples, clean and fresh, and then she knew she needed to distract herself from this woman so close to her, because wow, she could get lost in simply smelling her, and how creepy was that? So she forced her focus toward the cat. She hadn't been kidding. He *was* beautiful. She'd always thought all orange tabby cats looked the same, but this guy was his own cat. His stripes were zigzag. His feet were massive because they had extra toes. "He's polydactyl."

"Yeah, that's one of the things I liked about him when I saw him online." Ellis stroked a finger across one of his paws. "Look at these mitts." The cat blinked at her but didn't pull his foot away. Instead, he lifted himself up and pushed his face against Ellis's. She made a cute little sound of delight, and he did it again.

"He likes you," Cherry said.

"I mean, that's what that means, right?" Ellis blinked at her, the excitement clear in her voice. "A sign of affection?"

"Definitely. And his motor's running like crazy."

The cat nuzzled his head under Ellis's chin, and she turned wet eyes to Cherry.

"I think you've got yourself a cat, my friend." And the sight in front of her, this gorgeous woman holding a cat, with tears in her eyes and such love on her face…it put a lump in Cherry's throat that she wasn't expecting at all. She swallowed it down and tried to redirect things. "How old is he? Where did he come from?"

Ellis cleared her throat and took a moment, likely to gather herself. "Well, there isn't a whole lot of info on him. The shelter said he's been with a foster family for the past six weeks, but they just moved out of state so had to turn him back in."

"Oh, man. Poor Nugget."

"Right? Their paperwork says he's the best cat they've ever fostered, that he's loving and affectionate."

"Accurate," she said, pointing at him as he nuzzled Ellis.

"They think he's around five years old, but that's just an estimate. There's no records before the foster family."

Cherry reached out and touched the cat for the first time. "Wow. He *is* soft." His fur was like the softest blanket she'd ever touched. Light and velvety. He blinked his big yellow eyes at her as he watched her, purring the whole time, his head against Ellis's chest. "Yeah, he hates you. Clearly."

"Pretty sure this is my cat." Ellis said it firmly and punctuated it with a cute little nod.

"Pretty sure you're right." She watched as Ellis and the cat had a silent conversation with body language. "I'll get the woman for you." She headed for the door, intent on finding Lisa. When she glanced back through the window, Ellis and the cat were nose to nose. Ellis's lips were moving, and though she couldn't hear what was being said, the sight alone moved her in a way she didn't expect and couldn't explain. In that moment, somehow, she just knew her life was about to change. For the better? For worse? She had no idea. Only that change was coming.

A hard swallow.

The question was, was she ready for it?

CHAPTER SIX

Clouds had moved in by the time Ellis and Cherry stepped out of the Junebug Farms main building, but Ellis didn't care. She felt light on her feet. Excited. Like she'd turned the page on a new chapter of life, clichéd as that sounded. She inhaled deeply through her nose and stretched her arms over her head as if she'd just woken up.

"Wow," Cherry said from beside her. "That is a happy woman right there."

"Very much so." She turned and smiled at Cherry, taken again by just how gorgeous she was. Pulling her gaze away, she went over things in her head. Because how weird was it that they'd run into each other here? Ellis couldn't believe it when she'd seen her. What were the odds? Seriously. And her staying the whole time she'd met Nugget? Totally unexpected. And awesome. She turned back to Cherry, and those dark eyes mesmerized her once more. Redheads were supposed to have blue eyes or green eyes, not these gorgeous, mysterious ones the deep, rich color of coffee grounds.

"So, are you off to the pet store?" Cherry's smile was infectious, and Ellis was very aware of how much time her gaze spent on those full lips. How was she so beautiful? How was that fair to the rest of the world?

"Do you want to get something to eat?" Oh my God, did she say that out loud? *Holy shit. Fix your face! Fix it into something that doesn't look as shocked as you feel right now.*

But Cherry didn't frown. Or laugh at her. She didn't run screaming. She didn't narrow her eyes at her and squint in suspicion. Instead, her smile grew and revealed very white teeth, and she said, "I would love that. I'm starving."

And that's how they ended up in The Flip at a small table for two by a window, eating the house specialty and the reason for the name, crepes that were to die for. To. Die. For.

"I think it's interesting that you went savory, and I went sweet," Cherry said with a soft smile. Her crepes were filled with bananas and Nutella. Ellis's had potatoes, sausage, peppers, and onions. Cherry had taken photos of both plates before they dug in.

"That's so we each get some of both." She grimaced and glanced up at Cherry with her fork in midair, the presumption suddenly clear. "Do you share food?"

"Lucky for you, I want to taste your crepe more than I want to keep you from tasting mine." Pausing only for a second or two to blink at the obvious euphemism, she watched as Cherry cleared her throat and picked up her fork. They reached across and took a bite from one another's plates, ate in tandem, and then hummed in approval together. The laughter came next, and it curled its way right into Ellis, forged a trail around her heart, then headed south.

"So," Ellis said. She met Cherry's eyes as she chewed and had the sudden, overwhelming urge to know every single thing about this woman sitting across from her. Mentally talking herself into calming the hell down was harder than it should've been. "What do you do? I see you in the diner on your laptop, but I don't think I know what you do."

"I work for an insurance company. Claims adjuster. I visit clients who've had accidents, and I evaluate." Cherry glanced down at her plate, cut another bite.

"You like it?"

She watched as Cherry tipped her head one way, then the other. "It's okay. It's a decent company. Decent pay. Benefits. I don't have a degree, and they hired me without one, so I'm grateful for that."

"Me neither," Ellis said. She rolled her lips in and nibbled for a moment.

"You don't have a degree?" Cherry's surprise seemed genuine.

"I have half a business degree."

"Ha. Me, too." She lifted her glass of water. "Cheers to half degrees." They touched glasses and smiled, and Cherry asked, "Are you new at the diner? I don't remember seeing you, and I'm there quite a bit."

"I'm not actually a waitress," Ellis said, and for a split second, her brain tossed her an image of Michaela's freshly polished toenails. "I manage the place for the owner, who now lives in Florida. We had a couple of waitresses call out sick the day I waited on you, so I filled in. Not that Kitty couldn't have handled things on her own."

"Oh my God, that woman is *amazing*," Cherry said, emphasizing the word.

"She really is. She's become kind of a mother figure for me away from home."

"You're not from here?" Cherry put her elbows on the table and propped her chin in her hands, and Ellis could feel her attention. Actually *feel* it, as if it could touch her, run fingertips along her spine.

Ellis didn't talk about her family much. At least not on the first date. Wait, was that what this was? Were they on a date? Giving herself a mental shake, she tried not to wonder why she felt so comfortable with Cherry, who was essentially a complete stranger. "No, I'm from Pennsylvania. My mom died when we were young. And then..." She cleared her throat. "Five years ago, my younger sister got in a car accident. She was in a place in PA, but when my dad died two years ago, I found a better facility called Hearts and Hands and had her moved there. Here, I mean. In Northwood."

"Oh wow." Cherry swallowed audibly, and her expression showed sympathy, understanding, sadness. And before Ellis could even register it happening, Cherry reached across the table and covered Ellis's hand with hers. Cherry's was warm and soft, and Ellis instantly knew she'd remember this moment, the first time they'd ever really touched. "I'm so sorry, Ellis. That's awful. For what it's worth, I hear good things about Hearts and Hands. My roommate's grandma was there for a while. Really great, caring people."

Hang on.

"Your roommate?" she asked, going for nonchalant.

"Yeah, I have two. Adam and Shea. Adam is gay, single, juggles several jobs, and is a big sweetheart. Shea is a graphic designer, also currently single, but certain that Idris Elba is going to give her a call any day."

Ellis wasn't happy about the relief that flooded through her over the fact that Cherry likely wasn't sleeping with either of her roommates. She didn't want to analyze that. "I mean, if you're gonna get a call, you could get one from worse than Idris Elba, right?"

"Seriously. I'd take that call, and I like girls." Cherry flushed pink then, and Ellis wasn't sure if it was because of what she'd said or because of the way Ellis was looking at her. The eye contact was serious. Intense. Weighted.

"Me, too," Ellis said simply, then lifted one shoulder in a half shrug. *Yup. Nonchalant. That's me.*

Cherry grinned. "Glad to see my gaydar is in proper working order."

And then there was silence as they ate, but it was a happy silence. One filled with occasional glances and grins.

When Ellis had eaten all she could manage without exploding her entire stomach, she asked, "So, what about you? Are you from here? Family?"

"I am from here, yes." Cherry dabbed at the corners of her mouth with a napkin. "From Cleaver, just outside the suburbs, in the sticks. I never really knew my mom. She bolted when I was just a toddler, so it was just me and my dad. Who was not the nicest guy around, but he did the best he could with what he had."

"And where is he now? Still in Cleaver?"

"Nope. Been at St. Anthony's Cemetery over off Main for three years now."

"Shit. I'm sorry, Cherry." Cherry's shrug and clear indifference surprised her, though.

"Thanks. Like I said, he wasn't the greatest guy."

"But he was your dad."

"True."

"Siblings? Grandparents?"

"Nope. None. Just me."

"Seems we are quite a pair," Ellis said and smiled at her.

"Seems that way."

Gazes held and Ellis was struck again by how weird it was that they had clicked so thoroughly so fast. Given their circumstances, maybe the Universe wanted them to find each other. There wasn't a lot that Ellis took on faith, but she did believe almost anything was possible.

"Well," Cherry said as the bill came, and she snapped it up before Ellis could even think to grab it. "I should probably get home. And you have some cat supply shopping to do."

"I do! I almost forgot." She'd been having such a great time with Cherry, she'd totally spaced on the earlier part of the day. She had supplies to buy if she was going to welcome Nugget into her home the next day. "And next time I invite you to a meal, you have to let me pay."

"We'll see about that." Cherry's grin was flirty, and her dark eyes sparkled.

They walked out of The Flip together and saw that it had rained while they ate. Ellis gave an involuntary shiver.

"It's cooled down."

"April in Upstate New York, am I right?"

"Totally."

"Well." They stopped in the parking lot and stood between their cars. "I had a lovely time with you today, Ellis."

"Right back atcha."

Cherry made like she was going to open her car door, then turned back. "Do you want to exchange numbers?"

"Yes," Ellis said, so quickly they both laughed as they pulled out their phones. Numbers were exchanged, and Cherry sent Ellis a text with a cat emoji. Then she surprised Ellis by leaning in and placing a soft kiss on her cheek. When she pulled back, it occurred to Ellis that maybe Cherry had surprised herself, too. Her cheeks were red, and her eyes darted a bit.

"Okay. I'm off."

"Will you be at the diner next week?" Ellis asked, sounding more hopeful than she cared to admit.

"Definitely."

"Good."

Cherry did get in her car then, and Ellis stood and watched as she drove away, and she felt something she hadn't felt in a really, really long time.

Longing.

CHAPTER SEVEN

Editing was Cherry's favorite part of posting. She loved the creativity of it. The way she could take only the best parts of things and stitch them together like a master seamstress making the most beautiful of gowns, so the pretty things were front and center and the mistakes and blemishes were left on the floor in strips.

Sunday was dark and stormy, one of those days where you wake up and it's gray and cool, and you just want to stay in bed all day. She'd done that. She'd slept for an extra ninety minutes. Well, it wasn't full-on sleeping, but she dozed and relaxed and followed her brain as it meandered down different unrelated paths, the way brains do when they're untethered and given free rein to go where they want, even if it's to the high shelf or the back corner where things had been intentionally boxed up and placed out of view.

So, yeah, her brain went to one of those far-off places and found Ellis, and she let herself daydream for a few moments about what a great time they'd had yesterday, about the softness of Ellis's cheek against her lips, before she reeled it back in and forced her focus back to her computer screen.

"Hey, those posts on Insta from the Barkathon are great." Shea had popped her head around the doorframe of Cherry's room. "I want a dog now."

"You don't have time for a dog," Cherry reminded her, not looking up from her monitor. "You said so yourself. About thirty-seven times."

Shea's sigh was loud and put-upon. "You stop it with your facts and your logic. Just stop it."

Cherry grinned. "Sorry, Charlie. Reality is reality."

"Who's that?" Shea asked and came fully into the room.

"Who?" Cherry squinted at the row of photos across the top of her screen and then watched as Shea's finger poked through the air and landed on one particular blonde with an orange tabby cat. A photo Cherry had forgotten she'd taken.

"This very hot woman right here. With the cat."

"Oh, her. That's Ellis."

Shea tipped her head to the side, then moved to sit on the foot of Cherry's bed. "And who is Ellis, and why have I not heard of her before?"

Talking about Ellis hadn't really been in Cherry's plans for the day. She wasn't ready. She kinda wanted to keep her to herself for a while. But Shea was relentless. If Cherry knew anything at all, she knew that. Shea was a person who needed all the information all the time, and if she didn't have it, she drove you mad until she got it. Cherry knew from experience if she didn't tell Shea what she wanted to know right now, she'd have no more peace for her Sunday. She took a big breath, spun in her chair so she was facing Shea, and started talking.

"So, Ellis works at that cute little diner I like so much. The one I work at a couple mornings a week?" At Shea's nod, she went on. "She manages the place, so I've never seen her before, I assume 'cause she's in the back. But last week, she had to fill in for a waitress that called out sick, so that's when I saw her for the first time."

"She's super hot."

"Right? And…" She pressed her lips together as she tried to find the right words to describe how drawn to Ellis she was. "It was, like, this instant attraction." She snapped her fingers. "I mean instant. I've never had that before."

"Oh my God, I love this story so much already." Shea shifted her position so she was on her stomach on Cherry's bed, her chin propped in her hands, like they were two teenagers having a sleepover. "And?"

"I mean, we talked a little bit over a couple of days. Flirted some."

"Flirted? You?"

"Hey, I can flirt."

"I'm not saying you can't. I'm saying you don't. At least I've never seen it."

"Well, I did. And so did she. Just, like, fun. Nothing major." Using her toes, she pushed her chair around in a circle. "And then yesterday, I ran into her at the Barkathon."

"Just, like, randomly ran into her?"

"*Yes.* It was *so weird.* I went into the main building—which I never do, you know that."

"'Cause you want to take all the animals home."

"Exactly. I'd taken all the shots I'd planned on, and I don't know what it was that pushed me in that direction, but I walked in before I could stop myself. And there she was. Right there at the front desk. I saw her immediately. She was the first thing I laid eyes on."

Shea gave a little squeal. "This is the best story! And, honey, I hate to tell you this, but the Universe is talking to you. In a big way."

She didn't share Shea's beliefs about the Universe and fate and destiny and all that, but she did have to wonder. "She was there to adopt a cat." The rest of the story came tumbling out, from visiting with Nugget to Ellis asking her out to eat, the way the invitation just kind of fell from her mouth, surprising them both. "We went to The Flip and had a late lunch and ate off each other's plates and just talked and talked."

"You had, like, a day right out of a rom-com. I'm so jelly right now." Shea kicked her feet in mock frustration. "Are you seeing her again?"

"We exchanged numbers."

"Have you texted her?"

Cherry nodded. "I did last night, told her I had a great time. She said she did, too."

"This is amazing. You so deserve to date somebody *real*." Cherry was clear on Shea's stance around the whole fake online relationship thing. It was the same one Andi had.

"I didn't tell her anything about my social media brand."

"Really? Well. I'm not surprised." She'd expected Shea to criticize her. Scold her. At least roll her eyes at her. She did none of those things. "I mean, you can't really. Your social stuff says you have a girlfriend." Then she groaned. Loudly. "When are you gonna take care of that, by the way?"

"There it is," Cherry said, and it wasn't snarky, but her tone held a definite edge of being tired of this conversation. Because she was.

Shea flipped her body around so she sat up again and held out her hands in surrender. "Look, I'm not gonna give you shit about it today. You're very aware that you're lying, and you're very aware that you shouldn't be. I'm hoping maybe meeting a nice girl will give you the kick in the ass you need to fix things. I don't understand why you can't just be real online."

"Because people don't want real," Cherry said. Well, she *snapped* really, given they'd had this conversation what felt like a million kajillion times. "They don't want to see struggle. They want to see beauty and happiness and love, and they want to think they can have it, too."

Shea shook her head and stood, and Cherry could almost hear her argument, how people might appreciate her more if she was honest. And then Cherry would say they had no idea that she wasn't being totally honest and that's fine because nobody online is a hundred percent honest, and around and around they'd go like they had so many times before. Shea must've felt the same way because they just held each other's gazes silently. Finally, Shea threw up her hands and turned toward the door.

"Look, you do you. Okay? You do you. But mark my words—it's gonna bite you in the ass sooner or later." She mimed taking a huge, toothy bite out of the air. "Right in your cute little ass."

❖

I didn't start worrying about Mikey right away. That didn't start until she was seventeen and I was twenty-two and I noticed how painfully thin she'd become. I remember how our dad called her Pudge when she was little because she had this adorable tummy that stuck out a little bit. You know, like any little kid might have. The tummy didn't stick, but the nickname did, even as I watched her get thinner and thinner.

Rainy days were good for writing. The gray, overcast sky always put Ellis in exactly the right mood to let herself drift back in time. Back to before things went sideways. Back to before Michaela's life had gone off the rails, taking her father's and sister's with her. The book idea had been rolling around in Ellis's head for over a year before she sat down and actually mapped it out, made an outline for it, wrote a few sentences for each chapter from beginning to end. It wasn't a memoir because it wasn't really about her. Well, it was, but it was more Michaela's story. Ellis was just a secondary character. She had no idea what she'd do with it when she finished it. Most of her wanted to shop it around, look for an agent, get it published. But there was a small part of her heart that wanted to keep it. It was Michaela's story, after all, and it was Ellis's job to look out for her.

Yeah, 'cause you've done such a bang-up job already.

Her fingers stopped typing when that thought zipped through her head.

It wasn't new.

Her guilty conscience taunted her often with lines like that. Lines? No. Facts. They were facts. Ellis was the big sister. Fact. Big sisters are supposed to look out for their little sisters. Fact. Michaela had driven her car full-speed into a tree, and Ellis had had no idea whatsoever that suicide was something she'd ever even thought about. Sad, sad fact.

Yeah, it was time to stop now. She knew this. She knew when the blame began in her head, it was time to stop. She saved her work, closed the laptop quietly, and pushed her chair away from the table where she'd chosen to work that morning. Time to stop now.

"Okay, El, shake it off." She stood up, shook out her arms like a boxer, bounced up and down on the balls of her feet.

Because today was a good day. She wasn't going to let herself get pulled down by the situation she was writing about, which had happened more than once over the past several weeks. But not today. Today, she would pick up Nugget. There were apparently some final medical and housekeeping things that needed to be done by the shelter before he was cleared for adoption, which was why she couldn't take him home with her yesterday, so she did just what Cherry had suggested after they'd eaten. She'd taken time to get everything she needed for him—food, litterbox, bowls, toys—and now everything was ready for her to bring him home.

Her phone beeped then, and as if she'd been privy to Ellis's thoughts, it was a text from Cherry.

Got a cat yet? Except the word *cat* was replaced by a cat emoji.

Ellis smiled. She couldn't help it. She typed her answer immediately. *Headed there now!* She watched the bouncing dots, telling her Cherry was responding.

Jelly over here. Followed by a jelly jar emoji.

Ellis typed again as she gathered her bag and keys. *U2 could have a cat.*

Told u. No time. Rather live vicariously thru u.

She typed without overthinking, sent without editing. *Any time u want to come over and play u let me know.*

The dots bounced, stopped, bounced some more, stopped. Ellis watched them as her heartbeat pounded in her skull. What the hell had she been thinking, sending that? She sighed, slid the phone into her back pocket, and reached for the doorknob. The phone beeped again.

She stopped, swallowed hard, and pulled the phone out slowly and carefully, as if it was a bomb that might go off with too much jostling.

How bout 2nite?

She blinked. Refocused on the words. Blinked some more. Cherry wanted to come over. Like, tonight. She typed her response, holding her breath.

Perfect. We can order pizza. She sent a time and her address, and Cherry's happy response came complete with several smiling emoji and another couple cats. Of course.

A moment of breathing was needed then. Why did this make her so nervous? She'd dated before. Here and there. Nothing had ever really stuck, but that was because her focus had always been on Michaela and her situation. Getting her into the right facility. Making sure she had what she needed. But now, those things were taken care of. Hearts and Hands was exactly what her sister needed. She was well cared for. Close by. And the reality of it all was that it would be where she was until she died, whether next month or twenty years from now. Michaela was settled and not going anywhere, so maybe—just maybe—it was okay for Ellis to start thinking about her own life now.

She glanced around her tiny apartment. It was small, but neat. She didn't really need more than a bedroom, bathroom, small kitchen, and living room, and that's exactly what she had. But it was nice. The hardwood floors were in good shape. The kitchen appliances were fairly new. The countertop was granite. She was in the back corner of the building, so she had windows on two sides and got lots of natural light. She liked it here.

Setting her bag and jacket down, she did a quick fly through the living room, cleaning up books and fluffing the throw pillows on her couch. Her cereal bowl was in the sink, so she washed it, dried it, and put it away. Then she gave the place a last look, nodded once, and picked her stuff back up.

Time to bring Nugget home.

❖

Ellis didn't get super nervous until the doorbell actually rang. Then, it was like the sound triggered all the nerves in her body. Like an electric shock. Like she'd been tased. Her heart began to pound. Her palms got sweaty. With a glance at the open cat carrier on the floor, she asked, "Ready, Nugs?" The cat blinked his big yellow eyes at her, and she had to swallow down a lump three times before she felt calm enough to depress the talk button on the intercom.

"Hello?"

"It's me, ready for kitty lovin'."

Ellis stifled a laugh at the possible innuendo as she buzzed her in. She lived on the second floor, so by the time she opened her door, Cherry was halfway up the stairs. She carried a paper bag and wore a gorgeous smile, and watching her approach did things to Ellis. Made her feel happy and nervous and anticipatory all at once.

It also turned her the hell on.

"Hi," Cherry said as she reached the doorway, slightly out of breath. "You didn't tell me I'd have to climb a thousand steps to get to you."

"A thousand or sixteen. I see how you'd get them confused." She grinned and stepped aside. "Come on in."

Cherry passed her, leaving the scent of…was it vanilla? Caramel? Something sweet and warm, and Ellis felt her chin lift slightly as she inhaled when Cherry walked by.

"There he is," Cherry said and dropped everything so she could kneel down in front of Nugget's carrier, and her voice went up about three octaves as she began talking to him. "Hi there, handsome. You're home. What do you think? Are you gonna come out?" And with no further coaxing, Nugget stood up and walked right out of the carrier where he'd been sitting for the better part of an hour.

Ellis gave a small gasp. "He's out. How'd you do that?"

Cherry looked up at her with those big brown eyes and shrugged. "I just talked to him."

Well, I'd *go wherever she asked me to, so…*

She shook the thought away and watched as Cherry sat cross-legged on the floor and Nugget crawled up into her lap and got comfortable. "Yeah, I don't think he likes you."

"I mean, I don't really like him either, so we're even." Cherry dropped a kiss onto his little cat head, then scratched behind his ears, and his motor kicked on.

"Can I get you something to drink? I have seltzer. I made a pitcher of iced coffee—"

"Say no more and hit me with the iced coffee. Please."

"You got it."

As Ellis doctored up the coffee with Cherry's requested "One sugar and lots of milk, if you have it," she watched her. She still couldn't believe Cherry was here. Sitting on her floor. Scratching her cat. Looking around the room at Ellis's things. How had they gotten here? And what was the next step?

"Did you have pets as a kid?" She walked the coffee to Cherry, then sat on the floor next to her.

"Oh no. We could barely afford food for ourselves. My dad never would've allowed another mouth to feed." Ellis felt a wave of empathy for the vision of tiny Cherry her mind had conjured up. "You?"

"I always wanted a dog, but my dad was allergic. And once I was on my own, I worked a lot and had Michaela to take care of. Knew I didn't really have the time to devote to one."

"Cats are less maintenance."

"Exactly. Thus, this guy." She reached to scratch her cat. "Who seems to like you better than me."

Cherry nuzzled Nugget's furry head. "Nah. I'm just new. Well. Newer than you." She turned to look at her and those eyes…God, those eyes. Ellis couldn't help herself. She leaned in.

Cherry's lips were soft and slick and tasted like peaches. A second or two ticked by, and then Cherry kissed her back. Just a little at first. Seemingly hesitant. Uncertain. And then Cherry didn't just kiss her back, she *kissed her back*. And oh my God. It was gentle, but demanding. Soft, but hard. Yielding, but intense.

When was the last time she'd been kissed like that?

Like, ever? Had she *ever* been kissed like that?

She didn't think so.

Nugget jumped off Cherry's lap, which must've gotten her attention because she pulled away. When Ellis opened her eyes, Cherry was smiling at her.

"Um, wow."

"Same. Yeah." Ellis grinned at her. "Sorry about that. I—"

Cherry cut her off with a hand on hers. "Please don't apologize."

"No?"

"No. The truth is, I've wanted to kiss you from that first day you waited on me."

Ellis felt a pleasant wave in her stomach. And lower. "Seriously?"

Cherry tipped her head to one side, then the other and said, "I mean, the very first thing I noticed were your legs…so, after that, yeah."

Ellis was blushing. She knew it. She could feel it, the heat crawling up from her chest, rising over her throat and settling in her face. Her cheeks were hot. Her ears, too. "Well. That's…wow."

"Okay, the blushing? Stupidly cute." Cherry leaned in and kissed her again, this time softer. Slower. She ended it with a little flick of her tongue against Ellis's lip, and Ellis almost whimpered out loud. When she pulled back, their gazes held for a long time. Then Ellis swallowed and cleared her throat, then glanced around the room.

"Where'd my cat go?"

As if he understood her, Nugget came walking around the end of the couch, looking around the room as if for the first time. Which it kind of was. He walked slowly toward her, looked at her face for a long moment, then crawled into her lap.

"See?" Cherry said with a soft laugh. "He does like you. Told you."

"Finally. He's been sitting in that carrier for almost an hour. I was starting to think he wasn't ever coming out."

"Oh no, really?" Cherry reached over so she could give Nugget a scratch. "I get it, though. New digs and all, right? And cats are…I think they kinda work on their own timeline." She smiled and words came out of Ellis's mouth before she could stop them.

"Your smile just makes me feel all warm inside." And then the reality of what she'd said set in, and she froze in horror.

"You should see your face right now," Cherry said, laughing. "God, you're cute. Where did you come from?"

"Pennsylvania. I told you," Ellis teased. How could she be so nervous and so comfortable at the same time? It didn't make any sense, but she had no other description.

"You're funny."

"It's true. I *am* super funny."

Cherry laughed and bumped against her with a shoulder, and their gazes held for what felt like a really long time to Ellis. "So. Pizza?" Cherry asked. "I'm starving."

"Let's do it." Ellis got up to grab her phone. As she called up the app to place their order, she wondered if Cherry noticed her grinning like a fool. But she didn't care and just kept on smiling because this was easily the best evening she'd had in longer than she could remember.

A pizza with pepperoni and mushrooms was only going to make it better.

CHAPTER EIGHT

"Shea! Where are you, woman?" Cherry shut the door with her hip, her arms filled with her purse, lunch bag, and three boxes she'd picked up from the post office.

"How dare you demand my presence," Shea said with mock irritation, but her eyes went wide, and she hurried to help Cherry with her load. "What's all this?"

"I got *product*, baby," Cherry told her, unable to keep the smile off her face.

Shea squinted as she clearly tried to understand what that meant, and Cherry could see the exact second she got it. "Oh my God. Like, *product* product? Like, sent to you from companies product? No way."

"Yes way." Cherry couldn't keep the excitement from her voice. Hell, from her body. She was practically thrumming. She shrugged out of her jacket, still in her work clothes, and was way too aware of how much she wished Ellis was there right then. "I got a box from J. Jordan, who makes the mascara I reviewed a couple weeks ago. And one from Peak, an outdoor gear company, so I'm not sure what they sent. But the box is big."

"Babe," Shea said, and her eyes danced. "This is the goal. This is what you want. It's starting."

"*It's starting!*"

They squealed together like two sorority pledges, and then Shea got a knife so they could open the boxes.

"So, you'll use this stuff and then—the company hopes—you'll give it a positive review, and your followers will go buy it. Yes?"

"Exactly." Cherry sifted through the J. Jordan box. More mascara, a couple eyeliners. Some foundation, which she didn't wear, but also some moisturizer, which she did. "A lot here," she observed as she and Shea picked things up, examined them, and set them back down.

Shea sliced open the box from Peak. "Oh wow," she said as she pulled a smaller box from the big one. "Hiking boots."

"What?" Cherry said, her head snapping toward Shea. "Holy shit." It was, in fact, a pair of nice hikers, clearly high quality, with purple accents on the medium brown base. "Wow. These are gorgeous." She met Shea's gaze. "Look 'em up," she said, just as Shea had picked up her phone, likely to do just that.

"A hundred seventy-five bucks," Shea said after a couple minutes of typing and scrolling.

"What?"

"Yup."

"Wow." She pulled all the packing material out of the shoes, then slid her foot into one. "It fits like a damn glove. For my foot." She put the other one on, laced them up, and walked around the tiny living room. "These are amazing."

"You're gonna have to hike in them. Take 'em for a test drive."

"Definitely."

"Maybe your make-out buddy would go with you."

"Her name is Ellis," she mock-scolded her.

"Right. Pardon me. Maybe Ellis, your make-out buddy, would go with you."

Cherry watched her feet as she walked, liking the way the boots looked. "Maybe she would," she said quietly. Shea was teasing her now, but Cherry knew how she felt about the whole thing, and she wasn't in the headspace to deal with that right then, so she was relieved when the front door opened, and Adam came in.

"Sup, my bitches?" He dropped his stuff on the floor next to Cherry's. "What's with all the boxes?"

For the next hour, Cherry sat around the living room with her roommates, looking at Cherry's products and batting around ideas for her videos and reviews. Then Adam stood.

"Gotta go make myself beautiful," he said.

"Bartending tonight?" Shea asked.

He nodded. "You guys should come." Then he headed for his room, and Cherry knew he'd return in a cloud of Sauvage cologne, looking like a Disney prince. Coasters wasn't a gay bar, but much of its staff was queer in some way. Thus, so was the clientele.

"Wanna?" Shea asked, turning to Cherry.

She made a noncommittal sound and lifted one shoulder. "On a Monday? I don't know. I'm kind of tired. It was a *day*."

"Yeah, I get that." It was clear Shea was trying to hide her disappointment, and Cherry felt a pang of guilt.

"I mean, we could go for one. Right?"

Shea's face lit up, and in that second, Cherry knew she'd chosen correctly. "Just one. Possibly two. Maybe there'll be some dancing if the music is good."

Cherry nodded and gave her a grin. "Okay. Let's do it." She started packing her stuff back into the boxes, and when she looked up, Shea was focused on her. "What?"

With a finger, Shea made a gesture toward Cherry's phone. "Why don't you let your make-out buddy know where we'll be. I'd like to meet this woman you've been kissing lately."

"Kissed. I *kissed* her. We haven't *been kissing*. We *kissed*. Once." She toyed with the laces on one of the hikers. "Possibly twice." And she laughed because she knew Shea was teasing her. And also? What if Ellis did want to come out? She grabbed her phone to text, but her thumbs hovered. She glanced up at Shea. "How do I do this?"

"What do you mean?"

"Like, do I invite her. Actually say, *Come hang out with me and Shea*? Or do I keep it more casual? Like, *Here's where I'll be tonight, fyi*?" She blinked at Shea and felt the panic rising. "Help me!"

"OMG, give me that." Shea snatched her phone from her hand, typed quickly, and the sound of a text being sent filled the room. "There." She tossed the phone back to her. "Can we get ready now?"

As Shea turned and headed to her room to change, Cherry glanced down at the text.

Heading to Coasters with friends. I'd love to see you.

Well. That was surprisingly pleasant and simple. Too bad she couldn't come up with it on her own. With a roll of her eyes, she gathered up her boxes and hauled them all into her room so the living room didn't look like a recycling center.

❖

"Do I go, Mikey? I mean, I do, right? Or no? Maybe no."

Ellis stood in Michaela's room at the window, looking out on the impeccably landscaped yard that was bordered by some gorgeous woods. The brown of late winter and early spring had begun to fade, making room for the entrance of color. Green buds on the trees had begun to open, peeking out to see if the coast was clear. The bright yellow of daffodils springing up in flower beds and also in randomly unexpected spots, thanks to the squirrels who transplanted them. This view, this peaceful yard and gorgeous woods beyond, was one of the reasons Ellis had worked so hard to get her sister into Hearts and Hands. Yes, she knew Michaela probably didn't see anything and likely never would again, but just in case—*just in case*—she did ever wake up, Ellis wanted to make sure what she saw was lovely and comforting. Not some scary hospital walls or a parking lot out the window.

She watched as a squirrel ran across the yard with a mouthful of something she couldn't quite make out, and it reminded her that she wanted to get a bird feeder to hang outside the window. Michaela loved birds, even when they were kids.

"So?" she asked again, her eyes following the path of the squirrel. "What do I do? Go or not go?"

"You go. Absolutely."

The voice startled her, and she turned to meet Kendra's soft eyes. "I wasn't asking you," she teased.

"I know." Kendra came in, took Michaela's pulse, straightened her bedding. "Hi there, baby," she said softly as she ran the backs of her fingers along Michaela's cheek. "Your sister is asking for advice she doesn't really need 'cause she already knows the answer. But don't you worry, I got it covered." She met Ellis's gaze again and lifted one eyebrow. "Michaela and I agree."

Ellis clenched her teeth and made a face. "You think?"

"Girl, why are you treating this like it's a life or death decision?" She'd told Kendra about Cherry's invitation when she'd first arrived. She'd also told her last night about the previous day's kissing. Honestly, you'd have thought she told Kendra she'd won the lottery, the way she cheered and celebrated. "I've been there. It's not fancy. Just a bar. With drinks. You go, you have a drink. You see your girl. If you're not having fun—which I doubt will be the case, but if you're not—you leave. Easy peasy."

"Lemon squeezie," Ellis added with a soft smile, recalling what she and Michaela used to say as kids.

"Exactly."

Ellis looked at Kendra, this woman who'd become one of her very dearest friends in the world. She looked at Michaela, her unseeing blue eyes staring up at the ceiling, and felt the decision being made, almost as if it was out of her hands. "All right. I'll go."

Kendra clapped her hands together once. "Fantastic." She tipped her head to one side. "I'm proud of you. I know that wasn't easy. Or peasy. Or lemon squeezie. At least not for you."

"It disturbs me how you know me so well," Ellis said with a grin. But the truth was, she was relieved to have the decision made. It was just a bar. Just a drink. Nothing fancy. Nothing pressing. It would just be fun. A nice break from—

"I swear I can hear the wheels in your brain turning," Kendra interrupted. "Go. Now."

"But—"

"*Go.*" Kendra laughed even as she grabbed Ellis by the shoulders and steered her out the door. "Have a great time, and tell us all about it tomorrow." With that, she gave her a final nudge out the doorway of Michaela's room.

Ellis turned back, held her arms out to the sides, and wrinkled her nose. "Do I look okay?" She wore jeans and a lightweight yellow sweater. Black booties. Her hair was down. "I could go home and change…"

"You look fabulous, sweetheart." Kendra reached out, fluffed the ends of Ellis's hair. "I mean that. Her eyes are gonna light up when she sees you."

"You think?"

"I know."

"Thanks, Kendra." She gave her a big hug, inhaling her spicy scent, then let her go.

"I expect a full report tomorrow."

"Yes, ma'am." She turned and headed for the parking lot, and as she walked, she felt a smile blossoming on her face like the sun peeking out from behind a cloud. She was going to see Cherry now. No, it wasn't technically a date, but that didn't matter. She was going to see her, and that's all she wanted.

❖

Coasters wasn't fancy at all, but it had great lighting. It was one of the places Cherry liked to take photos the most because everything had this cool shimmer to it, bathed in an ethereal blue light. Shea had spotted a friend immediately and bopped over to say hi, so Cherry set her vodka tonic on the bar next to an art-deco-inspired napkin holder, blurred the background on her phone, and took a couple cool shots for future posting, the yellow from the lemon wedge adding a nice pop of color.

"Are you one of those people who documents every single thing they eat or drink?" The voice was unexpectedly close and sent an unexpectedly sexy shiver up her spine.

Cherry turned to meet sparkling blue eyes, made even more shimmery by the bar's lighting. "I mean, how else am I to remember what I ate or drank?" They smiled at each other, and the seconds seemed to slow—*tick, tick, tick*—before Ellis's face softened and she spoke.

"Hi, you."

"Hi yourself," Cherry said back, and something about Ellis's presence, her proximity, seemed to calm the world around her. Everything just…relaxed. Which was weird and also impossible, right? How could one person show up and settle everything so easily? Yeah, she was making it up. Had to be. "Want a drink?"

Ellis nodded and scanned the bar, and Cherry watched her make eye contact with Adam, who smiled and scooted over to them.

"Adam, this is Ellis. Ellis, this is Adam, one of my roommates."

They shook hands and Adam asked what he could get her.

"A rum and Coke?"

"You got it."

"On my tab, Ad," Cherry said, and he nodded without looking back as he grabbed the Bacardi off the shelf. Ellis opened her mouth, likely to protest, but Cherry stopped her with a hand on her arm. "I invited you. I buy."

"Oh, is that how it works?"

"That's how it works, yes." And more eye contact. Deliciously direct and sexy eye contact. She gave herself a mental shake and turned to put both forearms on the bar. "And how is my boyfriend, Nugget?" she asked as she took a sip of her drink.

Adam returned with a cocktail for Ellis, and she took a sip and nodded. "He's good. Starting to feel at home, I think." She angled her body so she was leaning against the bar and facing Cherry. She looked amazing, casual in jeans and short black boots with a yellow sweater, but there was an elegance about her, something classy. Cherry had to make a conscious effort not to stare at her like a creepy old bar regular who'd been there since early afternoon. "Missed you at the diner this morning."

Cherry groaned and let her head fall backward. "Ugh. Staff meeting. It was endless." She met Ellis's gaze. "Trust me, I would've much rather been in your diner drinking strong coffee and eating Cal's biscuits."

"God, those biscuits are life."

"Hey, bitch." Shea bumped hard into Cherry's shoulder, a clear signal she expected to be introduced.

Cherry closed her eyes and shook her head with a smile. "Hey, bitch." Before she could say more, Shea stuck her hand across Cherry toward Ellis.

"Hi. Shea."

Ellis took the hand, shook it. "Ellis. Nice to meet you."

"Oh, cool name." Shea gave her glass a subtle shake when Adam caught her eye, silently asking for a refill.

"Thanks. It was my grandpa's." It was clear she was proud of that fact, the way her eyes lit up and she stood the tiniest bit straighter. Something about knowing this personal tidbit about her warmed Cherry inside.

"It was?" Cherry asked.

Ellis nodded. "My maternal grandpa was Ellis. My paternal grandpa was Michael. My sister's name is Michaela."

"I love that."

"Clearly, my parents weren't going to let something silly like having girls keep them from naming their children after their fathers." She sipped her drink and looked around. "I like this place. I've never been here before."

Cherry turned and tried to see the bar through Ellis's fresh eyes.

"It's quirky," Ellis said. "Like it can't decide what decade to be in, so it's just gonna be in all of them."

She wasn't wrong—the bar was kind of an amalgamation of dozens of things. Not a strictly gay bar, but not straight. Totally inclusive, the decor consisting of both Pride rainbows and neon beer signs. There was a definite eighties vibe of brightly colored lights, but the actual bar itself had been updated only in the last couple of years, its surface still smooth and new. The barstools were also new, black with short backs on them, but the few remaining booths along the walls were clearly a good twenty years old, slices and scratches marring their vinyl seats, initials carved into the tables. And then suddenly, Lady Gaga's voice filled the space, and Ellis's grin grew wide.

"The sound system does not suck," she said, raising her voice so Cherry could hear her.

"It's new," she said with a nod, remembering two years ago when the bar went from a piano bar to a place where people could dance. The dance floor was the size of a postage stamp, and people filled it up in a matter of moments, making the small Monday night crowd seem much bigger than it was.

"Dance with me," Shea ordered and grabbed her hands.

Cherry shot a look to Ellis, who simply smiled like she was having the best time in the world, shooed her away from the bar, and lifted her glass in salute as Shea dragged her onto the dance floor, then wasted no time pulling her close enough to speak directly into her ear.

"Oh my God, Cher, she's *hot*."

Cherry felt her own smile grow and her face heat up because yeah. Ellis *was* hot. She'd known that all along, of course. But seeing her in the real world the past few times…the animal shelter, in her apartment…yeah. Her attractiveness had been impossible to ignore. And Cherry was starting to feel more drawn to her than she'd expected in the beginning.

When she looked back in Ellis's direction, she was chatting a bit with Adam, who had his elbows on the bar and was leaning toward her. Then they both looked at Cherry at the same time.

"Somebody's being discussed," Shea said, clearly seeing the same thing she was. When Cherry met Shea's gaze, she smiled at her and the teasing tone was gone. "She seems pretty great, Cher."

"She does, doesn't she?" The song morphed from Lady Gaga into the latest from The Weeknd, and she kept dancing. But her brain barely heard the music. The only thing it could focus on was the pretty blonde leaning on the bar, watching her dance.

What the hell was she going to do with her?

❖

Bars with flashing colored lights and loud music were not really Ellis's jam. She didn't dance. She didn't drink a whole lot. She'd much rather hang in a coffee shop or at the bar of a restaurant she enjoyed. Her presence at Coasters was a pretty good indication of what was happening between her and Cherry.

Cherry, who was dancing up a storm and, Ellis could easily admit, was fabulous at it. Her hips moved to the beat in a rhythm that was undeniably sexy. Arms up by her shoulders. Big smile on her face as she leaned forward to hear Shea and then respond. She was a sight to behold.

"She loves to dance."

Ellis turned to the voice. Adam, the bartender, was leaning on the bar and watching his friends, the affection clear on his face.

"She's really good." She wanted to talk more to Adam, be friendly, ask him questions, but she couldn't take her eyes off the dance floor. Yeah, this was going to be a problem. But that fun pang of anticipation hit low in her body, and her heart rate seemed to intensify, and she swallowed. Because, problem or not, she wanted this. She knew it as clearly as if there'd been a sign flashing above Cherry's head, a big neon arrow pointing down at her, all *This one! This one right here!*

The song changed again, and she watched Cherry wave off Shea, who quickly grabbed somebody else on the dance floor and never missed a beat. Cherry returned to the bar out of breath.

"Hey," she said, then picked up her drink, which Adam had refilled.

"You're a great dancer."

"Oh. Well, thanks. Do you watch *Grey's*? You know how they *dance it out*?" She made air quotes. "Turns out, that really does help. So whenever I'm stressed or worried or angry or...whatever, I dance it out."

Ellis nodded. "I do watch."

"You don't like to dance?"

With a grin, she said, "I got skipped the day they handed out rhythm."

"Oh no, I don't believe that. Everybody's got rhythm."

Ellis snorted a laugh. "Ha, yeah, I'm sorry to inform you that is *not* true."

Cherry laughed, a sound Ellis was rapidly beginning to adore. It was throaty, much deeper than you expected after talking to Cherry.

Because of the music, they didn't have much opportunity to really talk, and that was a bummer. What was not a bummer was being able to watch Cherry. Watch her dance. Watch her laugh. Watch her just… have fun and enjoy herself. For the first time in longer than she could remember, Ellis realized that having fun and enjoying herself were things she rarely did. More accurately, she existed. Simply existed. She *was*. And that had been okay for a long time. But Cherry made her yearn. Made her long for something more, and she hadn't been bargaining for that. Not even a little.

"Deep thoughts going on in there?" Cherry asked as she tapped a gentle fingertip on Ellis's forehead. "You look like something's on your mind." Her eyes were that soft, warm brown, with a little bit of sparkle from the mirror ball and the funky lighting. Her smile was tender, and Ellis could do nothing but smile back. She had no choice, like her smile was its own thing and did what it wanted.

"Just having a really good time," she said honestly. "Thanks for asking me to come."

"I'm glad you did."

Their gazes held, and Ellis had a moment of standing in a romance novel when the writer said something corny like *and the rest of the world faded away*. But that's exactly how it felt to her. Like the rest of the bar went all fuzzy, blurred out of focus, and the only thing she was interested in seeing was Cherry's smiling face. It was weird and wonderful and only lasted for a second before everything came screaming back into clarity, but Ellis knew it was a moment that was going to stay with her for a very long time.

A glance at the time on her phone made her grimace. "I hate to say this…"

"You've gotta go," Cherry filled in. "I figured. The diner opens stupidly early."

"It really does."

"Can I walk you out?"

"I'd love it if you did."

The evening had gone so quickly, and they hadn't had a ton of one-on-one time, and even when they had, it had been loud. It seemed clear that Cherry hadn't thought the invitation through and knew it, but Ellis didn't mind. At all. Any time spent with Cherry was time well spent. That was something she'd decided without realizing it, and as they walked out of the bar and toward the dark parking lot, she didn't even pause to think about reaching for Cherry's hand. She just did it.

Cherry looked down at their linked hands and smiled, then squeezed. "I'm glad you came," she said, then, as if privy to Ellis's thoughts, added, "Next time, let's go somewhere where we can actually hear each other talk, yeah?"

"I'd like that a lot."

"What about a hike?" Cherry seemed to blurt out the question, as if she didn't have control over it and it just wanted out.

"A hike sounds awesome. Much more my speed." Ellis pulled Cherry's hand up to her face and softly kissed her knuckles. "I'd love to walk in the woods with you."

"Yeah?" They'd reached Ellis's car and stopped next to the driver's side door.

Ellis leaned her back against the door and studied Cherry for what felt like a long time. Let her eyes wander over her face, that creamy ivory skin with the dusting of freckles across the bridge of her nose that she could see even in the dim lighting of the parking lot. Along the deep auburn hair that Cherry'd arrived with down, but magically whipped up into a messy bun once she'd started dancing. Down her body to the jeans with rips in various places. Back up along the simple black T-shirt that clung to her curves like it was designed to. Then all the way up to those dark, sexy eyes. It was amazing how she could still see them clearly, still feel like she was looking into the depths of them, even in the deep indigo of the night. She gave herself a shake, reminded herself that staring was rude, even if what she was staring at was achingly beautiful.

"A hike sounds amazing," she said again. "This weekend?"

Cherry nodded, but her eyes were on Ellis's mouth. Ellis could see that, and it sent a thrill through her, started a gentle throbbing low in her body. "I'll text you this week." Her words came out in a whisper as she leaned forward, and her lips met Ellis's. One of them whimpered, but Ellis wasn't sure which. Her hands found their way up to Cherry's neck, the sides of her face, and she pulled her in harder. Deeper. Opened her mouth to let her in, give her access, meet Cherry's tongue with hers.

The kiss was a study in push and pull. In give and take. In dominance and submission. Cherry pressed Ellis against the car door. Then Ellis would push back, and they'd be standing upright, nearly the same height. And then Cherry would lean in again, and Ellis would find herself trapped once more between Cherry's warm body and the cool metal of her car. Not a bad place to be stuck. Not a bad place at all.

They kissed for a long time. Despite her inability to distinguish complex things like up or down or right or left when Cherry was kissing her like this, she did know they kissed for a long time. When they finally wrenched their mouths apart and stood with their foreheads together, ragged breathing was the only sound. Then Ellis finally spoke.

"Your friends are going to think I kidnapped you."

Cherry nodded once. "Probs. I hope they don't pay the ransom."

Ellis laughed softly. "I promise I won't take it." She tucked an errant bit of red hair gently behind Cherry's ear.

Cherry seemed to take a moment to steady herself, and it took an obvious effort. Then she looked into Ellis's eyes, something Ellis felt all the way down to her center. She swallowed hard. Cherry's hand came up to her face, and she rubbed her thumb across Ellis's bottom lip. Grabbed it and gave it a gentle tug, then kissed her one more time.

This time, it was definitely Ellis that whimpered.

"Okay. Go." Cherry stepped back from the car, and Ellis found herself both grateful for and in anguish over the space she'd put between them. Cherry kept walking backward. "Go," she whispered again.

"Going," Ellis replied. And this time, she did get into her car, started her engine, waited until Cherry was no longer visible in the rearview mirror. Then she blew out a loud breath and dropped her forehead to the steering wheel. Wow. Cherry was so many things.

Not what she'd been looking for.

Not what she'd expected.

She met her eyes in the mirror, as a third *not* rolled through her mind.

Not someone she was willing to let go of.

She tipped her head as the words rolled through her brain.

Well. That's new.

Chapter Nine

The hiking boots that Peak had sent were amazing to look at. Cherry had spent several minutes Saturday morning gazing at her feet in the mirror, turning them at different angles. They were supportive, but flexible. Heavy, but breathable. She was looking forward to putting them to the test, and she snapped a couple photos to post before she headed to Tykeman Park to meet Ellis.

Ellis.

Yeah.

That situation was…it was so many things. It was exhilarating and terrifying and sexy and terrifying and energizing and terrifying and so much more. And also terrifying. Ellis scared the hell out of her. The fact that Ellis knew nothing of her online life scared her even more.

They'd texted every day since Monday's parking lot make-out fest, and Cherry had done some remote work at the diner twice that week. Lots of eye flirting and barely disguised innuendos. But they'd both been busy and hadn't had time to spend together all week, so hiking today would be the first time they'd been alone since the parking lot.

And Cherry was nervous.

"What the hell is wrong with you?" Shea asked when Cherry dropped a mug full of coffee all over the counter. "You dropped your phone in the living room. You dropped your hairbrush twice this morning while you were drying your hair. Now the coffee. Do your hands not work anymore? Are your opposable thumbs broken? When did you lose the ability to hold on to things?"

Cherry sighed quietly and didn't meet her eyes, and that was all Shea needed to figure out the very not-at-all complicated puzzle.

"*Oh*, it's Miss Ellis, isn't it? Today is hiking day."

With a slow nod, Cherry said, "It is. And I'm going to tell her today."

"You are?" Shea's tone made it super clear that this made her happy.

"I have to." Not only did she need to reveal her online life, goals, dreams, but she had to explain all the alluding to her girlfriend. All the *my sweetie*s and *my honey*s. That was going to be the weird part. That's what made her so jittery. "I have to," she said again.

"That's what I've been saying."

"I know."

"So…" Shea drew the word out as she tapped on her lips with a finger. "You're going to do the thing I've been saying you should do for weeks now. Would that mean that I'm right? Would you say that?"

Cherry couldn't help but grin, even though she tried to stifle it. She could feel the corners of her mouth turning up without her permission. "Yes, that's what it would mean."

"I think you should say it, though. Just to be clear."

A sigh. Still grinning, but a definite sigh. "Fine. You were right."

"Again, please. But say it slower this time. And like you mean it."

Cherry laughed openly now. "Fine." She leaned close to Shea. "You. Were. Right." Then she kissed her cheek with a loud smack.

"Music to my ears, those words. Absolute music to my ears." As Cherry left the room, she said louder, "You should say them more often, you know."

"Then be right more often," Cherry called back. And she glanced at the clock and her heart rate kicked up about twenty-seven notches because it was time. *It was time.*

"You're gonna be fine." Shea was next to her again, maybe sensing her worry. Maybe seeing her hands tremoring from across the apartment. Whatever it was, Cherry was happy to have her close again. "This is the right thing to do. Just be honest with her, and everything will be okay. Yeah?"

Cherry nodded, inhaled through her nose and blew it out through her mouth, and shook her arms out like a boxer getting ready to step into the ring.

"You got this, baby." Shea kissed her cheek. "Now go."

Twenty minutes later, her car slid to a stop in a parking spot at Tykeman Park. The entrance to the trails lay directly in front of her bumper, a sort of doorway into the woods that she knew would open onto a lovely nature walk the farther in she went. It was the end of April, and the weather was proof of that. Sunny and bright, peeks of early spring flowers giving the landscape little pops of color. The parking lot was next to an open field, and while it was mostly a lush green on that day, Cherry knew it would burst into color in another month or so, filled with summer wildflowers to attract the butterflies and the bumblebees. She smiled at a couple who exited the woods with their yellow Lab. Two cars over, a man was folding up a complicated-looking stroller while the woman with him held a sleeping toddler. When the woman turned so her back was to Cherry, the child's face was visible on her shoulder—blond ringlets and full lips, puckered in sleep, arm dangling loosely—and there was something about the beauty and the trust that sent a warm flush through her.

Of course, that warm flush was nothing compared to what her body did when Ellis's car slowed to a stop next to hers. Flush was an understatement. So was warm. Because there was nothing warm about how she felt when Ellis's sunglassed face turned and she felt the eye contact without even being able to see her eyes. It was heat. All heat. Very, very hot heat. Searing heat. Like fire. Like lava.

"Jesus," she muttered under her breath as Ellis got out of the car, shoved her sunglasses up onto her head, and smiled at her.

"Hey, you."

"Hey yourself." Did her grin make her look ridiculous? Yeah, she was pretty sure it did. Oh my God, what was happening to her?

"I am so ready for this," Ellis said, bending back down into her car and coming up with a water bottle and a lightweight nylon jacket. "I love being out in nature, but I never take the time to actually be out in nature." She came around the back of her car, and Cherry took in her tan shorts and navy-blue long-sleeve T-shirt. Ellis shrugged into a hoodie, which was also navy blue, and it took everything in Cherry's power not to stare at those legs. They were right there. On display. For looking at. And she felt like her brain and her eyes were literally in a battle. For a split second, her eyes won and she glanced down, then back up. Right at Ellis's eyes, which sparkled with knowing. Their gazes held for a beat as Cherry wondered if Ellis wore shorts on purpose, knowing what Cherry had said about her legs. And then Ellis fiddled with her water bottle as she asked, "Is there a plan? A specific trail you want to take?"

Okay. Good. Facts. She could deal in facts. That would help her focus her brain on something other than the gloriously female body in front of her and how badly she wanted to undress it. "Yeah, I thought we'd stay fairly flat. I'm breaking in these shoes."

"Those are amazing," Ellis said, looking down at the hikers. "These are, like, ten years old." She kicked up a foot to show Cherry her own hikers, but all Cherry saw was leg. Calf. Skin.

"Ready?" She had to move. Had to get walking or there was a very distinct possibility she'd throw Ellis up against the car and kiss her into next week. She made herself smile and hoped it wasn't creepy. Ellis didn't need to think she was following a potential serial killer into the woods.

"I've been ready for this all week," Ellis said, catching up to her and then bumping her with a shoulder.

And just like that, it felt better. Cherry felt herself relax, her shoulders drop, her hands unclench—she hadn't even realized she'd fisted them—and her head cleared. Just like that. And again, she wondered how Ellis did that. How did she just…settle things for Cherry? She wanted to ask, but the words stayed in her head. Probably a good thing for now.

They headed through the opening that led them into the woods. It was immediately chilly, as they'd left the sun behind for the moment, and Cherry stopped to zip up her puffy vest halfway, wishing she'd thought to bring something warmer to cover her arms.

"Cold?" Ellis stopped next to her and rubbed a hand up and down her arm. Then, as if she wanted to do so before she had a chance to think twice, she leaned forward and kissed Cherry's lips softly. Her smile was shy, and her cheeks had turned slightly pink. "I've wanted to do that since I pulled in and saw you standing there. I hope that's okay." Her nose wrinkled adorably.

"Totally okay."

They walked for several minutes in silence, but with occasional looks to each other. Looks that were filled with heat and possibility and promise. One thought echoed through Cherry's head on repeat.

How am I going to survive this hike?

❖

Was Cherry trying to kill her?

Not with the hike. No, the hike was cake. Mostly flat. Along a stream. Lots of trees that then opened into sunny clearings. Tykeman Park was gorgeous. But it didn't compare to her date. Cherry was… *stunning* was the only word that seemed to work, and even that didn't have quite enough shine or sparkle to do her justice.

It wasn't her clothes. They were nice, of course. Black shorts with several pockets and a purple Henley with a lightweight black down vest. The hikers were definitely cool, their purple accents matching Cherry's shirt, something she was sure Cherry did on purpose because when it came to fashion, Ellis had realized that Cherry knew what she was doing. The socks that were bunched at the tops of the hikers just left lots of leg to look at. And Cherry wasn't a typical redhead. She wasn't pale—she was almost olive skinned. Her legs were shapely—it was clear she either walked or ran a lot, or used to. And her ass—

"Doing okay?" Cherry asked, her voice cutting into Ellis's thoughts, thank God.

"I am. You?"

"Great." And she sounded it. Like she really was great. Her glance back to Ellis was heated, and she seemed to take a moment to find some words. At least, that's what it looked like to Ellis, like she was deciding what to say. She finally asked, "How's your sister doing?"

Ellis inhaled deeply, something she tended to do before talking about Michaela. "She's good. I mean, as good as she could be, right?"

"You said it was a car accident?" Cherry's steps slowed as she navigated her way along a rocky section of the bank of the stream. She glanced back quickly. "You don't have to talk about it if you don't want to. It's none of my business."

And something about that, something about the offer to *not* talk about it made Ellis feel the opposite. She wanted to talk about it, and that was rare. "I don't mind," she said and was surprised to realize she meant it. "Michaela struggled her whole life. Well, not her *whole* life. We actually had a pretty great childhood. But from the time she was a teenager on, she had lots of trouble."

"What kind of trouble?"

"Her looks. Her weight. Body image, though at the time, I don't think any of us really understood."

"Ugh. That's so hard."

"It is." Ellis did a hop-jump over a large protruding tree root. "Society is rough on women. It sets unattainable goals for us, then tells us we're failures if we don't reach them. Magazines, movies, models, television. And don't get me started on social media and how that skews our perception of ourselves. Yikes."

Cherry was quiet in front of her, so she assumed that meant she should continue.

"Anyway. Mikey struggled. Sometimes, she was happy, but mostly, she wasn't. Her weight went up and down. She got really thin. Then she'd gain weight." She paused as her brain tossed her a handful of images of her sister throughout their life, her body changing, her smile staying the same, her eyes always a little sad. Her voice went soft. "I always just thought she was beautiful."

"I'm sure she was," Cherry said, equally as quiet.

"Anyway, one day, my dad got a call that there'd been a car accident, that Mikey had hit a tree head-on."

"God."

"Yeah. Turns out they discovered in their investigation that she'd made no attempt to stop. There were no skid marks, nothing to indicate that she'd tried to steer away or hit the brakes." She cleared her throat and gave herself a moment for the emotion to settle before she allowed a bitter chuckle. "Clearly, she didn't count on the airbag."

"Ellis, I'm so sorry. That had to be so rough on you and your dad."

"I think it broke him," she said honestly and matter-of-factly. Cherry grimaced over her shoulder. "No, I do. He died of a heart attack, but I really think his heart was broken because of his daughter."

"Oh, Ellis," Cherry whispered.

"After he died, I went through the whole house and Michaela's apartment, had to get rid of things, decide what I wanted to keep. I found so much crap in Michaela's room and on her phone about dieting and the accounts she followed on Instagram and Snapchat and Tumblr were just…" She shook her head, still bothered by it all. "All these beautiful women wanting nothing more than to change everything about themselves." She sighed loudly. "The filters. The fad diets. The makeup. Telling her she should be or act or look a certain way, and most of the time, it was completely unrealistic. She never, ever looked in the mirror and saw what I did, how beautiful she was as a person. She never saw what she was. She only saw what she wasn't. It all just made me so sad."

"I can imagine."

"So." Ellis gave herself a mental shake. "You can imagine how much I'm not on social media and hate pretty much everything about it." She laughed and held up a hand, even though Cherry, walking in front of her, couldn't see it. "I know, I know, it makes me seem ancient, but I can't stand the deception online. There's so much of it."

She thought she saw Cherry nod but couldn't be sure.

"Anyway. Enough about that. How about this walk?" She frowned, annoyed at herself now for getting all preachy about things. "This place is beautiful."

Cherry stopped at a somewhat clear spot along the bank of the stream and seemed to just stare into the water.

"You okay?" Ellis asked as she sidled up next to her. She put a hand on her upper arm tentatively. "Listen, I didn't mean to get all judgy and weird just then. I think…" A bitter laugh escaped her lips. "I think I maybe have some unresolved issues around what happened." When Cherry looked at her, she made a face, and Cherry's surprisingly serious expression softened.

"It would only make sense if you did," Cherry said.

"Yeah." They stood quietly for a moment, just listening to the rush of water and the singing of birds overhead. "There's something about nature, isn't there?" Her voice was hushed. She didn't want to disturb the incredible sounds around them. "I feel like it can restore your faith in"—she shrugged—"life. Goodness. Show you that things you might think are huge are really just small drops in a bucket larger than you can possibly imagine."

"That's beautiful," Cherry said. "I love that."

Another half shrug and then Ellis looked down at their feet. "How are the new shoes?"

Slowly nodding, Cherry tipped her foot in different directions, held it at different angles. "Really, really great. Maybe a little hot, but I think they're waterproof, so that's probably why."

"Yeah? You should check and see." Ellis indicated the stream with her chin and grinned.

Cherry's smile grew, and something about seeing it after what felt like a long time of seriousness gave Ellis a sense of relief. Which she didn't quite understand. "I think I should," Cherry said, then reached out her hand. Ellis took it, the warm softness of Cherry's skin shooting a jolt straight to Ellis's center.

She swallowed hard.

Cherry stepped over a rock, then another, and set her foot directly into the water. She stayed shallow, as the boots were mid-cut, and she likely didn't want to finish the hike in wet socks.

"And?" Ellis asked.

Cherry tipped her head one way, then the other, as if deciding on her answer. Finally, she said, "Well, my foot is cold, but not wet. Very cold, in fact."

Her hand still in Cherry's, Ellis squatted down and stuck her hand in the stream…and yanked it right back out again. "Holy shit, that's freezing." She stood back up and tugged Cherry by the hand. "Come on. Out."

"Already?" Cherry teased. "How come?"

"Because if you fall in, I'm not jumping in to rescue you. Sorry. Too fucking cold."

"Fine. I see how it is." Cherry stepped back over the rocks, and her foot slipped. At least that's what Ellis thought happened because in the next second, Cherry was in her arms, Ellis having kept her from falling on her ass. When Cherry met her gaze, their noses were mere millimeters apart. "Oh. Hey."

"Hi," Ellis whispered, and she kissed her. Hard.

Cherry kissed her back without hesitation, and Ellis marveled at that. No uncertainty. No tentativeness. Just lips and tongue and hands and…

The loud snapping of a twig jerked them apart, and they turned their heads in tandem to see another couple—a man and a woman—walking by, on the trail rather than the bank of the stream, but clearly looking their way. Cherry waved at them, said hi, and asked them how they were doing.

"Not as well as you two," the guy said with a laugh and a thumbs-up. "Don't mind us. We're moving right along. As you were."

Ellis watched in fascination as a line of red inched up Cherry's neck and colored her face. But she was still smiling, and that made everything okay somehow. "So, PDA? Makes you blush?"

Cherry laughed and dropped her forehead to Ellis's shoulder. "I'm a redhead. Everything makes me look like I'm blushing."

"I disagree. You're not a typical redhead, and this is the first time I've seen you blush. It's really kind of adorable." And it was. Cherry lifted her head again, and those deep brown eyes held so much in that moment—promise, sensuality, expectation—that Ellis felt herself go a little light-headed. She had to take a step back with one foot to keep herself from falling right the hell over at the impact. Her mouth went dry, and she needed a beat to compose herself.

"Everything okay?" Cherry asked with a cute little tilt of her head.

"Mm-hmm," Ellis replied, then pecked her lips once before taking a subtle step back. Cherry gave her a look. Confusion? Uncertainty? Amusement? She wasn't sure. All she knew was that she needed to put a little space between them, so she could breathe again. Because that was the issue, wasn't it? Cherry literally stole her breath.

By unspoken agreement, they continued walking until they came to the cute little wooden bridge that crossed over the stream. They crossed it single file, Cherry still ahead. It turned the trail back on itself, so they were then heading the way they'd come.

Ellis forced herself to look around. To take in the trees and sunshine and nature itself. To inhale the scent of earth and sprouting flowers and spring. It was spring, and in Upstate New York, that was the marker for new beginnings, which wasn't lost on Ellis, the irony. The parallel to her current life situation. Was Cherry a new beginning?

As if sensing her pensiveness, Cherry slowed a step or two, so they walked side by side on the narrow trail, and something about Cherry's proximity seemed to calm things for Ellis. She couldn't explain it, but it simultaneously calmed her and freaked her the hell out. Which shouldn't have been possible, but totally was.

"I love this trail," Cherry said, her voice almost reverent. And then she inhaled deeply through her nose and held her arms out to her sides. When she dropped them back down, she bumped Ellis with a shoulder. "You having an okay time?"

"I'm having a great time. Thanks for inviting me." With a glance down, she asked, "How are the shoes holding up?"

"Amazing. Not a blister in sight." She kicked up a heel, then almost fell, and Ellis caught her. Again.

"Wow, you're really kind of a klutz, aren't you?" she said with a genuine laugh, and Cherry joined in. *Unless you're just trying to get me to kiss you again...*

"Maybe I just want you to kiss me again."

And who was she to deny the request of a beautiful woman? She kissed her again, softly, taking her time, sinking in. Nobody interrupted them this time.

The remainder of the walk back to the parking lot was made in very comfortable silence, and they held hands as they went. Ellis laughed to herself about how it felt both schoolgirlish and perfect at the same time, Cherry's warm, soft hand tucked snugly in hers. And when they finally reached Cherry's car, which was first in the lot, they turned to face each other, and she actually toed the ground, moved some pebbles around with her shoe, and then looked off into the distance.

"This was really nice," Cherry said, her voice quiet. "I'm so glad you came."

"I mean, can't have you breaking in new hiking shoes all by yourself. If I hadn't been here, you'd probably still be lying in the woods somewhere."

Cherry's laugh was cute, and her dark eyes crinkled at the corners, even as she looked away.

"So…it's the weekend," she began. The idea of spending more time with Cherry had been brewing throughout the walk. "Are you busy the rest of the day?"

"I've got some stuff to do, but my evening is open." Cherry leaned back against her car. "Wanna grab dinner?"

"Actually, I'd like to cook you dinner."

"Yeah?"

"Yeah."

"I didn't realize you cooked. I thought you were all manager-y."

"Listen, there's a lot you don't know about me." Her voice had turned a bit flirty, and she knew it. Let it happen.

"Yet," was Cherry's equally flirty reply. Then she leaned forward and kissed Ellis's mouth quickly. "Text me when, and what I can bring." Then she turned and got into her car, and Ellis was left feeling a little bit windblown, kinda tousled by the speed at which the plans had been made. She stepped back as Cherry backed her car out and left, and she decided she kind of liked that. The whirlwind. It was invigorating and energizing, and she'd never really been around anybody like that.

A deep inhale through her nose, and she headed for her car. If she was going to cook Cherry dinner tonight, she needed supplies.

CHAPTER TEN

Cherry hadn't taken enough photos in the woods. That fact was becoming clear as she sat with her phone and scrolled through the very limited selection. She did get a couple decent shots, both of the hiking shoes Peak had sent her and of the park itself. There was also one of Ellis that had very nearly taken her breath away. They'd been standing in a copse of trees, and the sun had to work hard to break through, individual rays pushing between leaves and branches, almost ethereal in their results. Ellis was standing near a big tree, her hand on its trunk, studying it, and Cherry remembered she'd been trying to ascertain which kind of tree it was. A ray of sunlight streaked across part of her face, leaving the rest shadowed, twinkling off her blond hair, highlighting the very light down on the side of her face near her ear, making her blue eyes sparkle a little extra. It was such a beautiful photo that she could hardly believe she'd taken it herself.

"Hey, bitch." Shea sauntered in and plopped down next to her on her bed. "Adam's cooking a late breakfast, so be nice and pretend to be hungry. And then tell him how good it was, even if it sucks, okay?" Before Cherry could answer, Shea leaned over to see what she was doing on her phone. "I am not ashamed to admit, that girl has me questioning my own sexuality."

The joke tugged Cherry out of her sexy daydream, which she needed because she had work to do before her dinner date. "She's ridiculously hot, isn't she? God."

"And things went well this morning?"

"The hikers were great. I'm about to edit some stuff together and give a little review."

She could feel Shea's eyes on her, and she didn't mean to audibly swallow, but she did.

"That's not what I meant, and you know it." Shea turned her body so she was facing Cherry. "You told her about Cherry on Top, right? And about the fake girlfriend?"

Another hard swallow before she met Shea's eyes. "I couldn't do it."

"What? Cherry. Come *on*. What are you doing?"

"No, you don't understand. She told me the details of her sister's accident." She reiterated the things Ellis had told her, emphasizing the issues her sister had had with body image and all the social media criticism she'd professed. "She hates everything about social media and has no accounts of her own. She hates what it does to women. She thinks people like me set unattainable standards."

Shea took a beat before saying gently, "I mean, she's not wrong, is she?"

Cherry was sure her shock was clear on her face. "I'm not *dangerous*, Shea. I don't make people want to drive their cars into trees. Jesus."

Shea put a hand on her leg, which was probably meant as comfort, but felt more like placating instead. "No, no, I don't mean that. Of course, you're not dangerous. I think…" She seemed to struggle to find the right words. "I guess I just mean there's a lot of truth to what Ellis said about social media."

Cherry wanted to argue. She really did. But the truth was, she hadn't thought about anything else since she'd left Ellis at the park, and she just didn't want to anymore. At least for a while. She waved a hand and didn't care if Shea saw it as agreement or dismissive. "It's whatever."

Shea stayed sitting next to her for several moments as she scrolled away from the shot of Ellis and back through photos of the hikers and the park and the trees and the stream. Finally, with a heavy sigh, Shea stood and left the room, and Cherry stopped focusing on her phone. Her gaze moved to the window, and she watched as the new leaves on the tree outside their building rustled in the gentle spring breeze. When she sighed and glanced at the doorway, Shea was there, leaning against the doorjamb, arms folded across her chest, but a sympathetic expression on her face.

"I really like her," Cherry whispered, and she could hear the helplessness in her own voice.

Shea nodded as she smiled softly. "I can tell."

"She's cooking me dinner tonight."

"Yeah? That's pretty romantic."

Cherry nodded. "She'll hate me when she finds out."

"You don't know that."

"How could she not, though? She blames people like me for what happened to her sister." God, saying it out loud made it feel so much worse, and she hadn't thought that was possible.

She expected Shea to come in and sit back down next to her, to talk her through, to make her feel better. But she did none of those things. Instead, she stayed where she was, and their gazes held across the room.

"Shea, when do I flip these?" Adam's voice called from the kitchen.

Shea mouthed, "Pancakes," and left to help. Which sent a wave of relief through Cherry because the direction things had been going just then was not a path she was ready to go down.

As if privy to the entire scene that had just transpired, her phone pinged with a text from Ellis.

Hey. Any food you hate? Allergies? I can't wait to cook for you! And then came a GIF of a kitchen on fire that made her laugh out loud.

And just like that, she felt better. Ellis was cooking her dinner tonight. At her apartment. Where things would go after that...She shook the thought away so as not to jinx anything.

She knew she had to come clean to Ellis. She knew it. She just didn't know how.

❖

"Why am I so nervous, Nugget?"

The cat was on the back of the couch, lounging and watching as Ellis stood in her very small kitchen and held her hands out in front of her, palms down. There was a noticeable tremor, and when she saw it, she closed them both into fists. Flexed her fingers. Shook her hands out.

She could cook. She wasn't worried about that. She'd become quite good after being on her own for so long. She had salmon ready to go into the oven. Sweet potatoes. Asparagus. She'd run it all by Cherry, and she didn't seem to be a picky eater at all.

The doorbell rang and she gasped as she glanced at the clock on the microwave. Six on the dot. Somehow, she'd completely lost track of time, because Cherry was there right when she'd told her to be. She took a deep breath and then gave her whole body a shake. *Here we go.*

She greeted her over the intercom and buzzed her in, and then, there she was. Standing at Ellis's front door, bottle of wine in her hands, looking…God, looking so absolutely breathtaking simply because she was her. She was dressed casually in jeans and a blue sweater, and her smile, well, it was completely clichéd, but it lit up the room. Easily.

"Hi, you," Cherry said as she held out the bottle. "I hope this works. I asked the woman at the wine store what goes with salmon." It was a bottle of semidry Riesling, and it would be perfect.

"This is great." She took the bottle and stood aside. "Please, come on in."

Cherry kissed her quickly on the mouth and walked by her, and the scent of vanilla and coconut made Ellis inhale deeply, quietly. Cherry went straight to Nugget.

"Well, hello there, my boyfriend Mr. Nugget. How are you today?" Cherry was clearly comfortable there and sat her butt right on the couch to love on Ellis's cat. And Ellis loved that, that she didn't hesitate. That she showed no uncertainty. Just walked in, plopped down, snuggled her cat. It was perfect in its ordinariness. Like a picture of normality. Of what home should look like.

Wait, what?

A shake of her head got her back to the moment, and she pasted on a grin. "Hungry? I'm just about to put the salmon in."

"Are you kidding? I've been thinking about this dinner all day."

"Really? Well, I'm flattered." She glanced over her shoulder as she bent to slide the salmon into the oven next to the sweet potatoes that had been baking for a while. "And also feel kinda sorry for you if this is the kind of dinner you think about all day."

"People who don't cook always look forward to being cooked for."

"No cooking for you?"

"I mean, I had to fend for myself growing up. I didn't starve, but

I also never got to the point where I *liked* cooking. And I kinda think that's the key to getting good." Her eyes had been focused on Nugget, but she glanced up, and there was a vulnerability there that Ellis hadn't seen before. It made her want to move around the couch and wrap her up in a hug. Instead, she slid the tray of asparagus out of the oven and gave it a toss before letting it continue to roast. "You like to cook, don't you?" Cherry asked.

"I do. But I didn't always." She set a timer and then held up the bottle of wine in question. At Cherry's nod, she opened it and poured as she spoke. "After my dad died and it was just me and Mikey left, I was kind of in the same boat as you. I was working two jobs and visiting Mikey at the facility, and I had to fend for myself, or I wasn't going to eat." She brought both glasses into the living area and handed one to Cherry, then took a seat next to her. "It didn't start as something I loved. Actually, it started out like a chore. It bugged me. I was irritated that I even had to do it."

"That's where I still am," Cherry said with a soft laugh, then held her glass up for toasting. "To you and the first dinner you cooked for me."

"The first of many." The words were out before Ellis had a chance to grab them, think about them, censor or even edit them at all.

But they didn't seem to bother Cherry. She just smiled and touched her glass to Ellis's. "Where's the bottle?" she asked, then got up to get it. She crossed the small room and arranged the bottle and their two glasses in a surprisingly photogenic way near the window, and it was still light enough for rays from the setting sun to cut through the Riesling and bounce off the glasses. She took several shots, and when she glanced back at Ellis with a grin, she told her, "Can't not take a photo of something so pretty, right?" And then she turned the phone toward Ellis and clicked off a couple shots of her, too.

She felt herself blush hotly and glanced down at her hands.

Cherry came back carrying both glasses, then bent down and kissed her softly on the mouth. Pulled back slightly and met Ellis's eyes and Ellis saw that Cherry's had gone impossibly darker. Cherry set down both glasses, then took Ellis's face in both hands and kissed her again. Slowly. Thoroughly. Taking her time and exploring. A soft moan filled the air, and it took a moment for Ellis to realize it was hers.

Cherry straddled her lap, her lips never leaving Ellis's as her ass settled into Ellis's hands, Cherry's hand sliding around to grip the back of Ellis's head as she pressed her tongue fully into her mouth.

The oven timer chose that moment to go off, and they jumped apart, startled. They both laughed and Ellis said, "I can't remember that timer ever sounding so loud or so obnoxious."

Cherry grinned and swung her leg over so Ellis was free, and she swiped one finger along the corner of Cherry's mouth, which was so fucking hot, it made Ellis let go of a little groan as she stood to check on dinner. "Killing me with that," she said as she shook her head.

"There's more where that came from," was Cherry's devastatingly sexy reply.

Another small groan.

Ellis only had a small, round table with two chairs, and she'd set it as nicely as she could with her mother's cream-colored dishes and deep green tablecloth. She hadn't gone so far as candles but now wished she had. Cherry brought the wine to the table, and she dished out the food.

"This looks amazing," Cherry said when Ellis set her plate in front of her, and she wasn't wrong, if Ellis said so herself. The salmon had cooked perfectly and looked like it had just been spatula'd off a television commercial and set on the bed of asparagus, and before Ellis's brain could even pull up the word *photogenic* again, Cherry was snapping a photo of her meal. "Absolutely gorgeous," she said quietly.

She refilled their glasses, then sat.

As they ate, it occurred to Ellis that she was both super comfortable and also incredibly nervous around Cherry. And how were both things possible at once? That didn't make any sense. But it was true. She didn't know how else to describe the way she felt. Nervously comfortable. Comfortably nervous.

"I'm so confused when I'm around you," Cherry said then, and Ellis snapped her head up in surprise.

"What do you mean?"

"I mean, I feel opposite things at the same time."

"Oh my God, me, too," Ellis said, a bite of her dinner on her fork in midair.

"Like…" Cherry set her fork down and looked toward the ceiling as if the answer was up there. "I'm super happy to be here. Relaxed. Comfortable. Nowhere else I'd rather be."

"Aw," Ellis said with a grin.

"At the same time?" Cherry held up one hand, palm down, fingers out, and the slight tremor was clearly visible. A clearly uncertain chuckle escaped her lips. "I'm shaking like a leaf because I'm nervous."

And the weirdest thing happened then. She couldn't explain it. But it was as if Cherry's nervousness canceled hers out. She suddenly felt completely, utterly calm. Relaxed. No nerves at all. Her gaze found Cherry's and held it. Cherry blinked at her, cheeks tinted pinked, and when her tongue peeked out to wet her bottom lip, Ellis felt an insistent flutter low in her body.

"Do you think maybe that's because there's a decent chance you'll be staying here with me tonight?" Yikes, did she say that out loud? Judging by the way Cherry's cheeks went deeper crimson, and the way her eyes got darker, and the way she swallowed so that Ellis could hear it, the answer to that question was a resounding yes.

And then Cherry seemed to pull herself together, to find her own control. She arched one eyebrow as she picked up her wineglass, and her eyes never left Ellis's. "I think that might be exactly the reason," she said quietly. Then she took a sip of her wine, and again, her gaze never left Ellis's and sweet baby Jesus on a skateboard, she'd never seen anything sexier in her entire life.

"I am so not interested in this food any longer."

"Me neither," Cherry said and stood. "Bring your wine."

With a glance over her shoulder and a sexy grin, she disappeared through the door to Ellis's bedroom.

CHAPTER ELEVEN

This was fast.

Cherry had never moved this quickly with anyone, and she never took the lead like this. Not once. Not that she'd had a ton of sexual partners, because she hadn't. She could count them on one hand. Okay, on three fingers. But she'd dated each of them for much longer than the mere less-than-a-month she'd been seeing Ellis. Hell, that she'd *known* Ellis. Less than a month! What the hell was she doing?

But when she turned back to the doorway and Ellis was standing there, all that hesitation, the uncertainty, insecurity, the sheer *insanity* of it all vanished like fog on a summer morning. Because there she was, this woman who'd had such an effect on her in only a handful of days. And she wanted nothing more than to touch her, to kiss her, to wring sounds from her and learn her body and watch her reactions. Study her. What she liked. What she loved. What would make her moan and writhe and beg, and the intensity of these thoughts pushed everything else out of her head. She set her wineglass on the nightstand, not taking even a moment to stop and take in the room, which was what she normally would've done. Look at the furniture, the colors, the style, all of which would tell her more about Ellis.

But there was no time.

Because if she didn't touch Ellis in the next few seconds, she was pretty sure she'd just burst into flames right there. Leave nothing more than a pile of ash on her bedroom floor.

Ellis stepped into the room, and the first thing Cherry noticed was that her bright blue eyes had gone dark. Hooded. When she blinked, it was slowly, her gaze never leaving Cherry's, and she took two more steps until there were mere inches between them. Ellis lifted her hand and brushed Cherry's hair off her forehead, tucked it behind her ear. They were very nearly the same height, Cherry only the slightest bit taller.

"God, you're beautiful," Ellis whispered, and the words sent a pleasant shiver through Cherry's body. Before she could reply—or even think about replying—Ellis's mouth was on hers. Instead of words, she made a sound. A whimper.

And then they were kissing. Hard. Making out. Deeply. Desperately. Yeah, that was the most accurate word. *Desperately*. It was like she couldn't get enough. She wanted more of Ellis. She wanted to get closer. To go deeper. To have more. She grasped Ellis's head with both hands and pushed herself as close as she could, dove in, pushed her tongue into Ellis's mouth, and this time, it was Ellis who whimpered.

That sound did things to her. Sexy things. Sexy, naughty things. And then she didn't think about anything else. She *couldn't* think about anything else. She merely acted, let her body lead the way. Her hands. Her mouth. She had no recollection of actually undressing Ellis, but she knew she did it because Ellis was suddenly naked, her bra dropping from Cherry's fingers to the floor. And oh my God, was she stunning. Cherry faltered then because the sight of her…*the sight of her*. Smooth pale skin and gentle curves and tousled blond hair and small, perfect breasts. The sudden feeling that hit her was a surprise: honor. It was actual honor, and she felt it in a wave. Honor and privilege washed over her as she reached out a hand to touch this gorgeous woman.

But Ellis caught her hand in midair, and the expression on her face was both sexy and playful as she waved one finger up and down in front of her. "Mm-mm. One of us is very overdressed. Hint—it's not me."

There was something indescribably sexy about undressing in front of Ellis in that moment. Cherry wanted to simply rip her own clothes off and throw Ellis onto the bed, but she forced herself to slow down. She pulled her sweater up over her head, then unfastened her jeans and left both items on the floor. Reaching behind, she unhooked her bra, intensely aware of Ellis watching her as she did so, and then her breasts were bare, and she swore to God she could feel Ellis's eyes on them. Roaming. Stroking. She swallowed hard and hooked her thumbs into the waistband of her underwear, slid it down her legs, and stepped out of it.

Both of them naked now, they stood quietly, looking at each other. This was new to Cherry as well. She'd had plenty of sex with her three partners, but it had always been right to the bed or the couch or the floor. There'd never been any standing naked in front of each other, so turned on you were sure you might spontaneously combust, your entire body aching to be touched. There'd never been any pausing to look. Just *look.* But that's where she was in that moment. On fire and desperate to have Ellis's hands on her, and there was that word again. Desperate.

Ellis was feeling it, too. Somehow, she knew that. A moment passed as they traveled each other's bodies with their eyes, but once their gazes met, it was as if something unlocked, as if the pause button was clicked off, and suddenly, they were on each other. Mouths crashed together and bodies pressed and breathing became ragged. Cherry didn't even realize they'd been moving until the backs of her thighs hit the bed and she tumbled backward onto the mattress, Ellis on top of her, the most delicious of weights. Her legs spread on their own, accommodating Ellis's hips, and when Ellis's stomach pressed into her center, Cherry understood how completely, almost embarrassingly wet she was.

"Oh my God," Ellis said, clearly also noticing. Her eyes met Cherry's and she asked, in the sweetest, most reverent tone Cherry had ever heard, "Do I do that to you?"

"You have no idea," Cherry said, then pulled her into a searing kiss as she wrapped her legs around Ellis's hips tightly.

Had it ever been this easy? This effortless? Because, while being with Ellis this way was exciting and erotic and sensual and completely blowing her mind, her crazy nervousness had all but abandoned her. Vanished like a thief in the night. She was exactly where she was supposed to be in that moment. And she knew it. She *felt* it. Somehow.

It became difficult to feel where she ended and Ellis began. It was like they were one being. Her hands were warm on Ellis's soft skin, and her tongue was waging a sensual battle with Ellis's in their kiss, and she was pretty sure that was Ellis's hand on her hip, her inner thigh, her—

She gasped as Ellis pushed into her. And then there was eye contact, hot and intimate, and Ellis's gaze never left hers as she set up a rhythm, slowly at first. Erotic. Cherry's hips started to move on their own, rocking, lifting into Ellis's hand, and it was like she had no say, no control. They just moved by instinct. She gasped when Ellis used her thumb to hit just the right spot, the rhythm picking up, and Cherry felt the orgasm careening toward her like a runaway freight train, barreling right for her, nothing she could do to get out of the way, not that she wanted to, and then it hit.

Oh God, did it hit.

Sparks and colors and sounds. Muscle tension. Arched back. Hips up off the bed. And sound. *Sound.* Cries. Moans. Whimpers. God, when did she become so vocal in bed? That was her, right? She barely recognized herself.

She came down slowly, needed time to recover. Her breathing was ragged, and her heart felt like it might pound itself right through her ribcage. And the entire time she was trying to regain control of herself, those blue eyes were trained on her, and Ellis was smiling like she'd just won the lottery.

"Wow," Ellis said quietly. "That was something else."

"Yeah? You should've been on this side of it." And Ellis's smile widened, and that did it. Cherry was suddenly recovered, at least enough to flip them—much to Ellis's surprise—so she was on top, Ellis looking startled and sexy beneath her. "In fact, let me demonstrate…"

❖

It was four a.m.

Ellis was awake. Awake, but sated. Warm. Thrilled. Smiling in the dark in the middle of the night like a weirdo. Cherry's breathing was deep and even. Had been for the better part of two hours now. She shifted in her sleep, winding herself even more around Ellis's body—which Ellis didn't think was possible—and snuggling her head in under her chin. Ellis tightened her grip and tried hard to remember the last time she'd been this physical with anybody. Ever. Once they'd begun, they'd had their hands on each other endlessly. *Endlessly*. Since Cherry had arrived, there'd barely been a moment that they hadn't been touching in some way. And it wasn't weird. It wasn't uncomfortable. It was perfect.

And then she was flashing back. This was how things had gone for her since Cherry fell asleep. She'd think about how different-slash-incredible-slash-inexplicably wonderful the night had been, and then her brain would toss her images of the previous hours and she'd relive them. And round and round and round.

The eye contact, though.

Yeah, the eye contact was a thing. A major thing for her. Ellis wasn't great at eye contact. It made her squirmy. Uncomfortable. She could do it, sure. She'd had job interviews and dates and such. She knew how important it was to look a person in the eye. But with Cherry? And in the midst of sex? It was easy. Natural. And kind of awesome. There was something so incredibly intimate about looking in another person's eyes while touching them in such an intimate way, and she realized that she'd never done that before. She hadn't had a ton of sexual partners in her life—a good-sized handful, maybe—but she'd never felt so connected to the other person. Not like she had with Cherry. Not like she still did with Cherry, and she pressed a gentle kiss to her forehead.

She must have drifted off at some point because the next thing she was aware of was the sliver of sun peeking over the horizon, viewable out her bedroom window. She was on her side now, and Cherry was snuggled tightly up against her back. Nugget purred loudly somewhere nearby, but she couldn't see him. She straightened her leg slightly—he was near the foot of the bed, and she nuzzled her toes up against him.

Comfortable was an understatement here.

Warmth. Safety. Comfort. She was experiencing all of it and didn't want to move. Like, ever. At the same time, she felt Nugget get up and pick his steps carefully until he was standing near her chest and touched his nose to hers.

"Oh, hey," she whispered to him, and he bumped her chin with his head. He meowed once to let her know it was time for breakfast, and she didn't want him to wake Cherry up, so she carefully slipped out from under her arm and then from under the sheets and stood, surprised and proud of herself for having managed such a feat.

Still naked, she grabbed a pair of joggers and an Old Navy T-shirt, dressed quickly, grabbed her phone, and herded Nugget out of the bedroom, closing the door behind them.

Spring in Upstate New York could be hit or miss, especially in the beginning. But it was already shaping up to be a beautiful day. The morning sky was a bright blue, white wisps the only signs of clouds. Out the living room window, she could see where Mrs. Carver, the woman who lived below her, had recently filled up her bird feeder. Chickadees sang happily as they ate, and a gang of sparrows were on the ground, cleaning up the leftovers, along with a pair of hefty gray squirrels. She lifted the window and watched for a moment, enjoying their cheer, and wondered if Nugget would want to sit on the windowsill later to stare at them. Or would that just be mean?

With a shrug, she headed into the kitchen to get him his food.

She set his bowl on the floor, filled the Keurig with water, and gave her phone a quick check, scanning the overnight report Hearts and Hands texted each morning. As usual, Michaela's night had been uneventful. Even though that had been the case every morning since settling her sister in, Ellis always had a brief moment of worry when she clicked open the text. It was a little silly, but it was regular.

"Morning," came a very sleepy voice from the bedroom doorway. Cherry stood there in a pair of Ellis's gym shorts and a white Nike T-shirt that was worn so thin, it left zero to the imagination, Cherry's nipples clearly visible. And giving her their own good morning greeting.

"Well, hello there. Coffee?" She tried unsuccessfully to keep her eyes off Cherry's breasts and got caught.

"Are you ogling me, ma'am?"

"I'm afraid I am, yes." Ellis grinned as she pulled two mugs from the cabinet.

"Maybe if you had shirts that were made of something more than tissue paper…"

"Maybe I very strategically placed that shirt where I knew you'd grab it. You don't know."

Cherry laughed and crossed the room—which only took a few steps, honestly—and came up behind Ellis as she popped a K-Cup in and hit the button. Wrapping her arms around Ellis's body, she pressed a kiss into her neck and squeezed her gently. "Good morning again."

Something about being hugged from behind, something about feeling Cherry's entire body up against hers, it did things to her. Sexy things. She turned in Cherry's arms and kissed her soundly on the mouth, which, of course, called up many, many happy details from the night before, and in less than a second or two, they were kissing deeply,

Ellis pushing Cherry up against the counter and bracing her hands on either side of her.

The coffee maker beeped its conclusion, and they pulled apart slowly, staying close enough that the tips of their noses brushed. "Last night was amazing," Cherry whispered.

"I wholeheartedly agree with that," Ellis said back and kissed her once more before reaching to switch out the coffee cups. She handed the full one to Cherry. "You have some time today? What should we do? Brunch?"

"Oh my God, I love brunch. Yes, please. Except…" Cherry looked down at herself. "I'll have to go home and change. Can we meet there?"

"Where?"

"Wherever brunch is?"

They took their coffee to the couch, and Ellis tried not to think about how completely normal, how utterly natural it felt to spend the morning drinking coffee and listening to the birds with Cherry. It was like they did it all the time. Like they'd already done it a hundred mornings.

Nugget sat on the windowsill chittering at the birds down below. "He doesn't seem agitated," Cherry said, tipping her head and watching the cat. "It's more like he's just…talking to them."

"Right? I was wondering if he'd, I don't know, claw the screen or shriek at them or something."

"Shriek at them? You haven't had many cats, have you?" Cherry's grin was teasing.

"Just the one," Ellis said, smiling back.

Cherry's phone pinged, and she picked it up from the coffee table and read the text. Her eyebrows knit into a V above her nose. She typed back quickly, then set the phone down.

"Everything okay?"

"Mm-hmm." Cherry nodded once. "Just Shea."

"Ah." She was lying. Ellis knew it. She wasn't sure how she knew it, but she did. She gave it five seconds to bug her, then decided she'd let it go. Cherry didn't owe her explanations for anything.

"How about we go to Carlson's for brunch?" Cherry's face lit up as she spoke. "They have bottomless mimosas."

"Listen, anything bottomless? I am in."

Chapter Twelve

Carlson's was never not busy.

"I've probably been here for brunch or lunch or dinner upward of twenty times," Cherry said to Ellis as they stood in a small crowd by the door near the greeter's podium. "It's like this every time. Packed. No matter what time. And I always feel like I somehow get the last table left." Owned by the Carlson family, duh, the restaurant had been a fixture in downtown Northwood for nearly fifty years. It was an area of the city that started out a bit sketchy when the restaurant first opened, then improved as the years went on, and was now part of Jefferson Square, one of the trendier Northwood neighborhoods. Carlson's definitely had staying power.

As usual, when she and Ellis arrived, the place was overflowing with people, and it looked like they'd have to wait. But the greeter waved them her way, grabbed two laminated menus, and ordered them to follow her to a small table for two in the corner by the window.

"See?" Cherry said in awe. "Again. Last table left. Every time."

"It's clearly a tradition you need to uphold," Ellis said as they sat.

"I mean, I can try." She caught Ellis's eye and it held. That sizzle ran between them, leftover from both last night and this morning when they'd gone into the bedroom to gather Cherry's things and had ended up back in bed. Cherry shifted in her chair, felt a subtle soreness in the muscles of her inner thighs, and she liked it. A lot. She could feel a slight heat in her neck, her cheeks.

"Flashing back, are you?" Ellis asked quietly, eyes on her menu, but a smirk on her beautiful face.

"*Maybe*," Cherry said, drawing the word out.

"Glad to hear I'm not alone." Ellis flipped her menu over. "What's good here?"

"Honestly, a better question would be what's not good here. And the answer to that would be nothing. I've never had something here that I haven't enjoyed. Ever."

"Well, that narrows it right down. Thank you for your help."

"Always happy to be of assistance."

The waitress came by, looking slightly haggard but smiling anyway, and took their orders for food and mimosas. The drinks arrived only a couple minutes later, and Ellis said, "I wonder if they have a pitcher of them made up back there."

"Can you make a pitcher of mimosas?" Cherry asked. "I guess I don't see why you couldn't. I just never thought about it before." She arranged their glasses so they were next to each other, but one was slightly in front. Then she moved the little bud vase on the table so it was behind the glasses, its single daffodil giving the photo a pop of color and accentuating the color of the orange juice. She angled her camera so the sunshine from the window next to Ellis created a ray shooting through, then bouncing off the glasses. "Gorgeous," she said quietly as she snapped the photo. She could feel Ellis's eyes on her. She liked that.

"Always after that perfect photo, huh?" The voice came from behind Cherry and startled her enough to make her whole body flinch. When she turned her head, Andi was standing next to her, her hand grasped in Julianne's. "Hey there."

Cherry felt her heart jump in her chest. Like, literally felt it bang into her ribs at the sight of Andi, who was now looking from her to Ellis and back. "Hey," she managed to croak out.

Andi stuck her hand out toward Ellis. "Hi. Andi Harding. This is my wife, Julianne."

Ellis's smile was warm and friendly. Of course it was. Why wouldn't it be? She shook Andi's hand, then nodded toward Julianne. "Ellis Conrad. Nice to meet you both."

The waitress showed up then—thank freaking God—with two plates of food, and there was a bit of a traffic jam, given the people coming and going, and Andi gave her a sympathetic look.

"Sorry! We'll get out of your way," she said, then ducked under the plate the waitress held up and gave a quick wave. "We'll talk another time."

And then Andi and Julianne were gone, and food was on the table, and Cherry felt a relief like she'd never known. And she hated herself for it.

"Oh my God, this looks so good," Ellis said, looking down at her Belgian waffle topped with strawberries and whipped cream. As she picked up her fork, she asked, "How do you know those guys?" She used her chin to point in the direction Andi had gone.

"Through work," Cherry said, which wasn't exactly a lie. "You're gonna let me have some of that whipped cream, right?" Yes, it was a massive change of subject, but Ellis didn't seem to mind.

"Maybe they'd let us just take it home and then we can do other things with it." Ellis winked at her.

"Maybe they will. Or maybe we can make our own."

"Or buy a can ourselves." At Cherry's puzzled look, Ellis added, "Easier to spray than to spread, if you get my drift."

And that was all it took for Cherry's mind to run away with her, imagining being in bed with Ellis, spraying whipped cream on her naked body, then licking it off…

"You did catch my drift, judging by that dreamy face you're making." Ellis forked a bite of waffle into her mouth and looked very, very pleased with herself.

She cleared her throat and knew she was blushing but didn't care. "Your drift was not hard to catch, trust me." She busied herself by cutting into her spinach and cheddar omelet and then took a bite. Even with her brain as preoccupied as it was, she had no choice but to stop and savor the food. "Oh my God, *so* good." She pointed her fork at her plate and raised her eyebrows in question. They traded bites. "I just want to say again how happy I am that you're not against sharing food."

"You've experienced the opposite, sounds like." Ellis popped a bite into her mouth and waited for her to elaborate.

"I went on two dates with somebody once who was very much against sharing their food. Not even a taste. Two dates was enough for me."

"I mean, part of the joy of going out to eat with somebody is that you get to taste their food, too, right?"

"Exactly."

"Exactly." Ellis pointed her fork at her to punctuate the statement. Then they ate quietly for a moment before she added quietly, "It's really easy with you. You know?"

Cherry looked up and into those eyes and yes, she knew exactly what she meant because she felt it, too. The ease. The comfort. The lack of worry. Well, the lack of most worry… "I do know," is what she said.

They ate the rest of their meals and had a second round of mimosas, and it was simple and casual and one of the best times Cherry could remember having over brunch. When the bill came, she snapped it up, ignoring all Ellis's protests.

"Nope. You cooked for me last night, and it was amazing. The least I can do is buy brunch."

With a sigh of defeat, Ellis said, "I get it the next time."

"Oh, there's going to be a next time, is there?" she asked, injecting a playful lilt into her tone.

Ellis leaned her forearms on the table and reached for Cherry's hand. Her voice held no such lilt. "I hope there are going to be many more next times."

So fast. God, so fast. The words shot through her head again, but somehow, the speed didn't scare her. Just like last night. She knew they'd moved *way* faster than she'd ever think was okay if Shea or Adam told her they thought they were falling hard for someone in less than a month. Somehow, though, she didn't care. Because it felt so perfect, even though she couldn't explain how or why or whether she should be running the other way as fast as she could. It just felt *right*. She squeezed Ellis's hand. "I hope so, too."

They stood up and gathered their things. Once out on the sidewalk, Cherry was reminded what a gorgeous day it was turning out to be. Bright sun, blue skies, low seventies. They fell in step, side by side on the way to the parking lot where'd they'd parked in adjacent spots.

"You got big plans for your day?" Ellis asked.

"That sounds like you're leaving me for today," Cherry said and hoped she didn't sound as clingy as she suddenly felt.

"I'm sorry," Ellis said with a frown. "I need to go spend some time with my sister."

"Of course," she said and gave her head a shake. "I'm sorry. Of course. Go be with your sister."

Ellis stopped her with a hand on her arm and turned her so they were face-to-face. She seemed to wait to speak until Cherry looked her in the eye, and then she said softly, "I had an amazing time with you. Last night. This morning." She gave her head a shake and looked off into the distance. "I don't know where you came from, but I'm really glad you're here."

And those words were everything, weren't they? Cherry felt herself warm from the inside, and she touched Ellis's face with her fingertips. "I'm glad I am, too."

❖

For the first time, Ellis understood what people meant when they said they were walking on clouds. She felt like she was floating along, her feet not touching the ground as she moved through her day. No control over the smile on her face that wouldn't leave, and when was the last time that happened? She drifted into the Hearts and Hands parking lot like her car was also floating, a vehicle from a cartoon future.

Inside, she waved to various staff and residents and residents' family members, all the while smiling and not looking like a weirdo. She hoped.

"Hello, dear little sister of mine," she said happily as she breezed into Michaela's room. Her sister was sitting in a chair today, which happened from time to time. She faced the window, her blue eyes open and unseeing.

Ellis went around to that side of the bed and pulled up a second chair so she sat in her sister's line of sight. As she did every time, she wondered if Michaela could see her. And if not, what *did* she see? Anything? Her own world? Ellis's joy slipped just a bit as she scooted her chair a little closer and brushed some hair behind Michaela's ear. "You look pretty today. Want me to do your hair?"

Michaela always had the most beautiful hair. Long and thick and a deep chestnut brown. She was always envious of Ellis's blond hair, but Ellis always loved Michaela's. She arranged her chair so she was behind her sister, then grabbed the brush from the dresser and began with long, gentle strokes. Michaela's hair had just the slightest body to it to keep it from being pin-straight, unlike Ellis's waves. People laughed that they hardly looked like siblings at all. Different hair color, different builds, differently shaped faces—until you got to their eyes.

They both had the exact same blue eyes. Same shape. Same shade of azure blue. From their mother.

Ellis could tell Michaela had had a shower that day. She smelled like soap and the cherry-almond lotion Ellis kept her supplied with. Her hair was fresh and soft and brushing it lulled Ellis into an easy, relaxed state, which let her mind drift. And of course, it drifted right toward the girl with sunset hair.

She continued brushing Michaela's hair for a while, continued to replay memories of Cherry, and the room was quiet. Finally, she set the brush down and told Michaela she was going to go get something to drink. "Be right back," she said and kissed the top of her sister's head.

In the community kitchen of the house, she was making herself a cup of coffee when she glanced out the window above the sink and noticed Kendra. Just sitting and watching the yard. Thinking she'd only been scheduled for the morning, she wondered if Kendra was decompressing before heading home. With a smile, Ellis made a second cup and carried both out to the back patio.

"Hey, you," Kendra said with a smile, which got bigger when Ellis handed her a mug. "You read my mind."

"You all done?" Ellis sat in the chair next to her.

"Yup. Just taking a few minutes before I head out." Then she sat back in her chair, making no move to leave, and they sipped and listened to the birds. "Gorgeous out today."

"It sure is. I love days like this." They were quiet for several minutes before Kendra turned to her. "What's new with you?" Ellis turned to her and smiled and felt the heat seep into her face. "Oh, there is definitely something new." Kendra's laugh filled the space.

"Well," she said softly, "I spent the night with Cherry last night." And there was a beat, a moment of stillness, just before Kendra let out what could only be described as a schoolgirl squeal of delight.

"Oh my God, that's amazing! I'm so happy for you." Kendra scooted to the edge of her chair. "And? Details, ma'am. I need the details."

"It was…God, Kendra, it was incredible. She's so…" She stopped and looked up at the sky as she searched for the right words. "She's easy. I'm relaxed with her. She makes me feel beautiful. And sexy. And wanted."

"And when was the last time you felt like that?"

Ellis was flooded by a wonderful warm feeling. "It's been a long time. A really, really long time." She told her the whole story. From the hike to the dinner invite to actual dinner to the limb-melting sex. She didn't stop talking for what felt like hours, couldn't stop if she wanted to. It was like the words had minds of their own and just kept dropping out of her mouth.

Kendra's grin made her feel less embarrassed about the babbling, and when she finally was able to get a word in, she reached across to Ellis's chair and closed her hand over her arm. "Ellis, I am *so* happy for you. You deserve this." She tightened her hold and ducked a bit to catch Ellis's eyes. "You. Deserve. This."

Her body kept doing things without her permission, and this time, it was her eyes. They welled up at Kendra's words, and she gave a quick nod. "I mean, it's not like we're in love or getting married. But I like her. I like her a lot."

"That's a good start right there." Kendra loosened her grip, patted Ellis's arm, and sat back again.

"It is, right?" A deep breath helped her shake off the emotion, and things went back to comfortable silence for a few minutes.

"Hey, how's the writing job you were talking about?"

A half shrug. "It's fine. Actually, I got another article to write up. Something about a grocery store that claims their meat is never frozen receiving a frozen meat delivery."

"Scandalous," Kendra said with an eye roll.

"I know, right?" She took a sip of her coffee. "You know what, though? It's kinda fun, writing these articles. I mean, if you don't want your stuff exposed, don't lie about it. Pretty simple."

Kendra snorted a laugh. "If there's one thing I've learned in my thirty-plus years of life, it's that nothing is as simple as it should be. Especially lies."

Later that night, as Ellis sat at her laptop working on the article for *The 11th Commandment*, she thought about Kendra's words. About lies being complicated. Were they, though? Was the truth really that hard? She tried to think about something big she'd lied about in her life. She wasn't perfect, duh, of course she'd told lies. Who hadn't? But most of the time, they were to save somebody's feelings. Like telling somebody their ugly haircut looked nice or that an outfit did *not* make them look frumpy.

Lies were what ruined Michaela. Lies about beauty. Lies about weight. Lies about fitness. Lies about what made a person attractive, popular, *worthy*. Lies about life in general. They were what made her feel less-than and ugly and gave her impossible, completely unattainable goals. They were what made her decide that not living at all was better than living as she was.

No. She wasn't convinced.

Life was complicated, yes.

The truth was not.

Chapter Thirteen

Focusing was hard.

It shouldn't have been. Cherry was good at this. Posting online was her favorite thing. The deciding on which photo worked best. Choosing the best lighting. Editing was a blast. She loved that part. And don't get her started on filters. They were so much fun to mess with. She'd gone through her park photos already but hadn't posted yet, so she was back at it. Sifting through. Shots of her feet in the hikers from Peak—damn, they looked good. A few nature shots—sunlight through leaves, the sparkling water of the creek. A few selfies in the park. But there was still that one shot. Of Ellis, rays of sunshine bouncing off her golden hair as she looked up at a maple tree. Cherry swallowed hard. Ellis had been unaware of the photo. Hell, Cherry hadn't even been aware she was taking it until she'd already pressed the button, heard the shutter click sound.

And now, here it was. That one shot. Taking all her attention. All her focus. Not allowing her to think of anything else except Ellis. Her face. Her hands. Her mouth. God, her mouth…

"Hey, bitch."

Thank the sweet Lord above for the interruption. She almost got up and kissed Shea because *thank you.* "Sup, bitch," she said back, forcing a smile onto her face and fake cheer into her voice. Which didn't work on Shea. It never worked on Shea.

"Why are you being a weirdo?"

"What? I'm not."

"Your eyes are all wide and your voice is high. What's wrong?"

"Nothing. Just editing my hiker shots." She turned back to the computer and clicked back on the shoes, sending Sunshiney Ellis back into the photo file.

"I thought you did that already." Shea came up behind her to look at photos over her shoulder. "Oh, that's a good one." She pointed to a particular shot she'd taken as she'd stepped up onto a fallen tree trunk. Shea watched Cherry work for a few more minutes, then dropped a kiss onto the top of her head. "It's Taco Tuesday, don't forget," she said as she backed out of the room.

"Got it," Cherry called, lifting a hand in a wave, but still not looking back at her. She was afraid Shea would be able to read her like a book, because now, not only had she still not told Ellis about her online persona, she'd slept with Ellis and hadn't told her, and she was drowning in guilt. She tried to shake off the uneasy feeling that had been creeping in, slowly but steadily, for the past week or two.

With a sigh, she switched from her laptop to her phone. Smaller screen, but easier to navigate the filters and editing tools. She posted the hikers, made sure to tag Peak and give her honest thoughts in review form. Maybe they'd send her more stuff. She swiped through her photos and came across the one of the mimosas. The lighting was perfect, and she'd used portrait mode, which made the edges of the flutes practically invisible, like the liquid was floating in the air all on its own. Too gorgeous to pass up. She posted it, along with a caption that read, *Beautiful cocktails, beautiful date, beautiful Sunday morning*, before she could second-guess herself.

The wonderful aroma of taco seasoning wafted into the room, and she forced herself to set aside the worry and the uncertainty of the situation and focus on the present. And the tacos.

In their tiny kitchen, Adam was stirring up the ground beef and seasonings while Shea was chopping up tomatoes and black olives and lettuce to put in little bowls so they could each build their own taco creations. It was what they did on the last Tuesday of every month, and it was one of Cherry's favorite things. 'Cause time with her friends was important. So were tacos. She wrapped her arms around Adam from behind and gave him a squeeze.

"Hey, handsome," she said and kissed his shoulder. Which was hard as a rock. She poked at it. "Wow. Been living at the gym again? Who is it this time?"

"It's Jared," Shea supplied before Adam could answer. "Successful Northwood Realtor and recent bar regular."

"Recent bar regular? Huh. I wonder what's drawing him there," Cherry said, tapping her finger against her lips and pretending to be all pensive as she munched on some cheddar Shea was shredding.

"It's a puzzle," Shea said with a shrug. "A mystery."

"I can't figure it out," Cherry said.

"You guys are hilarious," Adam said with a shake of his head and a not-very-hidden grin and some pink in his cheeks.

"My dude, are you *blushing*?" she asked.

"No," Adam scoffed.

"Totally is," Shea agreed.

"That's the most adorable thing I've ever seen," Cherry told him, then gave him a bump with her hip.

"Both of you can fuck right off," he told them, but his tone was teasing and the smile stayed.

"I hope that ground beef isn't from Becker's." Shea pointed her knife at the skillet.

"Why not?" Adam asked.

"I saw an article on that site, *11th Commandment*? Becker's says their meat is always fresh, never frozen, yet they have freezer trucks delivering meat there. They got caught. Broke the eleventh commandment, man."

"Ugh, I hate that site," Cherry said, getting more cheese out of the fridge. "Always up in everybody's business."

"You don't think people deserve the truth?" Adam asked.

Cherry looked at Shea, who wisely stayed quiet. "I mean, I do, but not if it means people spying on other people. They posted an article once about the gender of that one judge's baby before her family even knew about it. Invasion of privacy, if you ask me. And seriously, who cares?"

Shea grunted softly and Adam shrugged. "Truth," he said.

The three of them worked together to get all the taco fixings ready. Then they carried everything out to the living room, set it all up on the coffee table, and built tacos. Sitting on the floor around the table, they ate and watched *The Great British Baking Show*.

"I love this tradition," Shea said, and Cherry exchanged grins with

Adam over her head because she said the same thing on every single Taco Tuesday.

"Me, too," Cherry said. "Though I feel a little bad that we're eating something as simple as tacos while these people are making four-tier themed wedding cakes."

"And being nice to each other while they do it," Shea added.

"Speaking of being nice to each other," Adam said as he focused on Cherry. "How about you be nice to me and give me some details on your new girl? Since Shea seems to know everything and I know nothing, not even that you got laid on Sunday, because you didn't tell me." He crunched into a taco and stared at her expectantly as he chewed.

It was her turn to blush. She felt the heat in her cheeks and Adam's satisfied smile only confirmed it.

"That good, huh?" he asked.

"It's..." She glanced down, lifted one shoulder. "Yeah. It's that good. She's pretty incredible."

"Aw, look at you." Adam reached around Shea and gave Cherry's shoulder a squeeze. "I can't remember the last time I saw you this happy."

"It's been a while," Shea agreed. There was a beat and then she added, "Also, why aren't we drinking margaritas? Who was in charge?"

Cherry and Adam both fixed their gazes on her.

"Me? I was? Oh, shit. Sorry, guys." Shea jumped up and headed for the kitchen. "One pitcher of margs, coming up."

When she was out of sight, Cherry whispered, "Um, weren't *you* in charge of margaritas?"

"I don't know what you're talking about," Adam said, then gave her a wink before his expression grew more serious. "Really, though, I'm happy for you, Cher. It's nice to see you smiling."

She scooted closer and dropped her head to his shoulder. "Thanks, Adam." She was happy. It was true, and her friends could see it. That was huge. She wasn't a person who was terribly open with her feelings. Her childhood had taught her how dangerous that could be. For the most part, she was a fairly stoic person, so to have her friends actually notice and comment on her happiness...that was new. And it was thanks to Ellis.

Maybe the next Taco Tuesday, she'd join them.

"So," Shea said a little while later when they'd finished their tacos and were watching Brits make trifles. "She made you dinner."

"She did."

"Which means it's your turn to come up with a date." Shea nodded in expectation. "Yes?"

Cherry tipped her head from side to side. "Yeah, that makes sense."

Poking a finger toward the TV, Shea said, "Watching all these sweets reminded me of something I saw online yesterday. I think I've got your next date."

❖

Our mother was beautiful. Well, by societal standards, I mean. She was beautiful in general, but when I say by societal standards, I mean she was thin and blond and tan and everything Hollywood says points to beautiful. And I think that made it harder on Michaela because she wasn't built like our mom. She was built more like our dad. Solid. Muscular. Also beautiful, but not in the way she wanted to be. It made me sad for her then and it still makes me sad even now, as I sit near her bed and watch her unmoving face and her unseeing eyes.

Ellis stopped typing and glanced to her left to look out Michaela's window at the birds gathered on the feeder. Spring had shown up solidly, and the seasonal birds were slowly coming back. The goldfinches and grosbeaks flitted from tree to feeder and back again, and Ellis remembered how much her mother had adored birds. How she'd sit and have her tea on the porch and just watch, a gentle smile on her face.

"Any hummingbirds yet, Mikey?" she asked quietly. She'd recently picked up a hummingbird feeder, filled it with sugar water, and hung it off to the side of the yard, where it was still visible from Michaela's room. "They'll find it. Give 'em time. It's still early in the season."

Her phone pinged a text notification and she slid it out of her back pocket. Cherry. She felt the smile appear all on its own with no thought or permission from her brain. Cherry had that effect on her.

Hi, sexy. Just thinking about u.

She did that a lot, Cherry. Sent texts just to say hi or that she was thinking about Ellis or that she saw or heard or tasted something that reminded her of Ellis. It was new and it was nice and Ellis had no idea what to do with it, but she'd take it.

Yeah? How come? she typed back.

The dots bounced for what felt like a long time, but then she realized it was because a photo was loading. When it arrived, Ellis blinked at it in surprise.

It was a shot of her from their hike. She'd been looking at a maple tree, trying to figure out if it was in fact a maple tree. She hated getting her picture taken, always thought she looked surprised or alarmed or had crazy eyes. But this one? It was beyond flattering. The lighting was perfect, rays of sunshine filtering through the new leaves on the tree and beaming over her like small spotlights. They made her hair glow, looking much more golden than it was. Even her eyes looked gorgeous, big and blue as she looked toward the top of the tree.

Hello? Still there? popped through next, along with a grimacing emoji.

Still here. Just admiring myself a bit too much. And a sunglasses emoji. *You're quite the photographer.*

Dots bounced and then came, *All I did was hit the button. The subject was already beautiful.*

She stared at the text for a long moment, surprised by the use of the word beautiful, especially since she'd just been using it in her writing. She'd never considered herself beautiful, but the fact that Cherry did made her feel…Well, it did things to her. Sent flutters through her belly. Tightened everything lower than that.

Unsure of the right words, she sent a blushing emoji.

How's your sister? was the next text.

Fine. She used to say things like *same as always* or *the usual* when her dad asked, but at some point, that started to feel disrespectful. *Fine* wasn't exactly full of description and could even be looked at as off-putting, but it was the truth. Michaela was fine. She'd always be fine. She'd never be more than fine.

Good. Diner in the am. And then a GIF of a cat working on a laptop came next. *You'll be there?*

Her heart did that thing that writers called skipping a beat. She was pretty sure that's not what actually happened, but it did kind of feel that way. And hers always felt like that when she knew she was going to see Cherry again soon.

I'm always there, she texted back, added an emoji with swirly eyes, and then she made herself a reminder to snag two extra biscuits when they came out of the oven for her. Cal wouldn't mind. He never minded. He liked Cherry, too. *Having a good night?*

It's Taco Tuesday, so YES. Several tacos followed, enough so Ellis laughed through her nose.

Jelly over here.

Bouncing dots and then, *You're invited to the next one.*

I'm in, she typed back.

A few more back-and-forths and then Cherry got a phone call and had to go. Ellis went back to the book, but her focus was gone by then. Her head was filled with nothing but creamy skin and sunset hair, and it made her happy when she thought about how often that happened.

"Well, that's quite a smile you've got there, my friend." Evan stood in the doorway of Michaela's room, leaning on the doorjamb, arms folded across his chest. His dark skin made the lime green sweater he wore pop, and Ellis was so glad to see him, she jumped out of her chair and almost lost the laptop. Once it was put safely on a table, she threw her arms around him and hugged him close. "That's the best greeting I've gotten from anybody in a long time. Including my wife." Evan laughed and Ellis inhaled his scent, a combination of his aftershave and whatever fabric softener he and Kendra used on their laundry.

"I feel like I haven't seen you in weeks," she said, not wanting to scold him, but knowing it kind of came out that way.

"I know," he said and bowed his head for a second. "Work has been kicking my ass. I'm sorry."

"Forgiven. I'm just so happy to see your face." It was true. She was close to Kendra. Loved her. But Evan was like a brother and a best friend all rolled into one. They'd clicked immediately, both of them knowing they'd be friends for life. No idea why or how, just that it *was*.

"Hey, Mikey," he said and gently grabbed one of her toes, gave it a little wiggle. "How's your day going?" Something else she loved about him—he always, always said hello to Michaela. She probably couldn't hear him. Likely had zero idea about it or concern if he didn't say hi, but he always did. He never treated her like she was just a body lying there in the room.

"You here to pick up Kendra?" she asked, glancing at her watch and then widening her eyes. It was later than she thought, and she had to get home to feed Nugget.

"Yes, ma'am, but I wanted to come and see my two favorite sisters." He took a seat. "And I wanted to see how things were going. A little bird told me you've been seeing somebody pretty seriously. True?"

He was hurt she hadn't talked to him about it. She could see it on his face. And honestly? She felt guilty about that.

"It's happened so fast, though," she said, and it was the truth. Something she tried not to think about for fear of sending herself into a panic. "Like, crazy fast."

He shrugged. "Doesn't matter if it's right, you know?" He seemed to study her face, to look into her eyes as if trying to find something. "Is it right?"

"I mean…" She nibbled on the inside of her cheek. "I'm afraid to say."

"Don't wanna jinx it."

"Exactly."

"Fair enough. But you're smiling pretty big and you seem lighter. So I'm gonna guess that it's feeling right." He held up a hand. "You don't have to say it."

"You get me." And he did. It was part of why they got along so well. She rarely had to explain herself to him.

"I like seeing you like this." He waved a finger up and down in front of her. "Looks good on you."

"What does?" How was she acting any different?

"The smile. The spring in your step."

Her smile grew wider. She could feel it. And she knew that Cherry had altered her demeanor a bit, but she'd had no idea it was visible to other people.

"Like I said," Evan told her, "looks good on you." Her face warmed. "So does the blush," he added with a wink.

She covered her face with her hands and blushed some more.

Chapter Fourteen

It always amused Ellis when something like a regular, perfectly normal Wednesday was intensely busy at the diner. There was rarely any rhyme or reason to it. It just was, and it happened every so often.

Kitty was running around at double her usual speed, pro that she was. Cal was flipping eggs and pancakes and mixing biscuit dough like his life depended on it. The two other waitresses didn't stop moving, and Ellis stayed out front to help, wiping tables, filling water glasses, getting people seated. She didn't mind at all because if she was out front, she was able to steal looks and send winks to the hot redhead at the corner table who'd glance at her over the rim of her sexy glasses whenever she got the chance.

"You two are ridiculous," Kitty whispered at her behind the counter as she scooped pie onto plates. "All flirty and having eye sex with each other."

Ellis burst out laughing. "Excuse me?"

"And also, you're adorable and I'm jealous."

"That I'm not eye-sexing you?" Ellis winked.

Kitty barked a laugh. "Maybe twenty years ago, honey." Then she bumped her with a hip and left to deliver her pie, and Ellis had to give props to the customer, because who didn't want pie for breakfast?

As usual, things started to clear out a little after nine, nine thirty, until there were only Cherry and four other regulars left. The two retired gentlemen who met every Wednesday for coffee and gossip. The bearded guy with his AirPods in and the strawberry-blond woman that always had a book. She had today's propped up enough to see, the new Nora Roberts.

"Hi," Ellis said as she warmed up Cherry's coffee, then plopped into a seat across from her. "I'm the manager here, and I was hoping to get some feedback from you on your experience today."

Cherry slid her glasses off her face—something Ellis was shocked to find an undeniably sexy maneuver—set them down, then propped her chin in her hands, making a big show of choosing her words. "Well, I'm not gonna lie. The food is terrific. Those biscuits?" She gave a little full-body shudder. "To die for. The service is great, always. But today? My favorite thing today was the eye candy."

"Eye candy, you say?" Ellis cocked her head to one side.

"Yes, that sexy blond chick that flitted around pretending to wipe tables, but who was actually just out here to flirt with me? You know who I mean?"

"Hmm. Sounds vaguely familiar."

"Definite eye candy, that one. And very much appreciated. Made my morning much more pleasant. If you could pass that along to management, I'd be grateful."

"I'll be sure to send that directly to the owner," Ellis said and knew she was sporting a goofy grin.

"She should get a raise."

"I'll bring that up, too."

"And make many, many more appearances."

"Noted." It was Ellis's turn to prop her chin in her hand, and they sat that way, and it was something about them she was beginning to love—that they could just look at each other without words, and it wasn't weird or uncomfortable. She wasn't always great with silence. Maybe that was from all the time spent with her nonverbal sister, but she always felt like she needed to fill in the silences with her own voice, even when she didn't have anything to say. With Cherry? She didn't feel that. With Cherry, the silence was companionable. Easy. Plus, she liked to just look at her.

"Are you busy Friday night?" Cherry asked quietly, after they'd gazed at each other for a long moment.

Ellis shook her head slowly. "Nope."

"Would you go on a date with me?"

"Yup."

"Well, that was easy." Cherry's laugh was soft. Pretty. She picked up her coffee and took a sip.

"I'd go anywhere with you." The words were out before Ellis could think about them, filter them, catch them. Surprisingly, though, she didn't panic. She pressed her lips together, but then gave a small shrug. After all, it was true. And it didn't seem to surprise Cherry at all. She just kept smiling that smile.

"Same," she said.

"Do I get to know where we're going?" Ellis asked after a moment of delicious eye contact that made her seriously consider dragging Cherry by the hand to the back room of the diner and kissing her face off.

"You do not." And with that, Cherry began packing up her things. "I will pick you up at six thirty on Friday. Yeah?"

"Sounds great. I can't wait." And she couldn't.

"Good." Laptop in its case, purse closed, money on the table, Cherry stood and shouldered her bags. Then warm fingers grasped Ellis's chin, and Cherry kissed her softly on the mouth.

Ellis watched her walk away, lips tingling. Cherry went out the door with a little wave, and she tried to recall if she'd ever had a woman kiss her in public like that. Not that she wasn't out. She totally was. But there was something freeing about that kiss. Something natural. Something wonderful.

With a sigh that bordered on dreamy, she picked up Cherry's dishes and headed back to the kitchen.

"Well, that was adorable and sweet," Kitty said.

"I have a date on Friday," was her reply, and she could feel the lovesick grin taking over her face.

"Oh, nice. Where?" Kitty wet a rag in the sink under the counter and began wiping up the remnants of breakfast from the people who'd sat there earlier.

"I have no idea."

The rag stopped. Kitty looked at her, eyes wide. "A *surprise* date? Okay, that's romantic."

Ellis let go of a big sigh.

Kitty studied Ellis with her dark eyes for a beat before asking, "What's that face for?"

"I think we went backward."

Back to wiping, Kitty said, "Because you did the nasty right away."

She gritted her teeth and made a face. "Yeah…"

"So what?"

Blinking. *So what?* Lots of blinking.

Kitty glanced at her, then stopped wiping again and focused her gaze on Ellis. "Are there rules I don't know about? Something that says you can't have sex first and get to know each other later?"

Her shoes were very interesting all of a sudden. "I mean, no, I guess not. It just seems like…" She looked back up. "We're going about it wrong?" She said it like a question because that's what it was.

"Says who?"

"I don't know!" She gave a little foot stomp that made Kitty smile.

"Just breathe, baby. That's all you have to do. Okay? Just breathe. And let a beautiful woman take you on a date. And if you feel like it after that?" Kitty lowered her voice to a whisper. "Take her to bed. Again."

Ellis pursed her lips and slowly nodded as she pointed a finger at Kitty. "I'm rather fond of this idea. Good suggestion." Then she broke into a laugh.

"Hey, I only have your best interests at heart, you know."

❖

The early May day had been beautiful, but by the time Cherry picked up Ellis at her apartment, the clouds had rolled in and the sky had turned the slate gray of old ductwork. But it didn't matter because Ellis was in the passenger seat, and she looked absolutely edible in ripped jeans and a gray short-sleeved sweater. Her blond hair was down and held a gentle curl, and she smelled like peaches. Fresh, juicy, ripe—

"Now can you tell me where we're going?" Ellis asked, gazing out the window, but her hand on Cherry's thigh. And that hand was warm. No. Hot. So very hot. Driving became slightly more difficult with that hand there.

"I don't have to because we're here." Cherry slid the car into a parking spot and killed the engine.

Ellis was looking at the storefront of Vineyard. "I've heard of this place. It's a wine bar, yes?"

Cherry nodded.

"But it says closed for a private event." Ellis pointed at the chalkboard propped out front.

"Yup. We're part of that. It's a tasting."

And that's when Ellis's clear blue eyes lit up, and a smile blossomed wide across her face, both of which sent a flurry of flutters into the lower parts of Cherry's body. "I've never been to a tasting before." Her excitement was obvious, and Cherry silently gave herself a point, then remembered that it was actually Shea's point.

"Never? Well, good. And this'll be a fun one. Come on."

They got out of the car and headed into Vineyard, a small and super classy little space that Cherry always promised to visit more often and always forgot about. It was dimly lit and made of a lot of wood—walls, tables, floor. The bar was marble in swirls of black and white, and the tables were set up in a horseshoe with seats on the outside and a small head table at the opening. Each spot held a small plate and five empty wine glasses, as well as glasses of water and silver buckets spaced every three seats. Dump buckets, Cherry thought. There were also lists and tiny golf pencils for making notes. Four people were already seated.

Inside the door stood a cute brunette in a ponytail, her energy contagious before she even said anything. "Hi there," she said. "I'm Bridget. You have reservations?"

Cherry gave her their names and they were directed to sit wherever they wanted. She looked to Ellis, who didn't miss a beat and walked directly to where the horseshoe curved.

"This way, we can see the presenter, and we can people-watch the others without looking like we are," Ellis said in a whisper.

"I'm glad you have your priorities straight," Cherry whispered back as they sat.

"We have plates, so this must be a pairing kind of thing." Ellis picked up the paper and her eyes went wide. "No way," she said. And could she be cuter? She grinned like a kid and very nearly bounced in her seat. "Girl Scout cookies? This is a wine and Girl Scout cookie tasting?"

"It is." Jackpot. She owed Shea for this idea.

"Oh my God, I'm so excited." The last word was a tiny squeal. Yeah, she owed Shea *big-time*.

She arranged the glasses and used the portrait setting to take a couple cool shots before the wine or cookies came, and she planned to take several more throughout the evening.

Once all the seats were filled, a smiling blond woman stood at the small table. "I'm so happy you're all here. My name is Lindsay, and I manage this place. Who's in the mood for cookies and wine?"

For the next hour, they tried different Girl Scout cookies with different wines. All the pairings worked, some more successfully than others.

"Thin Mints are my favorites," Ellis told her as she munched. "But I don't think of mint as going very well with wine."

"No, but chocolate does." She swirled the semidry red in her glass, took a small bite of the cookie, then sipped. "Oh my God. So good." Ellis was watching her, eyes slightly hooded, lips parted, and everything south of Cherry's belly tightened, her brain sending her flashes of the two of them in bed. She felt her face heat up. Then she swallowed, cleared her throat, and had to force her eyes away.

"That was fun," Ellis said quietly, then sipped her wine with a bite of cookie and chewed, her face all mischievous grin.

All Cherry could do was shake her head and continue to blush like a schoolgirl. What was this woman doing to her?

That's how the evening went. Nibbling, sipping, making sexy eyes at each other. By the time they reached the fifth and final pairing, Cherry's underwear was uncomfortably damp, and she was so turned-on, she worried anybody who gave her a glance would know instantly.

The last pairing was Lemonades and a sparkling white.

"Okay," Lindsay instructed, "just like you've been doing, take a small bite of the cookie, then a sip of the sparkling, and let them sit together in your mouth for a second or two. This one's my favorite."

To say Cherry enjoyed looking at Ellis, watching her, observing her reactions and facial expressions, was a major understatement. She pulled out her phone and took a couple shots as Ellis followed Lindsay's instructions. She sipped the wine, and her eyes went wide, hilariously so. Cherry laughed in response and snapped several photos. "That good, huh?"

"Oh my God." Ellis picked up Cherry's cookie and handed to her. "Here. Do it. It's…I can't even. It's amazing."

If Cherry hadn't planned on partaking anyway, Ellis's face

would've convinced her. Easily. It was a strange realization, that. In that moment it became clear that Ellis could probably convince her to do just about anything. Had anybody in her life held that kind of power over her?

She took a bite of the cookie, tangy and citrusy, then sipped from her flute. The sparkling was fizzy and dry and holy Moses, the combination hit her immediately. Like a slap, but in a good way. Like a sudden party in her mouth. She felt her eyes go wide, and she looked at Ellis, who was grinning.

"See? Told you. Amazing, right?"

She nodded, and when she looked around the wine bar, everybody was having a similar reaction.

"Saved the best for last, didn't I?" Lindsay said to them, her smile knowing and very satisfied. "My fave." She clapped her hands together once. "Okay, that concludes the tasting. Thank you so much for coming, and feel free to hang out, order yourself a full glass. All the wines you tasted are available for purchase by the bottle." She held her arm out to the side toward the bar where a very attractive brunette stood next to Bridget from the door, both waiting. "Either Bridget or my lovely wife, Piper, will be happy to help you out."

Cherry blinked. Vineyard was run by a same-sex couple?

"How cool is that?" Ellis asked, reading her thoughts. "I mean, now we *have* to buy some wine."

Cherry nodded. "So, I'm not ready to go yet. Want to order a couple glasses?"

"If it means more time to sit here with you? Absolutely."

Their gazes held and that was another thing new to Cherry—perfectly comfortable eye contact. Looking into Ellis's eyes felt normal. Natural. Perfect.

"I'll get this," Ellis said after a long moment. "What do you want?"

As soon as she headed to the bar, Cherry rearranged dishware, glasses, any cookies that were left, and took a few more shots. She'd have a good bank of photos to choose from for posting tomorrow.

She watched the bar, watched Ellis chatting with the man standing next to her who was also ordering glasses of wine. She had such an easy sort of grace, an aura of sorts around her that just drew people in, as evidenced by the woman on the other side of her who joined in the conversation until the three of them were laughing and talking like old friends. That's who Ellis was, Cherry was beginning to realize. The one people gravitated to. The one everybody wanted to be friends with. And she, Cherry, was the one who was lucky enough to take her home.

Yeah. Falling for Ellis was a distinct possibility.

In fact, it was already happening.

CHAPTER FIFTEEN

I don't think I've ever been this happy, Mikey."

Ellis sat in her usual chair next to Michaela's bed, the latest Harlan Coben novel open on the Kindle.

"It feels good, let me tell you." She closed the Kindle's cover and sat forward on the edge of the chair, suddenly itching to talk to her sister. Even if she didn't comment back. "She's just…" She inhaled a big breath and let it out. Lifted her arms out to her sides and let them drop. "She's everything I've ever wanted. Smart and beautiful and kind and sexy. God, Mikey, it feels almost too good to be true." She paused and thought about what Michaela would say to her if she was actually participating in this conversation. What the next step would be. "You wanna meet her?" It had been more than a month now, and the reality was, if Michaela was her regular self instead of a shell of herself stuck in a hospital bed for the rest of her life, she'd have demanded to meet Cherry sooner than now. Probably after the second or third date. She'd be dying to size her up, give Ellis her opinion, decide if Cherry was good enough for her big sister. And Ellis would want that. She'd want Michaela's thoughts. Nobody knew her like her sister did. She'd see things Ellis didn't.

And now? That was never going to happen. Michaela was never going to offer up her opinion ever again. And if Ellis dwelled on that too long, it would break her heart all over again.

She stared at her sister. At the still-beautiful face. The eyes the same color blue as hers. She was pretty good at living in the moment, at not dwelling on the past or trying to predict the future. But every now and then, reality would hit her. Square in the face, like a punch.

Her parents were gone. Her sister might as well be gone. And Ellis was alone in the world. The lump of emotion sat like a rock in her throat, and she swallowed it down with effort just as her phone pinged.

Missed ur face 2day. Hiiiiiii.

And she smiled.

Okay, maybe not so alone after all.

She typed back. *Missed u2. Good day?*

They went back and forth, texting about their days, how busy, stories about coworkers, regular, everyday things, and Ellis was once again surprised by how nice it was to talk about ordinary, mundane things with somebody. She never realized how long it had been since she'd had somebody who was simply interested in her day. How weird was that?

Am I going to c u this weekend? she typed after they'd exhausted talk about their days.

The gray dots bounced. Then they disappeared and a couple minutes ticked by. Then they bounced some more and finally Cherry's words came.

Can't Saturday. Work stuff. Sunday?

Well. That was disappointing. But if it was work, what could she do, right? Not Cherry's fault.

Definitely, she typed. *Brunch again?* Then she added two champagne glasses.

Perfect. Can't wait to c u! And five smileys surrounded by hearts.

When was the last time she'd had somebody who couldn't wait to see her? Or maybe the more accurate question was, when had she allowed herself to feel that? To feel how much somebody else wanted to be with her? The answer to that was a long, long time. If ever. And then her mind went back to its earlier train of thought. Yeah. Maybe not so alone after all.

❖

Cherry was having trouble focusing on Saturday morning. She hadn't exactly lied to Ellis about working—this was work. Just not the kind of work Ellis probably thought when Cherry had told her she was working that day. So…a fib. Yeah. A fib was better than a lie, right? Smaller? Less deceptive? Wasn't it?

She released a quiet groan.

"You okay?" Andi asked, clearly catching the sound. She shut her car door, and they headed through the parking lot and toward the Northwood Arts Festival, which was set up in Ridgecrest Park.

She gave herself a mental shake. "Yup. All good. Just tired. I didn't sleep well last night." Another lie. God, they were just sliding off her tongue now. Who was she?

"Thanks so much for agreeing to do this with me." Andi led the way through the makeshift entryway, which consisted of braided twigs and flowers created by one of the artists there.

"Please," Cherry said with a snort. "Thank *you.* I'm really honored." Andi had asked her to come with her to walk through the festival and to hang at the LGBTQIA+ Pride Table to take some shots, shake some hands, say hi to folks. It would be a nice push for Andi's brand, but she would tag Cherry in many of the posts, and the likelihood of Cherry gaining a significant number of new followers from that was high.

She wasn't somebody who got recognized in public yet, but Andi often did. *Hey, you're that chick I see on TikTok!* This wasn't the first time she'd been somewhere with Andi when a random person came up to her to shake her hand or say hi or ask for a selfie with her. She always watched with a mix of pride in her friend and envy of her career. She wanted that. So very much.

"It'll be good to get some stuff posted from here, since I head to the mountains tomorrow for that sporting goods trip. Okay," Andi said, her voice chipper and fun, "cameras out." She had a great eye for interesting shots, but so did Cherry. For the next hour, they walked around the festival, taking selfies and shots of each other and video of various booths, of themselves, and of each other. Cherry had learned early on—from Andi, actually—that taking a stupid amount of footage to work with was best. *The more you have to choose from, the more likely you'll find something worth choosing* were her wise words at the time, and Cherry had never forgotten them.

"Hey, Andi," said one of the young guys behind the Pride booth. His name tag said he was Bentley, and Cherry thought what a cool name that was as he gave Andi a hug.

"Bent, this is my good friend Cherry Davis. She's got a great social media following and is really up and coming, so give her anything you've got, okay?"

"Hey, nice to meet you." Cherry stuck out her hand.

Bentley's grip was strong, his dark eyes soft and kind. "Any friend of Andi's, you know? Nice to meet you, too."

And that's how Andi did it. She introduced Cherry to everybody she knew, told them who she was, and asked them to treat her as they would Andi. Her generosity was one of the things Cherry loved most. Andi never treated Cherry as competition. She saw her as a colleague. A coworker. And she never refused to answer questions or give Cherry tips or point out something she might've gotten wrong.

They spent the next hour hanging with Bentley and two other Northwood Pride people behind the Pride table—an older lesbian named Jan and a nonbinary teenager named Ty. They talked to people who stopped, handed out Pride bracelets and pamphlets, and answered any questions they could, directing inquirers to Bentley if they couldn't.

"You're an influencer, too?" Ty asked Cherry at one point.

"Well, I mean, I'm not as popular as Andi, but that's my goal. Eventually. I'm Cherry on Top," she said, remembering what Andi told her about always mentioning her brand because sometimes people felt weird about asking.

"That's so cool," Ty said. "I'm on TikTok just doing random shit, but I think about streamlining more."

"Yeah? In what way?"

Ty tapped a finger against their lips as if searching for the right explanation. "In a helpful way? I'd like to talk about what it means to be nonbinary, to help educate people on pronouns. Stuff like that." They gave a shrug as their voice kind of trailed off, and Cherry recognized it as a shy uncertainty because she'd had the same thing not so long ago.

"Do it," she said with enthusiasm, remembering how positive and cheerleaderish Andi had been when she'd expressed a similar desire. "Why not? What have you got to lose? Nobody out there is you, right? There may be similar posters, but nobody is exactly you."

Ty seemed to take that in, roll it around. "I never thought about it like that," they said. "You're right."

"And I'm happy to answer any questions you have. Pointers. Stuff like that. Just message me."

"Really?" Ty's face lit up, their eyebrows rose, and a little splotch of pink formed on each cheek. Adorable. Seriously.

"Really."

"Hey, Cher, you ready to wander some more?" Andi interrupted them, and Cherry nodded. She squeezed Ty's shoulder.

"I mean it, okay?"

They nodded and smiled big, and Cherry felt like she'd done something right. She fell into step next to Andi as they left the Pride booth and wandered the festival, looking for more photo ops.

"You offer to help out Ty?" Andi asked as they stood in line at a food truck specializing in poutine that she'd been dying to try.

"They seemed like they could use a nudge."

Andi nodded, her hair, still lavender, swooping over one eye. "They're a good kid. I'm glad you stepped in." She reached for the paper bowl that was handed to her. It held a mountain of fries with curds of melty cheese in and on and around them, all of it smothered in brown gravy that smelled like heaven. "Oh my God, this looks incredible. Can you take a couple shots?"

That Saturday was amazing. It was everything Cherry wanted to do with her life, and she couldn't wait to get home and edit. Sift through all the shots, all the video, find the right stuff, use the perfect filters, and post. As she walked along next to Andi and took shots of her, posed so Andi could return the favor, she thought about how the day was damn near perfect.

But not quite.

There was one person missing, and though she tried to tuck it away, to not think about it at all, Ellis's face kept materializing in her mind, like a ghost coming into view. And she knew. Right then, she knew she had to fix things. Come clean. She could keep telling herself that you couldn't start a relationship without honesty, but she'd already done exactly that.

She needed to fix it. She owed it to Ellis.

❖

Mikey would love this, Ellis thought as she fingered a handcrafted artisan bracelet. Its tiny blue stones would look amazing with Michaela's skin tone, and bracelets were always her favorite piece of jewelry. It'd been a long time since she'd gotten a new one. She smiled at the woman in the booth.

"Isn't that the most beautiful color?" the woman asked.

"I'm not sure I've ever seen this exact shade before," she replied. "Kind of ocean meets sky meets…indigo maybe? Did you make it?"

A nod. "I did. Every piece here."

"Well, they're all beautiful." She handed the bracelet over to her. "I'd like this, please."

The woman took it and boxed it up as she said, "It's almost the same color as your eyes."

"It's for my sister, but she has the same eyes as me, so that's good."

She paid and thanked the woman, took a card so she could go online and see what else there was available. She hadn't planned to come to the festival, but as she was grabbing her mail that morning, she noticed a flyer tacked to the bulletin board near the mailboxes. Since she had a free day and wasn't seeing Michaela until later, it seemed like a fun thing to do. Who didn't love an outdoor arts festival on a sunny almost-summer day? Not to mention, she was pretty sure she could smell fried dough in the air and made a mental note to find the funnel cake truck ASAP. As she turned to continue her stroll, she caught a familiar figure out of the corner of her eye.

"What the hell?" she said quietly.

Down the fairway at a booth with some kind of jarred dip, it looked like, stood Cherry and that girl with the purple hair she'd met briefly at brunch last time. Annie? Amy? She racked her brain for details and finally remembered Cherry saying they knew each other through work. And Cherry couldn't see Ellis today because she had work stuff, she'd said. So it seemed to track. But Cherry was laughing, and they were feeding each other chips with the different dips, laughing and taking photos of each other and then photos together. Which seemed highly un-work-like. Ellis's stomach did a weird churning flip-flop that didn't feel good. At all.

For a split second, she thought about marching her ass right down the fairway and saying hi and asking what was going on. But something stopped her. Was it the familiarity? The way the two of them touched each other with no hesitation? The clear intimacy? Ellis nibbled on the inside of her cheek and had to admit to herself that she and Cherry weren't exclusive. They'd never had that discussion, and why would they this soon? It had literally been less than two months since they'd started seeing each other. Way, *way* too soon to talk exclusivity. Right?

But they'd had sex. More than once. And it was more than just sex. At least for Ellis. There had been emotions. She couldn't do sex without at least some of that. She'd assumed it had been the same for Cherry, but she realized now that that was stupid. You couldn't just assume things about somebody you've known less than two months, especially things as complicated and individual as emotions and feelings. Maybe that had been a mistake.

She watched for another moment, then turned in the opposite direction and headed back toward the parking lot, skipping the second half of the festival. And worse, funnel cake-less.

Sadly, her brain didn't stop once she was in her car and driving. Not that she'd expected it would. Her mind didn't work that way. Once an idea or a grievance or a worry got hold, it stayed, rolling around and around for hours. Or days. Sometimes weeks.

Her car was pointed in the direction of Hearts and Hands when her phone rang, and Aunt Tracey's number appeared on the screen.

"Hello, my favorite aunt," she said in greeting, the phone on speaker.

"I'm your only aunt, silly." It was always the same response, and something about that warmed Ellis with its familiarity. "I'm just calling to check on my girls. How's things?"

And right then, as she sat at a red light talking to her aunt, she decided she needed to get away. It was instant, like the snap of fingers, and the idea was suddenly there.

"Actually," she said, "I was thinking of coming for a visit. Like, soon."

"Yeah? Fantastic!" Her aunt's enthusiasm couldn't have been any clearer, her joyful laugh musical, and it made Ellis grin. "Come right now."

"Well, I was actually thinking of tomorrow. Would that work? I can't stay too long, just a day or two, but it'd be really nice to see you and Uncle Jamie."

"Sweetie, you don't have to ask. You never have to ask. You just show up. Okay?"

She felt lighter after the conversation. No, things weren't better. She was still bothered by what she'd seen, and she needed to talk to Cherry about it, but she needed a little time. She had to slow things down. She wanted to talk to Aunt Tracey face-to-face, see if she was overreacting or being possessive, and aside from Michaela, nobody knew her like Aunt Tracey.

Michaela.

This would be the first time she left her for more than a day. Would she notice?

The logical voice in her head shouted at her. *Of course, she won't notice. She doesn't notice anything.* But her heart worried.

And suddenly, there were so many arrangements to make. She needed to take time off from work. Just Monday and Tuesday, she decided. She'd return on Tuesday night and drive straight to Hearts and Hands to see Michaela. And she'd go there tonight and spend time with her before she left. She needed Mrs. Carver to feed Nugget.

And she needed to cancel brunch with Cherry.

Chapter Sixteen

"A zit? Really?" Cherry muttered. "What am I, fifteen?" She found the right filter and used it to smooth out her skin in the photo, and even deepened the tone a bit so she looked a little tanner. Then she altered the background and lighting, making it look a bit sunnier and easing the shadows just a smidge. In the photo, she and Andi each had a chip and that to-die-for chipotle dip, and their arms were entwined like a bride and groom when sipping champagne. The shot was fun and light and would get her a lot of hits, since Andi said to be sure to tag her when she posted it, which she was going to. Once she fixed her zit, she smoothed out her flyaways so her hair looked a little less messy. The summer always added some frizz. A little color to her cheeks and it was perfect. Thank God for editing software.

It was Sunday afternoon, and she was intently focused on her social media stuff because she was trying hard not to think about Ellis. She'd canceled brunch, said she was really sorry, that something had come up, and it wasn't that such a thing wasn't allowed or couldn't happen, because of course it was and of course it could, but it wasn't sitting right with Cherry. She had no idea why. There was just a feeling. A weirdness. An uncertainty that made her uncomfortable, itchy in her own skin.

"It's fine," she whispered to herself. "Quit freaking."

It was totally fine. She'd check on her later today and hit up the diner in the morning. NBD. They said their good nights that night, and Ellis was uncharacteristically short.

Cherry didn't sleep well.

The next morning, she decided to surprise Ellis, so she didn't tell her she'd be at the diner. It was Monday, after all, and Mondays were busy, so she tended to start them in the office. But Ellis had been on her mind all night, her responses to Cherry's texts all short and impersonal. Had she done something wrong? Said something? Missed a signal? Lord knew *that* was a possibility. She wasn't great at shorthand, especially early on in a relationship.

Whoa.

Was that what this was? A relationship?

She let that roll around in her head as she ordered coffee and a couple of Cal's warm biscuits from Kitty, then pulled her laptop out and made herself a little workstation. They hadn't talked exclusivity, but they had slept together. Granted, that had happened much sooner than Cherry was used to, but it had felt so right at the time. And still did. She gave a little snort because this was stuff she should be talking to Ellis about. Face-to-face. Instead of endlessly overthinking it all in her head.

Kitty came by with a plate of biscuits and her coffee. "How're you doin' this morning, honey?" she asked, and it always seemed like she really did want to know. She was broad and solid and had the kindest voice, and Cherry thought, not for the first time, that if she was ever sad or upset, she'd love to curl up in Kitty's ample lap and go to sleep there.

"I'm good," Cherry said. "How are you?"

"Oh, can't complain."

"Hey, can you let Ellis know I'm here?"

Kitty frowned. "She's not here today, hon. She took today and tomorrow off. I think she's out of town. Didn't she tell you?"

Ouch.

"Oh, that's right. She did. She did tell me, I just spaced." She made a goofy face. "Mondays, am I right?"

Kitty smiled back at her. "You let me know if you need anything else." And she was off to wait on other customers, leaving Cherry to sit there, fake-smiling, confused and hurt and a little bit ticked off. Ellis hadn't just canceled brunch yesterday, she'd literally *left town* and hadn't said anything to her. She'd be worried about Ellis's sister if she didn't know Michaela was actually here in Northwood. *What the hell, Ellis?*

She reached for her phone, ready to send a heated text, when she noticed a woman across the diner watching her. Cherry had seen her more than once—she was a regular, usually with a book. When the breakfast crowd filtered out and Cherry was on her third cup of coffee and really got down to focusing on her work, the book woman was almost always still there, sitting at her table, sipping tea—Cherry could see the tag and string hanging off the side of the cup—and reading. They'd never made eye contact, though.

Until today.

Something shivered through her, like fingertips dancing up her spine, and as the woman held her gaze, the feeling coiled in her stomach and sat there, making her weirdly fidgety. What the hell was that about?

She swallowed hard and had to make a conscious effort to tear her eyes away, even as the woman closed her book. She was still looking at Cherry, she could feel it, and the next time she looked up, the woman was walking toward her. Something about her was familiar, but she couldn't put her finger on exactly what.

"Hi," the woman said when she reached Cherry's table. The diner had cleared right out, and the two of them were the only ones left. Kitty was behind the counter, wiping a glass with a white rag and seemingly keeping an eye on the two of them, for which Cherry was grateful, because she was finally able to put a name to what she was feeling.

Fear.

"Hello," Cherry said back, and without invitation, the woman pulled a chair out and sat. "Um…" She cocked her head and watched as the woman folded her hands and placed her forearms on the table. Studied her hands, chewed her bottom lip, seemed to be looking for the right words. "Can I help you with something?"

There was something familiar about the woman. Cherry put her in maybe her early to mid-fifties. Short hair, sort of reddish blond. Brown eyes. Kind eyes, but eyes that had seen sorrow. Pain. How Cherry could tell that, she had no idea, but she was sure of it. When the woman smiled, there was a shadow of sadness to it.

"You're Cherry Davis." It wasn't a question, just a simple statement, and there was the sad smile again.

"I am." Was this a fan? Somebody who knew her from online? That was a rare occurrence, but it did happen, happened to Andi all the time. "Have we met?"

"A long time ago, yes." The woman looked down at her hands again. "My name is Lila."

"Li—" And it clicked. Every puzzle piece that she didn't realize was floating around in her head clicked into place with a loud snap. Just like that. She knew exactly who this woman was. "You're…" She couldn't make herself say the words.

Lila nodded and helped her along. "Yes. I'm your mother. Hi, Cherry."

❖

Torn between worry and comfort.

That's where Ellis was on Monday morning. Worry because she wasn't anywhere near Hearts and Hands, and if something happened to Michaela, it would take her a good four hours to get back to Northwood. Well, three and a half because she had a lead foot, according to her father. And comfort because she was at her aunt and uncle's home, and it was warm and welcoming and they were the only family she had and *they loved her*. So very much. She felt it the second she'd walked in yesterday.

That morning, she sat at the round table in the kitchen's breakfast nook, sipping delicious dark roast coffee and munching on a strip of crispy bacon as Uncle Jamie flipped pancakes and Aunt Tracey sat across from her. It was so warm and domestic and homey, and it made Ellis long for such feelings in her own life.

"I'm so glad you're here," Aunt Tracey said for about the millionth time, squeezing her forearm. "How'd you sleep?"

"Great. Though I've gotten kind of used to having a cat curled up near my head."

Aunt Tracey laughed. "I'm so glad you adopted one. I don't like the idea of you being alone in your apartment."

"Well, it's funny you mention that because I kind of wanted to talk to you about something."

Aunt Tracey gave an adorable little gasp and said, "Tell me you're seeing somebody."

Ellis laughed through her nose. "I'm seeing somebody."

Aunt Tracey clapped her hands together in clear delight. "You hear that, Jamie?"

"I heard," Uncle Jamie said, frying pan in hand as he approached the table and scooped pancakes onto their plates. "Tell us about her."

"Well, her name is Cherry."

"That's pretty," Aunt Tracey said, reaching for the syrup.

"She's got gorgeous auburn hair and big dark eyes and the most amazing smile. She's funny and beautiful and I really, really like her."

"Oh, sweetheart, I am so happy for you." Aunt Tracey passed her the syrup.

"I need your opinion, though." She nibbled on her bottom lip as she sorted through her thoughts, looking for a good place to start. "So, Saturday, she told me she had to do work stuff all day, so we couldn't get together." She told her aunt and uncle the whole story, right down to seeing Cherry and her friend, laughing and taking pictures and *feeding each other* at the arts festival, and how she left, canceled brunch, and drove to Cleveland.

Uncle Jamie scooped another round of pancakes onto a plate in the middle of the table, then took his seat and reached for the butter. "How come you left? Instead of going up to her and saying hi?"

Ellis inhaled and let it out loudly. "That is the question, isn't it? Because I'm ridiculous?"

"Yeah, I don't think that's it." Aunt Tracey chewed a bite of pancake and watched her carefully.

Ellis poked the inside of her cheek with her tongue before responding with what she knew was the truth. "Because I really like her, and I was afraid of what I might find out."

"You think she's sleeping with the purple-hair girl?" Aunt Tracey asked.

"The purple-hair girl has a wife. I met her last time we had brunch. So…I hope not?"

"I'm sure there are many possibilities here for what was going on," Aunt Tracey said. "But, sweetheart, the only way you're gonna find out is if you ask her." Her aunt pointed her fork at her. "Which you already know, so I'm not sure what this discussion is even about." She winked. "You have always had the habit of overthinking. You're an overthinker. Have been since you were a kid."

Ellis groaned. "Ugh. I know. You're right. It's what I do." A shake of her head. "I'm just not used to this. I don't know how to relationship. It's been so long."

"Love, respect, communication." Aunt Tracey reached for a slice of bacon. "The three most important things. Right?" She looked to Uncle Jamie for confirmation.

"Yes, dear," he said, then winked at Ellis.

"And knowing how to say *that*, right?" she asked with a grin.

"Exactly right." Uncle Jamie nodded and sipped his coffee.

They finished breakfast and sat chatting for nearly another hour before they stood from the table, and Ellis helped clean up. As she loaded the dishwasher, her brain kept replaying both seeing Cherry and her friend and also the conversation with her aunt and uncle. This wasn't difficult. She just needed to talk to Cherry about it. This was like one of those infuriating Hallmark or Lifetime movies where the whole conflict between the main characters could be resolved in five minutes with one simple conversation.

She'd been right the first time—she was being ridiculous.

I'll just ask her.

Ready to send a text, she jumped when her phone rang in her hand. She was even more startled to see it was Cherry.

"Hey there, I was just thinking about you," she said softly, by way of greeting.

"Hey," Cherry said, and Ellis knew in a split second, just by the odd tone of her voice with the one word, that something was off.

"What's the matter?" she asked, concern filling her.

Cherry sniffled. "I'm just…I don't know if you're far away, but when will you be home?"

"Baby, please tell me what's wrong."

"Can you come home?" The smallest voice Ellis had ever heard.

"Absolutely." No hesitation. No worries. Cherry needed her, and she was going to be there, no question. "Give me fifteen minutes to get my stuff together and say good-bye, and I'll hit the road. I should be home by two. Do you want to meet me at my place?"

Cherry agreed with more sniffling, whispered a thank you, and they hung up.

Aunt Tracey was worried. Ellis could see it in her eyes, on her face, but she didn't argue with her. Didn't try to get her to stay or ask her to examine more closely what she was doing. It was like she got it, like she understood that Ellis really had no other option.

Something was wrong, and Cherry needed her.

So she would be there.

CHAPTER SEVENTEEN

Ellis turned down her street at 1:47 and, as she approached her building, saw Cherry sitting on the front steps, scrolling on her phone. Cherry looked up, and the relief that washed over her face when she locked eyes with Ellis was palpable. Ellis felt it rush through her body like liquid as Cherry stood.

She pulled into the small parking lot in the back, into her assigned space, grabbed her bag from the trunk, and met Cherry in the front. They said nothing before Cherry was in her arms, holding tightly to her and not exactly crying, but definitely emotional.

"I'm so glad you're here," she whispered against Ellis's ear. "I'm so sorry to make you cut your trip short, but I'm just so glad you're here."

She extracted herself and held Cherry at arms' length. "Are you okay?" she asked, studying Cherry's face, then scanning her body. "Are you hurt or something?"

Cherry shook her head and then pulled her into another hug, and her grip felt like Cherry was worried she'd be whisked off into oblivion if she let go.

She tightened her arms around Cherry, felt her tremble slightly. "Let's go inside, and you can tell me what's going on."

Silently and holding hands, they entered the house, then climbed the stairs to Ellis's door. Nugget greeted them with some very loud, clearly annoyed yowls before apparently deciding to be forgiving and twining around their feet. Ellis was happy to see his food bowl was full and a note from Mrs. Carver dictating what times she'd popped in and how long she'd stayed. Cherry's hand was warm in hers, and she didn't let go, even once they were inside.

Ellis set down her bag and turned to Cherry, stared in expectation.

"Do you have any wine?" Cherry asked.

Ellis tipped her head.

"Whiskey? Vodka? Bourbon?" Cherry asked. "Moonshine?"

A chuckle bubbled up from her chest. "Fresh out of moonshine, but I have wine. Have a seat and I'll pour."

A few minutes later, she brought two glasses of cab into the tiny living room, handed one to Cherry, and sat down next to her. Sideways, so she could face her. She watched Cherry sip, gave her a moment, then said, "Please, please tell me what's going on. You've got me a little freaked. Are you sure you're okay?"

Cherry took a deep breath, her dark eyes cloudy with emotion. "I was at the diner this morning. You were not." She held up a finger. "Which is an entirely different story that we'll circle back to, but for now, I was at the diner this morning."

She grimaced, knowing she'd have to explain herself and okay with that. "And?"

"It was later in the morning, so it had cleared out and left just us regulars."

Ellis nodded, picturing the scene.

"Today, it was me and the lady with the short light red hair. You know the one I mean?"

"The book lady?" She nodded.

"She came up to talk to me." Cherry's face flushed, and her eyes darted. "Told me her name was Lila and that she…" She cleared her throat, very obviously having trouble continuing her story. Ellis set her wine down and reached for Cherry's hand, squeezed it, hoping to give her some strength. "She told me she's my mom."

Lots of blinking happened then. Staring and blinking. A couple *holy shit*s because what the hell do you say to something like that?

"Oh, my God, Cherry," Ellis finally managed. "Oh my God. That's…that's crazy."

"She said she'd been coming into the diner for weeks just hoping to work up the nerve to talk to me."

"How did she know to find you there?"

"I mean, she did a lot of other searching first, but she's been kind of following me for a while now."

"Following or stalking?"

Cherry paused, frowned. "Both, I guess?" She picked up her wine and took a huge swallow. "I am so confused, Ellis. I don't know what to do. I don't know how to feel. I don't know what she wants—I mean, she says she only wanted to meet me, maybe get to know me." Those deep brown eyes found hers and held them, implored. "Why now? What does she want?"

"I think…" Ellis looked down at the one hand she was still holding. "Did you ask her that?"

A big exhale. "No. I honestly didn't talk to her for very long, I was too freaked. She gave me her number, so I can call her if I want to, but Jesus Christ, Ellis, what should I do? The woman left me before I was even in school. And now she's back? Now? I'm thirty-two years old. She certainly took her time." Another sigh, complete with shoulders going up, then dropping. "I don't know what to do."

"Well, you don't have to do anything. Right?" Ellis spoke slowly, rolling her thoughts around as she did. "How was it left? Just that you'd contact her if you wanted to?"

Cherry nodded, the wetness that had filled her eyes spilled over, and Ellis had never seen anything she wanted to fix more than that. Cherry crying sliced at her heart.

"Oh, sweetie, it's okay. We'll figure it out. Come here." She opened her arms, and Cherry moved into them. Ellis held her tightly, rocking them back and forth in a gentle, easy rhythm, and Cherry silently cried in her arms.

Time ticked by. Nugget walked across both of them before deciding he'd stretch out across the back of the couch, and still Ellis held Cherry, the only sounds slight sniffles from Cherry and gentle soothing noises from Ellis.

Finally, Cherry sat up and Ellis loosened her grip. She reached for the box of tissues on the coffee table and held it in Cherry's direction so she could pull one out and blow her nose. After taking in a slow, deep breath and letting it out, Cherry turned to her. "I'm so sorry for dragging you back here from—" She shook her head. "I don't even know where you were."

"Cleveland."

A look of surprise, followed by a furrowed brow. "What's in Cleveland?"

"My aunt and uncle. I hadn't seen them in a long time, and I was missing them, so I decided to make a road trip." She braced.

"Without telling me at all."

There it was.

Ellis grimaced. "Yeah. I'm sorry about that. That was wrong. And selfish."

"I mean, you could've just said." Cherry seemed a bit more relaxed now, probably just glad to be talking about a different topic than her surprise mom. "I mean, I get that we're new, and we haven't really talked about any boundaries, so I can't be too mad. But it did feel kind of weird."

Ellis nodded. She needed to address the purple-haired chick, but this was not the day to do that. Cherry had enough on her plate, and seriously, she'd called her—not Purple Hair—when she was in need of a shoulder, and that said a lot, didn't it? "So, how do you feel? About your mom showing up? Not that I'm sure I should even call her that. Lila. Like, what did you say when she told you? I'm trying to imagine."

Cherry took a deep breath as if clearing out the emotion and trying to recall the moment. "It's weird because it's all gone sort of blurry. We made eye contact across the diner, and then she stood up and walked toward me and sat down across from me."

"I bet she's been working up the nerve all this time. She's been in the diner every morning for weeks." Now that Ellis knew who the woman was, her memory cleared, and she could recall just how often she'd noticed her.

"I think she might've said that. I'm not sure. Anyway, it was so weird because once she said who she actually was, I could suddenly see it. Like, see the resemblance. It's uncanny. I can't believe I never noticed it before."

"Yeah? I remember her hair, but it's much lighter than yours."

"It's the eyes. She has my eyes. Er, rather, I have hers." Cherry dropped her head back against the couch and groaned. "This is all *so weird*. And I'm so frustrated. God."

"I have an idea," Ellis said. She stood up and held a hand down to Cherry. "Come with me."

"Where are we going?"

"Someplace where you can let go of some of your frustration."

Cherry grasped her hand and let herself be pulled to her feet. "I'm all for that."

A few minutes later, they were in Ellis's car and pulling into the back alley behind Sunny Side Up. It was empty, just a strip of pavement with the brick side of buildings to the left and right, a large green dumpster tucked into a corner.

Cherry glanced at her. "Have you brought me here to murder me?"

"I thought it would be easier and less messy to do it here," Ellis deadpanned. "I mean, the dumpster is hella convenient."

Cherry blinked at her.

"Oh my God, stop it. No, you're not about to become a *Dateline* episode. I brought you here for another reason." They got out of the car, and Ellis fished out her keys as they approached the back entrance of the diner. Keying the lock, she said, "We're only open for breakfast and lunch, so there's nobody here right now."

She pulled the door open, punched her code into the alarm, and flicked on the light. They were in a back break room, and Ellis headed through the kitchen to a storage area on the other side.

"It's weird being here when it's closed," Cherry said, her voice barely above a whisper. "A little creepy, actually, like being in your high school when it's dark and empty."

"It'd be a good place for a horror movie, yeah?"

"I'm trying *not* to think that, El," Cherry said on a whine.

"Here we go." Ellis picked up a rack of glasses and turned to head back the way they came.

"What is happening right now?" Cherry asked, clearly confused.

"These all have chips or cracks in them. They're kinda cheap, so it happens often. I'm trying to get the owner to spring for better glasses. In the meantime, we put the bad ones here, and when it's full, we give it to the recycling guys."

"That's nice. But what are we doing with them?"

"You'll see." She led them back out the door, set down the rack, and then went to the dumpster and leaned into it until it rolled several feet down the wall, leaving a big open space of solid brick. She could feel Cherry's eyes on her as she popped back inside to grab a push broom and a dustpan, then handed Cherry one of two pairs of sunglasses she'd snagged from her car. "Put these on."

"What is happening right now?" Cherry asked again, but this time, she was curious and even a little amused. Ellis could hear it.

"Okay." Ellis looked at Cherry in the sunglasses, and she was both adorable and super sexy. "Those look great on you, by the way," she said in an aside. Cleared her throat. Back to the task at hand, please. She pulled a glass from the rack and handed it to Cherry. "Go ahead."

"Go ahead and what?"

Ellis pointed to the wall. "Throw it."

Cherry's eyes went wide with surprise which quickly shifted to delight. Ellis watched it happen and couldn't contain her own joy. "Seriously?"

"In my experience, I have found that the feeling of throwing something hard combined with the sound of breaking glass to be very, *very* satisfying when I'm frustrated."

The smile slowly crept across Cherry's face, and she turned toward the wall. Ellis slid the other pair of sunglasses over her eyes and jerked her chin at the wall.

"Ready when you are."

Cherry hurled the glass, and it shattered on impact, the sound echoing through the alleyway. "*Oh*, that felt good."

"Yeah? Well, there are twenty-three more here if you want to throw them all. Also? I find that yelling when you do it increases the satisfaction."

Cherry didn't wait. She took the next glass and roared—literally *roared*—as she hurled it.

"There ya go," Ellis said, finding her own satisfaction in just the watching.

Without taking a break, Cherry threw ten glasses in a row. Slightly out of breath and definitely a little flushed, she smiled at Ellis. "This is amazing."

"I thought you might like it."

"You've done this?"

A nod, but no words from her.

"One day, I'm gonna ask for details," Cherry said, pulling the next glass from the rack.

"Fair enough."

Cherry slowed her pace a bit, likely both from being tired and from realizing her glass supply was dwindling. And possibly emotion. She'd become quiet. Pensive. The corners of her mouth were turned down in a soft frown. When there were only two left, she pulled them both out and handed one to Ellis. "Together on three?"

Ellis positioned herself next to Cherry as she counted.

"One…two…three!"

They threw their glasses together, twin shatterings against the brick wall echoing down the alley as they stood there, shoulder to shoulder, Cherry breathing heavily.

"Ellis."

She turned and met Cherry's eyes, the sunglasses now pushed up onto her head, holding her red hair back so her entire face was visible. Sliding her own glasses off, she cocked her head.

"Thank you for this." Cherry leaned in and kissed her tenderly on the mouth. "It helped. A lot."

Ellis laid her hand against Cherry's face. "I'm glad. And you're very welcome." Another kiss, warm and comforting. "Want to grab dinner?"

"Yes, please. I've worked up an appetite."

"You have. Good job." She took the rack back inside while Cherry used the push broom to sweep up all the shards of glass that now littered the pavement. Together, as if they'd worked as a team for years, they picked it all up, put it in the dumpster, and rolled that back to its original position.

As Ellis reset the alarm and locked the diner back up, Cherry rubbed a hand along her back. "This was awesome. I feel better somehow. I mean, my issue hasn't gone anywhere, but…"

"You got rid of some of the stress." Ellis smiled and grabbed her hand. As they walked to the car, she said, "I'm glad."

On their way to the restaurant, Ellis glanced at Cherry a few times as she sat in the passenger seat. Her eyes still held a bit of worry, but there was a small smile on her face, and it occurred to Ellis that Cherry hadn't picked up her phone once in the entire time they'd been together that day.

What purple-haired chick?

CHAPTER EIGHTEEN

Cherry was *so* behind on posting content.

One of the very first things Andi had taught her was that if she wanted to stay relevant, she needed to post regularly. It didn't have to be a lot. Didn't have to be a complicated video that took hours of editing. Didn't have to be a series of any kind, or anything with tons of explanation. Just a photo would do. And she'd taken zero yesterday. She'd have to delve into her stockpile, the random photos she took all the time and saved to use on a day exactly like this one.

It was just about the beginning of June, and it was unseasonably hot, and Cherry was frustrated. With herself and with her moth—um, Lila. Not because anything had happened. It hadn't. Lila hadn't contacted her. She hadn't contacted Lila. Lila hadn't shown up at the diner again since that day. Part of Cherry was relieved. The rest of her? Kind of pissed. Because what the fuck? She'd walked in, dropped a bomb like *I'm your mother who abandoned you almost thirty years ago, hi*, and then she just sat back and waited?

Which, Cherry had to admit, was the right thing to do, the waiting. Lila couldn't push. Couldn't press. Wasn't in the position to. But man, Cherry hated having the ball in her court. She had no idea what to do with it. Worse, she had no idea what she *wanted* to do with it. So she stood there.

Ellis had been amazing all week. Supportive but not pushy. Available to talk, but she never pried. Cherry brought the subject up once or twice, but they shut it down again when her brain felt overloaded. "It's okay to sit with it," Ellis had said the other night. "For as long as you want to. There's zero hurry here."

She'd been in her car all day, driving from client to client to check out accidents and vehicular damage, and driving always gave her mind time to wander. And when it wasn't focused on Lila, it was focused on Ellis.

"Oh, Ellis," she sighed now quietly as she headed home. While it was very common for her to wish the apartment would be empty as she drove home, for the first time in longer than she could remember, she hoped everybody was home. She'd had more than enough time with her own thoughts for the day. She wanted to be distracted by the thoughts and jokes and comments of others for a while.

It had been a long day, and she'd worked two hours longer than usual. Ellis was visiting her sister, so Cherry had the evening to herself. The level of her exhaustion hit her hard as she pulled into the parking lot and cut her ignition, taking a moment to lean her head against the headrest, blow out a breath, and just *be* for a few moments. Her brain actually hurt.

Distraction was definitely on the menu that night because when she walked into the apartment, three faces greeted her. Shea, Adam, and a man she'd never met before.

"Sup, bitch," Shea said, and Cherry saw the stranger's eyes widen just slightly in what was likely surprise. It made her grin.

"OMG, what a day." She dropped her laptop case and purse onto the floor, crossed the living room to the only open seat—a beat-up recliner—and dropped into it like a rag doll. "Is there alcohol?"

Shea made a *pfft* sound as if she'd asked the stupidest question in the world—and she kind of had—and stood. "Wine, beer, or hard?"

"Surprise me," Cherry said with a wave of her hand, and Shea disappeared from the room. Meanwhile, Adam's eyes were on her, like he was waiting his turn, and she noticed his hand on the other man's thigh. When she met his gaze, he smiled widely—almost too widely—and it occurred to her that this introduction was important to him. She sat up a bit and gave him her attention.

"Cherry, this is Jared," Adam said, and Cherry took the time to look at him. He was older than them, maybe in his late forties or early fifties? Handsome in a distinguished way, the slight gray at his temples and the crow's feet in the corners of his blue eyes really the only indicators of his age. He was sitting, true, but he looked fit, and his clothes were neat. Jeans, a light blue oxford, the sleeves rolled up to reveal muscular forearms covered in dark hair, brown loafers with no socks. He stood and held out a hand, so Cherry stood, too.

"It's a pleasure to meet you, Cherry," Jared said as he enveloped her small hand in his large one. His skin was surprisingly soft, his grip firm but not crushing. "I've heard a lot about you."

"Uh-oh," she said, then laughed.

"Only good things. I promise."

"Well, it's nice to meet you, too. I've heard about you as well." They sat back down, and Adam blushed furiously, which she so wanted to tease him about but decided to save it for later.

"Voilà," Shea said, and a glass appeared in front of her face.

Cherry took it and sipped. "Amaretto sour," she determined. "Perfect. Thank you." The drink was cold and sweet and delicious. Once again, her best friend knew exactly what she needed. "So, Jared, what do you do?"

"I own a payroll company," he said, and they spent the next hour, the four of them, talking about marketing and clients and the ins and outs of working for small businesses, which they all did.

Cherry watched Adam's face as Jared spoke and had to swallow her own huge grin. Adam was clearly entranced, obviously smitten. *Do people even say smitten anymore?* The thought made her happy, and then Shea was asking her a question.

"What are you grinning at?"

Cherry blinked several times, as if coming out of a trance. Which she kind of had. "What am *I* grinning at? I'm grinning at Adam grinning at Jared." They all laughed, and Adam's blush returned. This time, Jared saw it and closed his hand over Adam's, and that's when Cherry noticed that Jared was just as enamored with Adam as Adam was with him. The thought made her warm from the inside, so happy that her dear friend had found somebody worthy of him.

"That's how you look when you talk about Ellis," Shea pointed out.

Adam nodded. "Truth."

"Where is she, anyway?" Shea asked.

"Is Ellis the girlfriend?" Jared asked Adam, who nodded.

Cherry was both touched and a little freaked that they'd discussed her love life. "She's with her sister tonight," she said, and when she looked to Adam, she could tell he'd already given Jared the details. He nodded.

They spent the rest of the evening laughing and talking and getting to know Jared, who turned out to be a really cool guy. Cherry liked him, liked the way he looked at Adam. The age difference had been a concern at first, but Jared never seemed to talk down to Adam or treat him like he didn't know as much, and she was relieved. Adam tended to gravitate toward older men but had yet to find one that treated him like an equal.

"Anything from you-know-who?" Shea asked quietly later on as they sat side by side while the guys talked with each other.

She shook her head.

"And how do you feel about that?"

She shrugged. "Honestly? I have no idea how to feel."

"Do you think you'll call her?"

Another shrug. "Depends on the day." And it did. "A couple mornings, I've woken up and been sure I wanted to contact her. I have so many questions, you know?" She glanced at Shea, who nodded. "And then the anger will creep in, and I think, no. Fuck her. She gets no part of me, not even my rage. And around and around I go."

"What does Ellis think?"

"She supports whatever I want to do. I've told her I'm gonna call, and she says okay and to let her know if I want her to be there. And then I tell her I chickened out, and she says okay and to let her know if I want her to be there."

Shea smiled. "Sounds like she's being very careful not to push you one way or the other."

"She is." Cherry knew that. Was grateful for it. Most of the time. "I guess there are times when I wish she *would* push. I feel like I need somebody, anybody, to just tell me what to do. You know?"

"I do." Shea shifted in her seat, almost like she was weighing what she had to say. When her eyes met Cherry's, there was a softness there, and her love was clear. "But you know we can't do that, right? That this is up to you and only you? And that we'll support you either way? Because we love you?"

Surprised to feel her eyes well up, Cherry swallowed the lump in her throat and nodded vigorously. Because she did know that. She did know how lucky she was to have people who cared so much about her. Supremely lucky.

If only one of them would point her in the right direction because she was stuck.

❖

"And she just showed up out of the blue?" Evan's eyes were wide as he listened to Ellis tell the story of Cherry's mom. "Like, no warning or anything? After how many years?"

"I think, like, twenty-eight or nine?" Ellis scrunched up her nose as she tried to remember the math. "She said she was barely past being a toddler when her mom left."

Evan frowned and shook his head. "Ugh. Man, how do you do that? How do you just leave your kid?" He was sitting in Michaela's room with her, his feet propped up on the wide windowsill, crossed at the ankle, while he waited for Kendra to finish her shift.

"I don't know." She joined him in the head shaking. "I don't understand it." And she didn't. Her heart ached for little toddling Cherry Davis, who had no idea her mother would just disappear one day and leave her. "I mean, my mom's gone, too, but she didn't choose to leave. That's the difference."

"That's a huge difference." Evan snorted a sarcastic laugh. "I don't have kids—"

"Yet," Ellis added with a grin.

"Yet. But I can tell you right now as I sit here, I will sure as shit never abandon them. Not on purpose."

"Same."

Evan took a moment. "I'm trying to decide if she gets points for trying now." He pursed his lips. "You said she's been coming into the diner?"

With a nod, Ellis said, "Yeah, but I'm not sure for how long. We just considered her a regular, you know?" She shrugged. "I didn't think anything of it. Nobody did. She always had a book, and I thought she was just a woman who needed to get away from her house to read." It sounded kind of silly now, she knew.

"When she was actually scoping things out."

"Evidently." Ellis sighed. "I wish I'd been there when she made her move." She hadn't told anybody else about that weekend, seeing Cherry and Purple Hair—what the hell was her name again?—and she'd pretty much put it out of her mind since then. But she did wish she'd been in the diner the morning Cherry's mom had decided that was the day she was going to approach her, that she'd been there to offer support. Coulda, shoulda, woulda, as her father would say. She mentally shrugged.

"I guess she gets a little bit of credit for that. Like, she didn't just pop in, all, *Hi, remember me? The mother who left you when you were little?*" Evan made a face. "Though, she kinda did exactly that."

"Right? Just because she took the time to prepare…"

"Cherry didn't get any."

Ellis pointed at him. "That."

Kendra walked in then, her pace quick as it always was, but her aura calm. Even when she looked thoroughly exhausted—like she did then—she was still relaxing for Ellis to be around. It was a true gift.

"What are we talking about?" Kendra asked, her bags over her shoulder, her white uniform still looking fresh, even after a nine-hour day.

"The mom," Evan told her with wide eyes.

Kendra nodded, as Ellis had already given her the gist. "Yeah, that's a piece of work right there, isn't it?" She shifted her dark gaze to Ellis. "What's she gonna do? She decide yet?"

Shaking her head, she told her no.

"That's a tough call, for sure." Kendra glanced at her husband. "You ready, baby? I feel like I got run over by a semi, and then it decided it forgot something, shifted into reverse, and ran over me again."

"That's a rough day, right there," Ellis said with a grin.

Evan got to his feet and gave Ellis a hug, then took his wife's bags off her shoulder.

"Chivalry is not dead," Ellis said.

"Not in my house," Kendra agreed. Then she, too, hugged Ellis. "Don't you stay too late, missy." She walked around the bed and pressed a kiss to Michaela's forehead. "I'll see you tomorrow," she whispered. With a wave to Ellis, the Jacksons headed home, and it was just Ellis and Michaela.

A glance at her phone said it was just after nine. She thought she'd have gotten her next *11th Commandment* assignment by now, but sometimes the info didn't come until after midnight. She needed to head home. Nugget would be hungry for his wet food, but he had plenty of dry, and she wasn't ready to leave Mikey just yet. That happened sometimes. Every so often, there'd be a day when she was visiting her sister and just felt like she should stay. There was never a particular thing that happened, just a feeling. A tug. A pull on her heart, and more than once, she'd wondered if it was somehow some form of Michaela talking to her. Telepathically or mentally or psychically. There was no real proof, of course. Having a feeling didn't mean anything concrete. But whenever she felt that tug, she stayed. She didn't wonder over it, didn't question it. She just stayed.

She got out her laptop and made herself comfortable in the chair next to Michaela's bed, stretched out her legs, and used the rolling table as a desk. Her phone pinged and indicated a text from Cherry.

Hi cutie! Doing ok? Met Adam's guy 2nite. Still here. Nice. Might b kinda drunk. The text was followed by a couple of drink emoji and one with a goofy, overserved-looking expression. She grinned. In the almost two months she'd known Cherry, she'd never seen her intoxicated. And if your long-lost mother showing up out of the blue wasn't reason enough to get plastered, she didn't know what was.

As long as ur home, she texted back. *All good here.*

The dots bounced for a few seconds, then stopped, then bounced some more, then stopped. Cherry was clearly trying to find her words. When they finally arrived, they were simple.

I don't know what to do.

Ellis didn't need to ask what she meant or who she was talking about. *Then you do nothing. Until you do know.* She wished she had an easy answer for her, but it was the best she could do.

Right.

No more dots came, and Ellis assumed she'd gone back to her guest and roommates, which was okay. She was feeling a little in her head, as Michaela used to say when she got all pensive and quiet.

"What would you do, Mikey?" Her voice was soft but still felt a little loud in the silence of the room. She inhaled slowly and let it out bit by bit. "It's a tough call for us, isn't it? God knows I'd give anything at all to be able to talk to Mom one more time. Wouldn't you?" That had been the first thought she'd had when Cherry had told her. *You have your mom back! You're so lucky!* But then she remembered that their situations were, in fact, not the same. That Ellis's mom had left *unwillingly* and Cherry's mom had *chosen* to leave. Huge difference there.

"What if Mom had left us? Just woke up one day and decided she didn't want to be our mother anymore? Can you imagine? Can you even begin to imagine? 'Cause I can't. Not even a little."

And maybe that was the reason she was having trouble watching Cherry waver. It wouldn't—for one single second—occur to Ellis not to want to connect with her mother. However, she had zero idea what it was like in Cherry's shoes. Not just to be abandoned by your mother, but to be left with your father who was, in Cherry's words, not a nice guy. No, she couldn't even begin to imagine what that must feel like. And because of that, she had no right to judge. Or even have an opinion. "Nope. My job is to be supportive of this person I care about." She turned to look at Michaela, whose blue eyes were watching something unseen on the ceiling. "Right? It's not my decision to make. I know that."

And she did. Didn't make it any easier, but she knew.

Half an hour later, she'd drifted off in the chair and her phone pinging woke her up. A good night text from Cherry.

Sweet dreams. Mtg tomorrow, so no diner. Boo. And a crying emoji.

Sleep well, she texted back, and an emoji blowing a kiss. Then she sat up and stretched her arms above her head. She'd stayed later than she'd intended, and guilt settled on her when she thought about her poor cat.

"Gotta go, Mikey." She gathered her things together, then gave her sister a kiss. "See you soon."

Out in her car, she found herself thinking about Cherry again, about how it hadn't taken long at all for her to become such a huge part of her day. Hell, of her life. She started the engine, then pulled out her phone and texted once more.

I missed you today.

She added a heart emoji, and then headed home, smiling big.

CHAPTER NINETEEN

Tuesday was already a bear, and it was only eleven thirty in the morning. For whatever reason, lots of people had crashed their cars in the days before, and Cherry found herself driving all over town to check claims, examine damage, go over details.

She'd managed to send a text off to Ellis midmorning to see if she could meet for a quick lunch. Because honestly? Seeing her face even for just five minutes would go a long way in helping Cherry get through the rest of her day. Maybe they could do dinner or something.

Driving from client to client was when she did most of her thinking, and luckily, she'd been able to shove Lila to the side for the moment because Ellis had been on her mind a lot lately. She'd used the previous night—meeting Jared and spending time with him, Adam, and Shea—as sort of a test for herself. Not that Ellis spending time with her sister meant Cherry wasn't allowed to see her. She totally could've pushed the issue—she knew that already. Ellis would've made time for her, like she had when Cherry had called her back from Cleveland. She'd dropped everything because Cherry had asked her to. That spoke volumes about her reliability and trustworthiness. Not to mention it was a pretty big clue that Ellis was feeling the same way Cherry was about them. No, she had wanted to test *herself* last night. Spend the evening away from Ellis, on her own with her friends, and be fine. And she had. She was. But she'd missed Ellis like crazy. More than she'd expected to. And that had been eye-opening. When had she become this person, this girl whose most prominent thoughts revolved around the person she was seeing casually?

That was the important word, right? *Casually*. They were seeing each other *casually*. Okay, Cherry could admit that she was dying to have sex with her again. Because OMG, they were good at it. Playing it cool was much harder than she thought it would be. Part of her just wanted to dive headfirst into Ellis, into a relationship with her, be her girlfriend, spend holidays together, all that stuff couples do, and that was surprising. Given her upbringing, the whole idea of the happy life, white picket fence thing tended to be kind of a joke. But part of her thought about it. Often. The other part? Yeah. The other part knew there was much more they needed to deal with. Talk about. Take apart.

She noticed the little red number one on the screen in her car, meaning she had a text, and she hit the touchscreen so the car would read it to her.

"*Ellis Conrad said, Near the lake across from diner twelve fifteen.*"

Cherry chuckled at the lack of inflection or emotion in the robotic car voice. It made it sound like Ellis was clipped and stoic, two things she definitely was not.

At twelve ten, she pulled into the diner's parking lot, which was only half full. Sunny Side Up served lunch, and it was good, but not nearly as popular as breakfast, so she wasn't surprised by the lack of customers. It was likely why Ellis had time to meet her.

She trudged across the little street to the lakeshore, the area busy with other folks walking or meeting up or having lunch. There were lots of shops and little businesses in the area, and summer was prime time for lakeshore activity. She found Ellis sitting alone on a bench that faced the water, and even just seeing the back of her blond head made Cherry's stomach do a little flip-flop of gleeful anticipation.

"God, am I glad to see you," she said as she sat next to Ellis, close enough so their thighs touched.

Something was wrong.

She could tell instantly. The air felt off. The atmosphere. The energy Ellis radiated.

"What's the matter?" she asked, then immediately added, "Is Michaela okay?"

Ellis didn't look at her, just at the phone she held. "My sister is fine," she said quietly, then did some scrolling and held the phone toward Cherry. "Who's this?"

Cherry took the phone and squinted at the photograph, which was slightly grainy. Two women were sitting at a small outdoor table in a restaurant, their hands clasped across it. Both were brunette.

"Scroll. There are several." Ellis's voice held no emotion at all, weirdly similar to the car's robot voice. What the hell was going on?

She scrolled and very clearly felt the bottom drop out of her stomach. The second photo was less grainy, much sharper. Sharp enough that she recognized one of the women, and this time, they were kissing. It was Julianne, Andi's wife. She didn't recognize the other one.

"Um," Cherry swallowed, and her stomach churned, "I think that's Andi's wife, Julianne." Oh, poor Andi.

"It is. I had to do some research last night. Your friend Andi has a significant online presence."

Cherry could hardly breathe.

"Interestingly, when I wandered through her social media accounts, I found several posts that tagged an account called Cherry on Top. And I was curious, so I took a look."

Oh fuck.

Cherry felt sick and was almost certain she could hear walls crumbling down around her.

"Let me ask you a question." Ellis continued to stare out at the water, and her voice was low. Quiet, but not in a soft way. In a steely way. In a clearly angry and hurt way. "Do you have a girlfriend?"

"What? No!" Cherry blurted before she had time to think. Then, "No, I don't have a girlfriend."

Ellis looked her in the eye for the first time since she'd sat down, and her blue eyes widened in disbelief for a split second before her whole face shuttered again. "Not according to Cherry on Top." The sarcasm was clear.

"I can explain that," she said, but Ellis was clearly having none of it.

"You can explain what? How we've been seeing each other for nearly two months—eight whole weeks—and not only did you neglect to tell me that you're an LGBTQ+ influencer with several thousand followers, but you have a girlfriend, and you talk about her all the time on your socials?"

"No, that's just it. I don't. I don't have a girlfriend. She's pretend. I pretend to have one."

"I'm sorry, you *pretend* to have a girlfriend?" Ellis's eyes were almost comically wide. "Why the fuck would you do that?"

"To get more followers," she said quietly. Miserably. "Andi gets so many views on her posts that feature her wife…" She sounded ridiculous and she knew it.

"Yeah, well, Andi's wife is clearly banging somebody else, so something's not working."

She had no idea what to say to that, and then her eyes welled up, which was all she needed. She felt helpless as she literally felt everything she'd wanted slipping through her fingers. And it was her own fault.

"I can't believe you didn't tell me any of this."

"In my defense, you're not exactly a fan of influencers and social media in general." Okay, that came out a bit too snarky, and she grimaced.

"Did you just think I'd never find out?" Ellis was clearly incredulous. "Were you just *never* going to tell me?"

"No, I was." Ellis shot her a look that said she clearly didn't believe that. "I planned to, but I kept putting it off and putting it off and then…" She shrugged because she didn't really have an acceptable ending to that sentence.

"And then two months went by."

"I'm sorry," she said and was annoyed when her voice cracked. "I'm so sorry. I just…I didn't know how to bring it up after you talked about your sister."

Ellis gave a small nod. "I scrolled through your pages. I spent a lot of time last night and this morning doing that after my assignment came and I saw the pictures and recognized your friend with the purple hair."

"Your assignment?"

A nod. "I write for *The 11th Commandment*."

Cherry gaped at her in disbelief. "That online tabloid rag that airs people's dirty laundry? You never told me that."

Ellis's eyes flashed at her. "I guess we're even then."

Cherry felt her own anger zap through her but managed to keep her mouth shut because no, they weren't even.

"Your posts are…" Ellis shook her head as she looked off over the water. "They're not even you. They're…altered. Filtered. Airbrushed. And fake. Way too perfect. And"—her shoulders dropped, and she sighed and looked completely defeated—"maybe that *is* the real you, and the one I've spent two months with is the fake version. I don't even know at this point."

"No, no, that's not true." Cherry sounded desperate, and she knew it, but she didn't care. Because she *was*. She *was* desperate. Desperate to keep from losing this woman who sat next to her with the most disappointed eyes she'd ever seen.

"Which isn't?"

"The online version. I doctor that up so much. I use filters and editing and airbrushing and—"

"Fake girlfriends."

"And *a* fake girlfriend. Yes. One."

Ellis looked at her then. Held her gaze. And Cherry felt like she was searching inside her, looking for her soul, coming up empty. "But why?"

How could she answer that? The truth made her sound horrible. Vain. Self-centered. And she couldn't lie. Not again. She could never lie to Ellis again. She *would* never lie to Ellis again. She lifted her shoulders and let them drop, then sighed. "It's what I've wanted to do for a long time."

"Be a phony?"

Ouch.

What could she say to that? Ellis didn't understand, couldn't. And Cherry couldn't blame her, after what happened to her sister. Grasping at straws, she tried to explain. "Be better than me. I grew up with not a lot of money and not a lot of love. Nobody saw me. I kind of floated through school. I don't think my teachers could've picked me out of a lineup. I kinda thought that was going to be my entire life. Just floating through, disturbing nothing, being noticed by nobody. Then, I managed to get partially through college, and I became friends with Shea and Adam, and they helped me build some confidence. Shea especially helped me…be less hard on myself. She turned me on to Instagram and Snapchat and TikTok, and I really got into social media. I followed different influencers, and Shea told me all the time that I could easily do that. So I gave it a shot, and I was surprised to find out that I *really* loved it. And I was good at it. I *am* good at it."

Ellis said nothing, looked completely unimpressed, but was listening, so Cherry went on.

"As time went by and I gained followers, I started to realize that it was something I could do more. Maybe actually make a living at, down the line. A career. This may come as a surprise, but working at an insurance company isn't my dream job." The stab at humor fell short. Way short. Cherry continued, "I met Andi at a beerfest. I'd been following her for a while and tried to emulate things she did. She's kinda my idol in all of this."

"Influencing is not really doing her any favors, though, is it? If her wife is cheating on her?"

Yeah, that was an extra bit of information she hadn't even begun to digest yet. Poor Andi. "I guess not," she said quietly and the wind was suddenly completely gone from her sails. Explaining anymore just seemed silly. "I'm really sorry, Ellis." A beat of silence went by, then another. "I don't know what else to say. I'm so sorry I kept this from you."

Ellis had barely looked at her this whole time, and that continued. She stared at the water, at the people walking by, at the dogs on leashes. Anywhere but at Cherry. Her throat moved as she swallowed. It was when her eyes welled up that Cherry reached over and put her hand over Ellis's. Ellis pulled hers away.

Another ouch.

"I don't…" Ellis shook her head. "I don't even know what to do with all this. It's about the last thing I ever expected."

Cherry nodded, words leaving her head like dissipating steam. The lump in her throat felt huge, the size of a peach, just stuck there.

Ellis continued to shake her head, just slightly, like it had become a tic. "I just…I don't know." And then she stood up. Again, she didn't look at Cherry, and that really started to sting. "I think I need some time, Cherry."

And that was it.

She sat there as Ellis rounded the bench and walked away. Just walked away.

Get up. Get. Up. Chase her. Don't let her leave.

The thoughts shot through her brain like bullets, but her body remained still. Seated. Because she knew this was on her.

The best thing that had ever happened to her, and she'd blown it.

She'd blown it.

Story of her life.

She was used to this. Used to finishing at the end of the pack. Used to being overlooked. Used to having an average—sometimes less than average—life. This was just par for the course.

All of that ran through her head, train cars of negative thoughts, chugging away like they always had. But it wasn't the same as always because she knew that this was on her.

Her eyes welled up and the tears spilled over, rolling silently down her cheeks as she sat there looking out over the water, wanting to scream at the people who were laughing and enjoying their day while she sat there, her world crumbling.

This was on her.

Chapter Twenty

Shea somehow managed not to say *I told you so*. Not when Cherry initially told her what had happened. Not when she told her she'd texted Ellis several times and had gotten no response. Not at all. Cherry had no idea how she wasn't bursting at the seams to say it—it was certainly warranted. But she didn't, and for that, Cherry was grateful. She knew Shea had been right all along. She just didn't need to be reminded of it.

She had texted. She knew it was risky, but it was better than stomping right into Sunny Side Up and demanding to talk to Ellis. She'd said she needed some time, and Cherry had no choice but to respect that.

But she'd texted.

Three times.

All apologies.

Zero responses.

Now she sat in her room, flopped back on her bed, her phone in her hands, scrolling through her own stuff, then Andi's stuff, then her own, then Andi's, then to *The 11th Commandment*. She found three articles written by an E. Conrad. Mystery solved. She wanted to click off, but she was curious and ended up reading all three articles.

Ellis could write.

It was another thing she'd had yet to learn about her, and that only served to remind her how very new they were and how much there was left to get to know. And how she'd likely blown her chance.

The articles were good. Very well-written. Neutral and not at all judgy, which was surprising for the type of site it was, but not surprising given what she knew about Ellis's mind and, now, her ability to write.

She hated *The 11th Commandment* and all similar ilk. It was one thing to expose a company's lies to the public, but shining a spotlight on somebody's personal life was just not cool. And with that thought, she clicked over to Andi's Instagram, scrolled her photos, especially the ones that featured Julianne prominently. She knew Andi was on her trip to the Adirondacks, not due back for another couple days, and this was certainly going to change things if she was having a good time. She wondered if she should call her. Warn her.

Shea chose that moment to rap on the doorjamb and come in with a plate of cheese and crackers, and a glass of ice water. "Hey," she said as she took a seat on the bed next to Cherry's hip.

"Hey."

"I know you're probably not hungry, but I need you to eat a little something, okay?"

Instead of answering, she asked a question. "Should I tell Andi?"

Shea set the plate and glass down on the nightstand and then met her gaze. "Would you want to know?"

Cherry sighed.

"I mean, if I was married, and you found out my husband was cheating on me, wouldn't you tell me?"

"Would you want me to tell you?"

"Hell, yes!" Shea's eyes were wide, and her eyebrows rose toward her hairline. "I'd be pissed at you if you didn't."

"I was afraid you'd say that."

"Why?"

"Because how the hell do I tell Andi this?" Cherry pushed herself up so she was sitting and grudgingly took a cracker. When Shea didn't respond, she said, "I'm serious. What do I say? Specifically. Like, what words do I use?"

Shea sighed and gave her a nudge to move over. When they were both sitting side by side on Cherry's bed, backs against the headboard, Shea shook her head. "I think you just be as gentle as possible. Right?"

"I mean, I guess?"

"But you have to tell her before the article comes out. The last thing you want is for her to be caught off guard, scrolling along on her phone, and catch it in her mentions. Or worse, find out via a comment from a follower. Which is most likely how it would happen, right?"

Unfortunately, Shea was right about that. The speed with which information—especially negative information—traveled online was staggering. There was no way Andi wouldn't hear the news as soon as the article posted. No, Shea was right. She was Andi's friend, and as such, she needed to protect her as best she could. She had no idea when Ellis would deliver the article, and if she already had, when it would be posted. Realistically, that could happen at any moment.

"Goddamn it," she muttered. "I hate this. I hate all of it."

Shea wrapped an arm around her shoulders. "I know, sweetie. I'm sorry." And if there was a perfect place for her to insert an *I told you so*, it was right then. But she didn't.

Cherry leaned her head against Shea's shoulder. "I'm such a fool."

"We all are at some point. I still love you," Shea said with a squeeze, and she pressed a kiss to her temple.

They sat there in silence for several minutes, just being together. Cherry's brain had been a whirlwind of thoughts and excuses and blame and pleas and everything in between since lunchtime that day.

Shea reached toward the plate and grabbed a cracker topped with cheese. "Eat."

"Yes, ma'am." She put the cracker in her mouth, chewed it, and hardly tasted it at all. When her phone pinged a text announcement, her head snapped toward Shea's. Could it be Ellis? Finally?

Slowly, she picked up her phone and turned it so the screen faced her. Not Ellis. Lila.

Shea was looking over her shoulder and blurted, "Holy shit, I totally forgot about her. But…didn't you ask her not to contact you?"

"Yup." Cherry sighed. "The one I want to contact me won't. The one I don't want to deal with is texting. What the actual fuck, Shea?"

Shea squeezed Cherry again. "Oh, honey, you've got a hot mess going on, don't you?"

Cherry set the phone down with a groan because truer words? Never spoken.

❖

Michaela's room was quiet.

Not that it wasn't always quiet. But usually, Ellis talked more to her. Or Kendra came in to chat. Or Evan hung with her for a while, and they talked. But Kendra was off that night, and she'd texted briefly with Evan earlier, and she just wasn't in the mood for chitchat.

Cherry had sent a few texts apologizing. God, so much apologizing. Which Ellis both appreciated and was annoyed by. Because why do such a thing in the first place? If Cherry hadn't lied, if she hadn't hidden a huge part of her life from her, she'd have nothing to be falling all over herself apologizing for now. So, yeah. Ellis was irritated.

The article was written. All she had to do was give it a quick proof and send it to the editor. Turned out that Cherry's friend Andi—that was her name, finally!—was pretty well-known in social media circles. A few hundred thousand followers on TikTok, more on Instagram. *She* was the news here. Seemed her vids about being a lesbian in today's world prominently featured her wife and how happy they were, how wonderful their life together was, and they offered marriage advice. Ellis had scanned Andi's socials for over an hour. The vids had descriptions like *How to listen to your partner better*, *How to make a romantic dinner in less than thirty minutes*, *Keeping the lines of communication open*, and *Honesty is the best policy*. She'd snorted at that last one, said to Mikey, "Yeah, Cherry must've missed that one." She was relieved that Cherry wouldn't be mentioned in the article because the focus of it was on Andi, not her fellow influencers. It was one time Cherry would probably be glad she only had a fraction of Andi's followers.

"Seriously, how do you toss your advice around like that and not know your wife is cheating on you?"

She knew she was concentrating her irritation on Andi's situation in order to keep from looking more closely at Cherry's. She was aware. She'd spent much more than an hour on Cherry's page. Cherry on Top, it was called, and apparently, that was her brand. Ellis had to admit that she did a nice job with photos and vids, and she sat there in Mikey's room watching video after video, scanning photo after photo, and the thing she noticed the most was that none of them even seemed like the Cherry she knew.

Or did they?

She scrolled a bit more, noticing the filters used on Cherry's selfies, her skin unnaturally smooth and pink. She paid extra attention to shots that mentioned the mysterious FG, as Ellis had started calling her in her head: Fake Girlfriend. If she went way back, she found posts with somebody named Alyssa who seemed to be an actual girlfriend, and commenters loved her. Asked questions about her. Commented on how pretty she was, what a cute couple she and Cherry made. Then, about two years ago, she seemed to simply disappear. Wasn't mentioned. And the comments were relentless. *Where's your hot girlfriend? Did you guys break up? What happened? Your posts are boring now, bring back Alyssa!* Ugh. Poor Cherry. Ellis was surprised to find herself feeling sorry for Cherry when she thought about her reading through all the things her followers said. God, people could be so mean.

Then several months ago, Cherry started mentioning her *sweetie pie* taking the picture, now and then. There were a couple videos where she appeared to be talking to somebody off-screen. More photos taken by *my honey*. And the tone of the comments changed, too. Now, the followers wanted to see the new girlfriend. Wanted to know if she was as hot as the last one. And Cherry's number of followers started to increase quickly. Significantly.

It was kind of ridiculous, really, how nosy people actually were.

How did Cherry not notice that? Or did she, and she didn't care? These people didn't care about her. They were entitled assholes who got off on spying on other people. A sliver of sympathy slid into Ellis's heart, and she thought about how sad it was to think you had to invent somebody to love you for the sake of appearances.

She scrolled some more, stopping on shots she'd breezed by the first time, and that's when she realized that the shoes Cherry had worn on their hike together were given to her by the sporting goods company that made them. She could see that now, could see Cherry's review of them. She recognized some of the shots from the park that day, the sun coming through the trees, Cherry's feet in the water, and that sliver of sympathy vanished. Seriously? She'd been working that day and didn't think to tell Ellis.

"God, so many lies." She shook her head, feeling nothing but utter sadness.

She knew she should probably talk to Cherry, but she wasn't ready. She knew that. She was too mad. Too hurt. Too disappointed. The last thing she was in the mood to do was talk to Cherry. Saying something she couldn't take back would be a definite possibility.

Still.

Cherry had her mom to deal with. That was gonna be rough, and she could probably use somebody to lean on.

A shake of her head.

"No. She's got roommates. She can lean on them."

That was cold. Harsh. She knew that, knew she'd said it out loud because she was trying to be mad about it. But there was no fire, no anger. Just defeat.

CHAPTER TWENTY-ONE

Cherry sighed as she scrolled through Andi's TikTok. Since the article had gone live on *The 11th Commandment*'s website, Andi had lost over a third of her followers. In a twenty-four-hour period. Wow, lesbians hated infidelity. She'd told Andi who Ellis was, that she was the person she'd been seeing, and she'd tried to apologize for not being able to stop Ellis from writing the article.

Andi had been understandably shocked, and Cherry hadn't spoken to her since. Thinking about their friendship wasn't something she could do at the moment because it made her sad. Even though what had happened wasn't her fault, she was inextricably attached to it all. She hadn't been obliged to tell Andi who E. Conrad was, but she felt like she should. She knew Andi was going to need time to recover, but she hoped their friendship would still be intact afterward. It had been on her mind for hours.

And don't even get her started on the subject of Ellis. Another person who hadn't returned any of her texts. It had been three days now, and she was shocked by how much she missed her. It was a literal ache in her heart, and she didn't know what to do with it. She'd cried. She'd thrown things. She'd screamed into a pillow. And now? Now, she was simply numb.

Unfortunately, she had to set all of that aside because she had more pressing issues to deal with as she pushed through the Dunkin's double doors.

Lila was already at a table, tucked in the corner, her hands wrapped around a cup. Cherry didn't know her well enough to be able to tell from across the store if she was nervous, but she kind of hoped she was. Because Cherry definitely was.

It was late morning on Friday, and for whatever reason, her workload was lighter than usual, but she hadn't told Lila that. Rather, she'd scheduled this meeting at ten thirty in the morning so she could use her job as an excuse to leave. This was gonna be short and sweet—that was the plan.

Seeing Lila sitting at the corner table made the butterflies in her stomach grow until it felt like she had boomerangs bouncing around in there. Which pissed her off because she was the one with the control here. She stopped at the counter and ordered herself a cup of coffee she was reasonably sure she wouldn't drink and tried to remember what Shea had said.

You're in control. You set the pace. You can stand up and leave anytime you want to. Remember that.

She gave a slight nod to herself as she paid for her coffee and grabbed the cup. She glanced down at her feet, took in a slow breath, counted to five as she let it out, then headed toward where Lila sat.

Lila's face lit up. There was no other way to describe it. Her smile grew. Her eyes sparkled—dark eyes just like hers, Cherry noticed again. She stood partway up, like a gentleman standing in a lady's presence, then sat back down.

"Hi, Cherry," she said, and Cherry was surprised by the softness of her voice. The gentleness of it. "I'm so glad you came."

"Well, I thought twice." She gave her head a twitch and corrected herself. "No. I thought about seventeen times."

Lila smiled sadly. "I understand."

"Do you?" It came out snarky, and Cherry only felt bad about that for a split second, but Lila nodded.

"Absolutely. You owe me nothing, and I'm very aware of that."

"Good."

Silence reigned for a moment or two. Finally, Lila inhaled a huge breath and let it out very slowly through her nose before saying simply, "What do you want to know?"

Wow. Carte blanche, huh? Not what Cherry was expecting, but she was up for it. She could feel twenty-eight years of pent-up anger, hurt, and resentment starting to bubble up.

"Why?" It was all she said. All she needed to say.

A slow nod, as if that was exactly the question Lila had expected. "Well. None of it is a good excuse now that I look back. And I doubt any of it will make you feel better, but I promise to be as honest as I can." She cleared her throat. "I was young. Too young to be a mother." She held up a hand, stopping Cherry's protest on her lips. "No, it's not an excuse, and it shouldn't have mattered. But I was lost. I was selfish. I was *terrified*." She stared at her cup as she added the next part very quietly. "I felt trapped."

"Excuse me," Cherry said, as she stood and hurried to the ladies' room. Once there, inside a stall, sitting on the lid of the toilet, she gritted her teeth so hard her jaw started to ache. "I will not cry, I will not cry, I will not cry…"

God! Her mother was a selfish bitch. Oh, she had a baby and then felt trapped? Too fucking bad. *You don't just run out on your kid.* She snorted a sarcastic laugh. She hadn't even made it through five minutes of Lila talking before she'd bolted, and that wouldn't do. She was not a wimp. She was tough. She was strong. She'd made it this far without a mother—she wasn't about to let one fact clobber her.

She gave herself a shake, exited the stall, fixed her makeup in the mirror, and headed back out into the shop where Lila still sat at the corner table, looking out the window. When she turned her head and met Cherry's eyes across the room, she smiled sadly and waited until Cherry came back and reclaimed her seat.

"I'm sorry," Lila said softly.

Cherry nodded. "Where did you go?"

Lila tipped her head. "What do you mean?"

"When you left me with Dad. Where did you go?"

"Oh. I went south. I didn't really have a plan. I just…ran. Ended up in Durham. In North Carolina."

Cherry nodded again, slowly. "And what did you do there?"

Lila turned her eyes toward the window and gazed out. "I floundered for a while, bounced from shelter to shelter until I found a job, then another job, then ended up the office manager for a dentist." Cherry found it easier to look at her when she wasn't gazing back. She was fifty if Cherry remembered correctly, but she looked a bit younger. Great skin and gentle eyes and young-looking hands all contributed.

Her hair was a much lighter red than Cherry's, but the short cut was stylish, hip even. She turned back and caught Cherry looking. "Once I was making money and had an apartment, I called your father. I wanted to see you."

Cherry blinked at her several times as she frowned because what? When? When had she called? Her father had never told her that. According to him, she'd run away, and he'd never heard from her again. End of story. "What?"

Lila nodded. "Yeah. I called several times."

"He never told me that."

"I suspected that." Lila cleared her throat. "He said that you were doing great and that I'd disrupted your life enough by leaving, and I had no right to disrupt it again by popping back in." And that's when her eyes welled up, unshed tears shimmering in the late morning sun beaming through the window. "And I was only twenty-three at that point. Young and stupid and decided he was probably right. So I wrote the letters instead."

More blinking. "Letters?"

This time, Lila looked stricken. "He didn't give you my letters?" Her voice held a tone of quiet horror as realization seemed to sink into her brain. "Oh God. Oh my God."

Cherry sat there and watched the expressions on Lila's face. Watched her eyes fill with tears. A tiny prickle of sympathy began to form, niggling at her as she witnessed Lila's emotions.

"I sent you letters," Lila said quietly. "So many of them. And birthday cards and Christmas cards." She stared in Cherry's eyes. "He never gave you *any* of them?" When Cherry slowly shook her head, a small, strangled sound came from Lila's throat. "Oh, that son of a bitch. God, no wonder you hate me."

Her initial reaction was to say, *I don't hate you*, which was what you said when somebody says, *You hate me*. But she didn't. She swallowed the words. Because the truth was, she had hated Lila for a very long time. Years and years. And one misunderstanding wasn't about to erase all that anger.

But.

Yeah, there was a *but*, and she had to admit it. Lila looked crushed, clobbered by this new information. And Cherry was tough, she'd had to be to survive living with her dad and his damage, his anger, but seeing Lila taking in this new information put a nice, solid crack in her protective shell.

Lila looked up at her then, her eyes wet, her face flushed. "I'm so sorry, Cherry. I'm so sorry. I should've tried harder. I should've kept calling. I should've driven up here. I…"

Excuses. That's what they were. But Lila seemed to know that, seemed to understand how they looked. How they sounded. And she didn't push any farther. She just shook her head, wiped her eyes, and sipped her coffee.

A moment of silence, as if neither she nor Lila knew what to say next. Finally, Lila met her eyes.

"So, this has been a lot." Cherry's sarcastic chuckle seemed to give Lila a little energy, and she offered a sad smile. "I would love to see you again, talk some more, maybe share a meal, but I also think we could both use a break right now. I know I could."

Cherry nodded. "It's been a lot," she agreed, grateful that Lila had made the call she had.

"I'm going to leave things in your court, though. I…" Lila sighed heavily. "I did not expect things to go the way they did, and I know I've apologized twenty-seven times, but at this point, I feel like I'm just going to keep doing that, and I'm betting you're getting tired of hearing it." She held up a hand like a traffic cop. "Don't answer that." And she gave a sad little laugh and stood up. Once she'd gathered her purse and shrugged it onto her shoulder, she met Cherry's eyes. Her hand reached out toward Cherry, as if she was going to grasp her arm but thought better of it. "I hope you contact me. I'd love for you to contact me. But I understand how hard this all must be." Her dark eyes filled with tears again, and she blinked them back. "I really do hope to see you again."

With that, she gave one nod and headed across the floor and out the front door. She must have been parked out back because Cherry couldn't see her get into a car.

Wow. That was a lot of information in a short amount of time. She wasn't sure what to do with it all, so she stayed where she was, sipped her now-cold coffee and felt it hit her stomach like a punch of acid, and stared out the window at the street beyond. The day was hot but overcast, and the dull sky reflected her mood at the moment.

There had been letters?

What the actual fuck, Dad?

She knew he'd struggled after Lila left, and she knew she'd reminded him of her, which made his life hard. But had he actually kept it from her that her mother tried to connect with her?

If nothing else, Cherry Davis prided herself on her toughness. On her ability to let emotional things bounce off her. TikTok was rife with endless trolls and people who had nothing better to do than crap on others. She had her fair share of them in her comments. She laughed them off. Growing up, she'd had to have a steel exterior to survive her father's mood swings. His temper tantrums. And she'd done it. She'd survived. Some would say she'd even thrived.

But this?

A car pulled out of the parking lot then, and she could see Lila behind the wheel, and that shone a spotlight on this current crisis she'd been handed.

This was heavy. This felt like weight on her shoulders that she wasn't sure she could hold. Her knees were buckling because, holy shit, her mother had sent her letters that her father had never let her see.

What the hell was that?

And suddenly, the tough exterior cracked some more. It was almost like she could feel it, the shell surrounding her beginning to weaken, the knowledge that it would soon crumble completely and leave her open and vulnerable almost as bad as the cracking itself. Her eyes filled with tears. A hard lump took up residence in her throat, and she was glad she had her back to the rest of the Dunkin' so nobody could see that she was on the verge of tears.

She felt lost. Lonely. Hurt. And the only person she wanted to talk to about it didn't want anything to do with her.

And that just made it all so much worse.

❖

Ellis had submitted the article late—and with a slight hesitation—but she'd sent it.

The fallout for Andi had been swift and harsh. Ellis had watched, she hadn't been able to help herself, checking in on Andi's socials every couple of hours. And she felt guilty as she watched the number of followers get smaller and smaller, as if it was Andi's fault and she shouldered the blame for having an unfaithful wife. True, she had a huge number of followers, and she did get many messages of support, but she'd lost, like, a lot of them. Ellis grimaced as she closed out of Instagram on her phone and tried to ignore her own hand in the whole mess.

She'd checked on Cherry on Top as well, the big red cherry with the stem looking so happy and cheerful, and more guilt set in. Cherry had definitely lost some followers, too, and Ellis wondered at that. Guilt by association? Because they were friends and somebody decided they no longer liked Andi, did they not like Cherry as well? Ellis didn't think she'd ever understand this influencer community.

Interestingly, as of this morning all the posts that featured Cherry's girlfriend were gone, and all captions referring to her sweetie or honey or better half had all been edited. Somebody had been hard at work cleansing her accounts.

Cherry hadn't been in the diner all week. Ellis knew because she'd checked. This morning, she'd pretended she needed to look at the walk-in fridge, and Kitty totally called her out.

"She's not here." Kitty didn't look at her as she wiped a coffee mug dry and set it on the shelf.

"Oh, I wasn't…" She let her words trail off because it was clear by Kitty's *mm-hmm* that she was on to her like white on rice. She'd hurried back into her office.

The lunch rush had died down, and the doors had been locked, and her staff were doing their final cleanup before they knocked off for the day. She was sitting at a table in the dining area with a laptop, working on orders and paperwork. Her office in the back had no windows, and sometimes, it made her feel better to sit out front and absorb some daylight. She was doing just that when her phone rang. Evan.

"Hey, loser," she said by way of greeting.

"Sup," he said, and she could tell by the background noise that he was driving.

"On your way to a meeting?"

"Out of town," he told her. "Just wanted to check in, see how you're doing. I saw the article."

"Yeah."

"It's a good one. Nicely written."

"Thanks," she said, and a niggling feeling began to gnaw at her stomach.

"I checked her accounts after I read it. Man, she's hemorrhaging followers." He didn't accuse her, but the tone was there.

"Well, that's not on me." She didn't quite snap it, but almost. He didn't respond right away, and she made herself inhale slowly and count to five. "I'm sorry. I'm not mad at you. I'm mad at…others."

"Cherry."

"Yes." She swallowed a sudden lump. *And myself*, she thought but didn't say out loud. Something she wasn't ready to examine. Yet.

"You okay?" Evan could read her like a book, impressive for a guy. Kendra said the same thing about him.

A sigh. "Yeah."

Evan gave a chuckle. "That's not an *I'm okay* yeah. That's an *I'm totally not okay but don't want to talk about it* yeah."

He was not wrong.

"I don't think I wanna work for *The 11th Commandment* anymore." She blurted it, surprising herself.

"What? Seriously?" He was surprised, too.

"Yes, seriously," she said with a laugh. "I just realized it this very second. I hate them. I hate what they do to people. I mean, I'm okay with them uncovering when companies screw up. But the personal stuff? People having affairs or hiding their sexuality? No. That's between those people and their loved ones." She braced, waiting for Evan to lambaste her, but it didn't happen.

"Thank *fucking* God," he said instead, and she was so surprised that she barked a laugh.

"Tell me how you *really* feel," she said.

"I fucking hate that rag." Evan's disgust was clear. "I didn't say anything because I knew you were excited to get the gig, and you said you could use the money, but yeah. That thing sucks." She sensed he wasn't finished, and she was right. "I mean, yeah, it's terrible that somebody's getting cheated on, but does it really need to be spread all over the internet? Does it have to negatively impact her career? 'Cause it has, thanks to that piece of crap that calls itself a news outlet." A horn beeped in the background, and she was reminded that he was driving.

"Please be careful," she said automatically.

"I have you on speaker. No worries." There was a beat of silence before he went on, but his voice got noticeably softer, and she had a feeling what was coming. "Don't you think Cherry would've told you eventually?"

Yup. She knew it. "I mean, she had two months, Ev." There was a definite edge to her voice.

"I know." And he sighed like he was disappointed in Cherry. Which he should be, right? He *should* side with Ellis.

What she didn't tell him was that part of her was second-guessing her choices, her decisions. Not that she didn't have a right to be upset, because hell yes, she sure did. And there was still definite anger with Cherry. Definite anger. Righteous anger.

But.

Yeah. There was that word.

But.

But she wished she'd handled things differently.

But she wished she hadn't played a part in the mess that Andi Harding was now submerged in.

But she wished her guilty conscience had shown up *before* she'd hit send on the article.

But none of that had happened, and she'd done what she'd done, and there was no taking it back now.

She and Evan finished their conversation and hung up, and Ellis found herself staring out the window instead of finishing up her orders. The staff was gone, the diner was locked up, and still, she sat. The sun was shining, and people milled about in it, soaking it up. The small section of the lake she could see from her seat glittered a cheerful blue, three boats floating across her view. It was summer. It was warm and fun and happy, and she should be outside, laughing and enjoying the weather, not sitting in the empty diner, working late and kicking herself for her poor judgment, wondering what the girl she still really liked was doing, and wanting so badly to text her that she literally had to sit on her hands for several minutes until the urge passed.

Instead of texting Cherry, she wrote up an email to *The 11th Commandment* and thanked them very much for the opportunity but said she couldn't justify the havoc their stories wreaked on the lives of some people, and she regretted to inform them that she was resigning as one of the staff writers. Then she proofed it, signed it, and sent it.

And just like that, a weight lifted. Well, not all the weight, because the truth was, she carried a ton of it. But some. Some of it lifted.

She sighed and closed her laptop and couldn't stop her brain from wondering how Cherry was.

She was still wondering later that night as she sat in Michaela's room and read to her from the new Lisa Scottoline novel she'd downloaded. She started and stopped a few times, her brain trying to handle several topics at once.

A quiet laugh puffed from her nose as she realized she'd read the same sentence out loud three times. "Sorry, Mikey. Having some trouble focusing." She closed the Kindle's cover on her finger and stared out the window, then sighed. A big one.

It wasn't long after her pause that Kendra came in to check on things. Ellis hadn't expected to see her. "I didn't think you were working tonight."

"Switched shifts with Omar. With Evan out of town, might as well, right?" Ellis nodded but could feel Kendra studying her. She perched on the edge of the bed, put a hand on Michaela's leg, and stared at Ellis for a moment before speaking. "Talk to me," she finally said, spinning a finger around in front of Ellis's face. "What's that look?"

She'd already fended off Evan. She didn't have the energy to keep Kendra at bay as well. "Why couldn't she just be real, Kend? What's so hard about that?"

Kendra took a moment. She tilted her head, gnawed on the inside of her cheek. "Don't you think she was being real with you?"

"What do you mean?"

Kendra took a deep breath. "Let's be honest, okay? You don't like her online persona because of this girl right here." She tapped gently on Michaela's thigh. "That's not on her—that's on you."

"But she lied to me."

"She didn't, though. She didn't lie. She just didn't tell you everything. And that wasn't cool, no, but don't you think you're being a little hard on her? How many times has she sent you an apology text now? A million?"

That brought a reluctant smile. "A couple million, yeah."

"You have all the power here, you know. Maybe it's time you let her talk to you, yeah? Maybe you need to explain why you overreacted."

"I didn't overreact!"

Kendra said nothing, just watched her face.

"Shut up," she said, but there was no venom. She knew Kendra was right. Her own brain had been telling her the exact same thing. She set the Kindle on her lap and stared out the window.

"Just give her a chance, maybe."

"Maybe…"

"At least think about it." Kendra stood and dropped a kiss on the top of Ellis's head. Then she headed out the door, presumably to check on her next patient.

Give her a chance. Seemed simple enough. The question was, though, had she missed that chance?

CHAPTER TWENTY-TWO

Cherry stood with her hands on her hips and stared at the bright yellow garage-type door of the storage unit. She'd rented it several weeks after her father had died. Selling the small run-down shack they'd lived in meant she'd had to clean it out, and while she'd thrown most things right into a dumpster, there were a few things she'd boxed up to keep. Since she rented an apartment with two other people, she didn't have the extra space to stack a dozen boxes and a couple pieces of furniture she'd kept out of sentiment, so a storage unit it was.

She hadn't been back to it in years. Literal years. She got an invoice each month, paid it, and never gave the unit—or its contents—another thought.

With a sigh, she slid her key into the Master Lock and popped it open. The door opened loudly, clearly not used to sliding up and down on its track, squealing in protest.

Must hit her right in the face, as if it was a physical thing and not just a smell. Dust, old cardboard, and neglect all combined to create the air of *forgotten*. Cherry frowned.

She didn't really want to be here doing this, but her conversations with Lila, the shock and disbelief on her face and in her voice, had stayed with her for more than twenty-four hours, playing on a loop in her brain. She'd gotten very little sleep, and when she woke up Saturday morning, she knew somewhere in her being that she would end up here today, before she'd made a plan or even considered it. She just knew. She almost texted Ellis to ask if she'd come with her, but the idea of Ellis saying no was just too much to bear, so she managed to close out of the open text and slide her phone into her pocket. Now, she was there. Alone.

Boxes were piled in no conceivable order. Haphazard. Some against the side wall. One stack of three toward the back. There was a rocking chair, the one her mother had rocked her in as a baby, before deciding to head for the hills. Some sliver of sentiment must've made her keep it. There was also a step stool, clearly handmade, painted white with little cherries on it. Her late grandfather had made it for her. A dresser and night table and bed frame all stacked next to the other wall. Her childhood bedroom set, also a gift from her grandparents.

God, she'd lost so many people, and not for the first time, she let herself wonder what her childhood would've been like if her grandparents hadn't died early. If she hadn't been left with an angry, heartbroken dad who had zero help and very little knowledge about raising a little girl.

Shaking that off, she went to the boxes. Neighbors had helped her pack things up, so she had no idea what was in which box. Luckily, each one was labeled by room, so that would narrow it down a bit.

The kitchen boxes had all the dishes and utensils they'd had. Not a lot of happy memories tied to those. Her father didn't cook and had no desire to learn. Suffice to say, she'd eaten a lot of pizza in her young life. *A lot* of pizza. Boxes marked *bedroom*, *bathroom*, *basement*, *kitchen* again—she moved them all until she came across two that said *bedroom closet*. Since she'd taken the box from her closet when she moved in with Shea and Adam, these two were definitely from her father's bedroom closet, stuff that had been in there that wasn't clothing or shoes. She took the boxes off the pile and set them in the center of the unit where there was space directly under the bare bulb hanging from the ceiling. Pulling off the tape that sealed them shut was easier than she expected, as it had lost its stickiness over the years.

She hadn't packed these boxes, had no idea what was in them. She'd been forbidden to go into her father's closet as a kid. From going into his bedroom at all, actually. His roar was terrifying, and she'd only needed to hear it once to keep her from ever venturing near his room again. She'd ridden out many a nightmare by her little shaking self because she was too afraid to wake him up in the night. She didn't know a lot about his room, but if there were personal things or things he hid from her, this was likely where they'd be.

Getting lost in memories would be easy, she knew, as she pulled the rocking chair closer so she didn't have to sit on the floor of the dirty, musty storage unit. She brushed the dust off the seat with her hand, then sat and opened the first box.

All his clothes and shoes had been donated or thrown away—he didn't have anything even close to new or fancy, just jeans, flannel shirts, and the like. She'd taken three of his shirts, washed them, and hung them in her own closet for memory's sake. No, they didn't get along at all, but he was still her father, and she thought she might want something of his down the line. They still hung in the far reaches of her closet, and she hadn't taken them out since that first washing.

The first box didn't contain much. A few photo albums she didn't have the energy to flip through. Some spy novels. His favorite. A shoeshine kit, which made her snort a laugh because not only had she never seen him shine any shoes, but all he ever wore were his steel-toed work boots. What would he have shined? A toiletry kit was also there, almost empty save for a razor, some tweezers, and a small travel-sized bottle of Brut, the cologne he slapped on once in a while. She unscrewed the cap and took a whiff...and was instantly transported back to that old, run-down house and her childhood. She closed her eyes and could see her father's smiling face. He didn't smile often, and she was grateful that was the memory that hit her. She gave herself a shake and put the cologne back.

The second box only contained a few things as well. A framed photo of her grandparents that she didn't remember and decided to take with her, so she set it aside. A small tool kit with a hammer, flat-head screwdriver, Phillips-head screwdriver, tape measure, and pair of pliers. She also decided that might come in handy and set it next to the photo. The last thing in the box was another box, also sealed shut with tape. This tape was different, and she figured whoever had packed up her dad's closet had simply tossed this box in without looking inside. She pulled the tape off and flipped the flaps open. A pile of envelopes filled her vision.

Her heart began to pound as she read her own name and address on the top one.

"Oh my God," she whispered as she picked it up. Reaching into the box, she sifted all the envelopes through her fingers. There were dozens. *Dozens*. Maybe a hundred or more in all. Different sizes.

Different colors. Different weights and thicknesses and postmarks. A few had been torn open, but the majority of them were still sealed. Never opened. Never given to her. Tossed into a box and left there for decades. The only thing that was the same on every single one of them was her name in her mother's flowery handwriting.

"Oh, Dad, what did you do?"

She dropped them, covered her mouth with both hands, and felt the emotion boiling inside her. She wanted to read them. She also wanted to put them away and pretend she'd never found them. Her eyes filled, which pissed her off, because she'd made a vow a long, long time ago not to give her mother any more of her tears. She'd given far too many as it was. But now?

What about now?

Because while this pile of mostly unopened letters didn't change everything, it certainly changed *some* things. Yes, her mom had still left, but she hadn't ghosted her. She'd done what she could at the time to stay in contact. She'd sent—she sifted through them again, scanning dates on the postmarks—roughly six or seven letters a year for God knew how many years.

What had her father been thinking? On what planet was it a good idea to let your child think her mother wanted nothing to do with her, rather than explain the intricacies of divorce? Maybe not when she was five, but how about when she'd gotten older? As a teenager? When she was old enough to understand some of it? How in the world did he think completely erasing her mother from her life was the better option?

She felt sick and, for a horrifying moment, worried she might throw up right there in the middle of the dingy storage unit. But she pulled herself together and literally swallowed down her hurt, her borderline rage at *both* her parents now—though she had to admit she'd softened the slightest bit over her mom.

Several minutes passed, and she stayed in the unit, on her mother's rocker, and just blinked into the gloom while she let her brain absorb the new knowledge. And then, as if poked by a cattle prod, she plunged her hand into the box, grabbed one envelope, and pulled it out.

It was a soft mint green with a Hallmark gold seal on the back. Clearly a card. It was postmarked the year she turned ten. She tore it open before she could talk herself out of it and slid a birthday card out. A teddy bear holding a bunch of balloons graced the front, and a big pink number ten floated above it. When she opened the card, a twenty-dollar bill slipped out and settled into her lap. Her mother's handwriting spoke to her from inside.

> *To my little Cherry Pop—*
>
> *I know you're probably too big now for teddy bears, but this one reminded me of Sherman. Remember him? You had him when you were two and he was about the same color brown as the bear on this card. I hope you have a terrific birthday. Use this to buy yourself something fun. I can't believe you're ten years old! I love you and miss you so much. Call me anytime. I'd really love to talk to you. It's been so long. 919-555-6723. Happy birthday, my sweet girl.*
>
> *Love, Mommy*

The tears were flowing freely now. She opened five more. Each card or letter had the same phone number printed at the end. She'd had access to her mother for years and years and hadn't known it. And this time, that feeling of being sick wouldn't be swallowed down. She bolted from the chair and out into the daylight to a nearby garbage can where she emptied her stomach until she was dry heaving nothing but air.

❖

Later that afternoon, alone in the apartment—Shea was out of town visiting her parents and Adam was working—Cherry sat on her bedroom floor, the pile of cards and letters fanned out between her knees. She hadn't opened more, since the few in the storage unit. Hadn't been able to find the strength she'd need to do that. She'd looked at all the postmarks, and she'd put them in chronological order, but that's as far as she'd gotten.

She needed to open them. She owed Lila at least that, didn't she?

When her phone pinged a text notification, she didn't think twice. Probably Shea checking on her, as she'd done three times already that day. But when she glanced at the screen, she felt a jolt of surprise.

It was Ellis.

A little gasp left her lips without her permission and she quickly opened the text.

Been thinking about u...not sure I should tell u that, but there it is. U ok?

Apparently, Cherry had turned into a waterworks that day because her eyes welled up as she read the text again. Should she respond right away? Wait a bit and let Ellis stew? She snorted. Why? Why wait? She typed.

Hi! So glad to hear from u. Ok is a relative term. Been a really weird day...

The gray dots only bounced for a second before Ellis's text came back. *Tell me.*

Those two words warmed her in a way she didn't expect, and the tears spilled over and down her face as she cried for what felt like the sixty-third time that day. She cleared her throat, wiped a hand across her cheek, and typed.

Found out yesterday that my mom tried to contact me, but my dad wouldn't let her. She said she sent letters for years and never heard back...

Ellis replied with a simple: *OMG.*

But wait...there's more. She typed the rest, and it felt good to lay it out. *2day, found all the letters. Unopened. In my dad's stuff. 167 of them.*

This time, it wasn't a return text. The phone rang in her hand. Ellis. "Hey," she said as an answer.

"Where are you?" Ellis asked.

"Home."

"Tell me the address. I'm coming over."

It wasn't presumptuous. It wasn't bossy. It was comforting, and as soon as Ellis said the words, Cherry knew that's exactly what she wanted. She rattled off the address, and Ellis promised to be there in twenty.

When the doorbell buzzed, Cherry was still sitting on the floor in her room, and she looked up in surprise. Had twenty minutes gone by already? A glance at her phone said yes, in fact seventeen of them had. And she'd just sat there, lost in her own thoughts, clearly zoned the hell out.

She jumped up and went to the door, buzzed Ellis in, unlocked her door, and waited. When it pushed open and Ellis stood there, Cherry's breath left her lungs. Just left without a parting word or a good-bye.

"Hi," she said, and she scanned Ellis's form without actually meaning to, taking in the cropped jeans, washed-out light blue tank top, her blond hair in a ponytail. She smelled like warm peaches, and Cherry didn't even try to be subtle about inhaling her scent.

Ellis said nothing. She simply opened her arms and held them out for Cherry to walk into.

Which she did. Because hello? Of course she did.

And Ellis held her.

The circle of Ellis's arms was warm and soft, and Cherry felt safe there. That was a realization that surprised her because when was the last time somebody had made her feel safe? Ever? She inhaled deeply, and when she spoke, her words were muffled by Ellis's shoulder. "I feel like I've been doing some sort of losing time thing. I thought I'd just hung up from you, and the doorbell rang. I sat there for seventeen minutes and totally spaced out."

Ellis released her from the hug, but held her upper arms as she looked her in the eye. "Well, how could you not? This is big stuff." She blinked. "A hundred and sixty-seven letters? Seriously?"

"Seriously. I counted them." She grasped one of Ellis's hands and led her to the bedroom where the fan of envelopes still sat on the floor. "She left me roughly twenty-nine years ago and, from what I can tell, averaged about six letters a year." She waved vaguely at them.

"Holy shit."

"Yeah."

Ellis looked from the letters to her. "Are you okay? How did you find these? I assume you didn't know about them, right?" She frowned. "I'm sorry. That's a lot of questions, and if you want to tell me to mind my own business, I get that."

"Ellis." Cherry felt herself soften, just from saying her name out loud. "We have things to talk about, but right now? I'm really, *really* glad you're here." She gestured to the envelopes. "I've only opened a few so far." Then she gritted her teeth and grimaced.

"Do you want to open the rest?"

"I do. I also don't."

"Perfectly understandable." Ellis pursed her lips in obvious thought, and Cherry smiled. Squeezed the hand she still held. "Want coffee?" Ellis asked.

"I want alcohol," was Cherry's reply.

Ellis grinned. "I figured. Just wanted to make sure it was your idea and not mine." She glanced over her shoulder into the apartment. "Whaddaya got?"

A few minutes later, they were both seated on the floor with glasses of Shea's white wine. She wouldn't mind. In fact, she'd have insisted. Cherry took a healthy sip, set the glass down, and shook out her body.

"Ready?" Ellis asked. She'd taken the fan of envelopes and neatened them into a pile that she now had on the floor near her.

Cherry nodded. Ellis handed her the top envelope. A deep breath and Cherry sliced it open.

They took their time. Cherry opening one letter at a time, reading it to herself, then handing it over to Ellis—who clearly wasn't going to read them, judging by the way she folded the first one up. "You can read them."

"It's okay," Ellis said. "This is your private stuff between you and your mom. And I know you and I have been…" She shrugged, maybe not wanting to put a label on what they'd been.

"You can read them," she said again. "I trust you."

Ellis's smile and the way her face changed at the words made Cherry relax even more. And it was true—she did trust Ellis. She blew out a breath and was on to the next letter.

In the end, most of the letters were very similar in tone and message. Lila loved her and missed her and wished Cherry would call, here's the number. The earlier ones talked about her new life in North Carolina and how she'd made a room for Cherry if she ever came for a visit. As time went on, the letters got shorter. Simpler. The same message, but in fewer words, as if Lila was slowly giving up. Cherry's tears flowed pretty much nonstop, and they'd finished the bottle of wine. Lila had sent twenty dollars for every birthday and fifty for every Christmas. The letters had stopped three years ago—likely because Cherry's father had passed away and the house was no longer his address. All told, there was one thousand eight hundred twenty dollars in cash in a pile near her knee.

"Do they still mark things Return to Sender?" she asked.

Ellis scrunched up her nose. "Good question. I don't know. Why? Oh, 'cause the letters stopped after your dad passed away."

"Exactly."

"You could ask Lila." The suggestion was gentle. Cherry had relayed the story of their conversation as they went through the pile, how she'd started out so angry and how Lila was a little bit defensive until the fact of the letters was revealed. "Does she know you found them?"

Cherry shook her head. "I haven't had any contact with her since our conversation. She may have assumed my dad tossed them. I did."

Ellis nodded as if she understood. Did she? "What are you gonna do now?"

A big sigh slipped from Cherry's lungs. "I mean, I want to call her. I should call her. I will call her. I just…I need to absorb all of this first, you know? It's…"

"It's a lot," Ellis said with a snort. "Like, *a lot* a lot. Wow."

"It is, right?" Cherry laughed softly. "I was worried I was making it too big a thing."

"What?" Ellis barked a laugh. "Too big a thing? It's a *huge* thing. No, you can't possibly make this into too big a thing. Don't worry about that."

They laughed together for a moment at the ridiculousness of the entire situation. When the laughter died down and they were just smiling, Cherry met Ellis's gaze. "I'm really glad you're here. Thank you."

Ellis stayed for a while longer, but somehow, they'd silently agreed it wasn't the time to talk about their issues. Cherry was too exhausted, too mentally overloaded to deal with one more thing, and Ellis seemed to get that. She made a mental note to thank her for that, down the road. When Ellis left, they hugged in the entryway for a long time. Just held each other. No kissing. Nothing sexual. Just comfort. It was exactly what Cherry needed.

The second she shut the door behind Ellis, it was as if any scrap of energy she had left just vanished. She went back to her room, crawled under the covers, and was asleep in seconds.

CHAPTER TWENTY-THREE

The week came and went before Ellis even realized it. On Sunday morning, she'd actually forgotten that the diner was closed and she had a day off from work. She went in anyway. There was always something that needed to be done. And also, she needed to try to focus her mind on something other than Cherry Davis.

She was failing miserably at that, staring off into space and doing a hell of a lot of sighing, when the back door to the diner opened—right next to her open office—causing her to jump up out of her chair in frightened surprise.

"Relax, baby girl, it's just me," Kitty said, chuckling as Ellis pressed a hand to her pounding heart.

"Jesus Christmas, you scared the hell out of me."

"Sorry about that. Just swinging by to pick up a batch of biscuit dough Cal made for me. Having my mama and sisters over today for a barbecue." Her eyes scanned over Ellis's desk, likely taking in the scattered papers and open laptop. "You wanna come? You're more than welcome, and Lord knows there will be plenty of food."

"Oh, that's really nice of you. Thank you. I'm good."

"Mm-hmm," Kitty said, arching an eyebrow. "That's why you're in here on a Sunday, working." When Ellis didn't say anything, she asked, "Why aren't you off doing something with the redhead?"

Ellis thought about shooing it away, waving a dismissive hand and laughing about how that was over, and it hadn't really been much of anything anyway. She really did. But something in her stopped the words from leaving her lips. Kept her waving hand on the table. Made her roll her lips in and bite down on them in thought…just a quick moment of thought…

And then she sighed again, dropped down into her chair like her legs had given out, and spilled it. She just spilled it all. She told Kitty everything, from beginning to end, leaving nothing out. When she finished, she was literally out of breath.

"Well." Kitty found a folding chair, unfolded it, and sat down in front of Ellis's small desk, as if the story was too heavy for her to keep standing. "Wow."

"Yeah."

"I mean"—Kitty shook her head, her eyes wide—"wow. That is a *tale*."

"I know, right?"

"And the solution for you is to come in to work on a weekend and, what, write orders until your eyes cross and fall out of your head?"

Ellis grimaced, feeling sheepish as she admitted, "I mean, I was gonna do some cleaning, too."

"Girl," Kitty said and somehow managed to make that one word sound both scolding and loving at the same time. "What am I gonna do with you?"

Ellis let go of yet another huge sigh, then whined, "I don't *know*," dragging out the last word to about five syllables.

"What do you want from this girl?"

"I don't know that either."

Kitty gave a snort. "Well, don't you think you'd better figure that out? And if the answer is nothing, then you leave her the hell alone. But if it's something…" She tilted her head like Ellis should already know the answer.

And she did.

"I want to be with her. I want us to try. We are so good together, and I want to see where we could go. But"—she swallowed, unsure why it was hard to say this—"I want her to be real. I don't want the fake, filtered, artificial Cherry on Top. I want the *real* Cherry. If she can't be real with me—"

"She's been real with you," Kitty corrected.

That was true, she was beginning to understand. Both Kendra and Kitty had said the same thing, and Ellis was starting to get that they were right. "Yes, but she kept the rest hidden. Lied about it. Sort of."

Kitty nodded. "And does she know this is what you want from her?"

Yeah, there was that, wasn't there? Because they hadn't talked since she'd been over to see Cherry and watched her reading her mom's letters. They'd texted a bit, sure, but they hadn't *talked*. Not about them. "I mean, she knows it was a problem for me."

"But have you told her you're still interested if she's willing to do this one thing?"

"I haven't told her that, no. The whole thing with her mom was a distraction."

"Mm-hmm."

"I hate when you make that sound."

Kitty shrugged. "It's just a sound."

"It's a judgy sound."

"That's because I'm judging you."

Ellis dropped her head to her desk and slowly banged her forehead against it while groaning. It made Kitty laugh.

"Honey, you know what you need to do here. Nothing good ever comes from hiding your feelings from your partner." Kitty waved her hand in front of Ellis. "Case in point."

A groan. She'd been doing a lot of that lately. "I know. I know. You're right."

Kitty sat up and cupped a hand to her ear. "Say that again, would you? I can't hear it enough."

"You. Are. Right." Ellis laughed then. She couldn't help it.

"You're damn right, I'm right." Kitty pushed herself to her feet. "I'd love to stay and solve all the world's problems, but I have a barbecue to host." She moved to the large walk-in refrigerator, went inside, and came out with a silver bowl covered in plastic wrap. The biscuit dough, Ellis presumed. "And if you change your mind, come on over to my place, okay? You can bring your redhead."

"Thanks, Kitty. I owe you."

"You owe me nothing." Kitty stopped on her way toward the door and turned to meet Ellis's gaze. "It's okay to say what you need. Totally allowed, okay?"

"Okay."

"And it's okay to be happy. You *deserve* to be happy. Okay?"

That one was harder for her, but Kitty clearly wasn't leaving until Ellis smiled softly and said, "Okay."

“Okay.” And with one nod of her head, Kitty was off.

Ellis sat there in the silence of the closed diner for long moments after Kitty left, her head a whirlwind of thoughts and feelings and emotions.

You deserve to be happy.

She hadn’t been in therapy since they’d moved to Northwood. She hadn’t taken the time to find a local therapist, if she was being honest. But that line about deserving happiness was one her last therapist had touched on with her and something she had lots of trouble swallowing, given how badly she felt like she’d failed her sister.

And now, in addition to that little gem of self-recrimination, she had the very sharp feeling of being torn. Torn between running as far and as fast away from Cherry Davis and her toxic online life as she could, and staying put, trying, talking, working. Because she could bitch about and complain over and protest against Cherry’s influencer dreams, but number one, they were Cherry’s dreams and Ellis had no right to quash them, and two, she had feelings for her. Deeper feelings than she’d had in a long, long time. Years. Deeper feelings than even she cared to admit. That was probably why the discovery of Cherry’s online life was such a blow.

She picked up her phone. She suddenly wanted to check out more of Cherry on Top. She hadn’t looked in quite a while, so maybe it was time. Maybe she needed to watch more and try her best to open her mind. At least a little. A touch.

“Maybe, like, just a crack,” she said quietly to the empty office. She navigated to Cherry’s TikTok and saw there were a couple new videos. She hit one, and the screen filled with Cherry’s beautiful face, and Ellis felt everything in her soften a bit at the sight. Dammit. She was clearly in her bathroom with her phone propped up or on a tripod or something because both her hands were free. She put a headband on and pushed it back so her gorgeous red waves were all off her face.

“Hi, loves, Cherry here. It’s Saturday evening and let me tell you, it’s been a hell of a week for me. I’ve learned some things. I’ve discovered some things. I’ve realized some things. I thought I’d share them with you in snippets because I’ve decided I’m gonna veer a bit onto a new path here.”

At this point, Cherry pulled out what looked like a wipe of some kind and began moving it over her face, taking off her makeup. Ellis blinked in surprise.

"No more filters, first of all. I'm not sure why we've become a country—a world—that thinks the only thing that makes a person beautiful is perfection. I am not perfect. Far from it. See this?" She poked a finger at a now-visible blemish on her cheek. "That was a zit that I picked at last week. What the hell, Universe? I'm thirty-two years old. Can't I be done with zits now?" And then she smiled that smile, and the screen practically lit up as she continued to remove her makeup.

"A lot of you saw *The 11th Commandment*. I know you did, 'cause I got lots of comments, and I'm gonna set the record straight in another post, so stay tuned, okay?"

Ellis grinned because the subtlety of the marketing there was kind of brilliant. *You're watching this video, and I'm doing something I've never done before, but I don't want you to go anywhere, so I'll tease a future video just to keep you on the hook.* She had to give Cherry kudos. She knew how to keep her viewers wanting more.

"But in the meantime, we're gonna do a bit of shift here." She finished removing all her makeup, then looked right at the camera for a beat or two. "This is me. This is it. This is how I look without makeup or filters or special lighting. Just me. In my bathroom." A shrug. Then, she held up a finger and gave a crooked smile. "Now, does that mean I'm going to stop wearing makeup? Please." She gave a cute little snort. "But I'm no longer using any filters. Hashtag #nofilters is taking on a new meaning over here at Cherry on Top." Her expression grew serious, enough that it made Ellis lean slightly closer to the phone in her hand. "We're going for real. Okay? Real talk. Real life. Because that's what's important. That's who we are. We are all *real people*." She let that sit for a beat, then let that beautiful smile loose again. "Until tomorrow, loves. Peace." And she held up two fingers and tipped her head to the side.

Ellis hit pause.

Real talk. Real life.

Well. Wasn't this interesting?

❖

"Hey."

Shea stood in the doorway of Cherry's room a couple days later, her shoulder against the doorjamb, arms folded across her chest, and the sight of her best friend always made her world feel a bit less crazy.

"Hi," Cherry said, sitting on her bed. She toed off her shoes and sighed with relief. "How was your day?"

"Busy. But good. Yours?"

"Same. Well, except for the good part. Amanda is gonna send me over the edge soon, I swear to freaking God. She's such a micromanager. Seriously, just leave me the hell alone, and let me do my fucking job." She fell back dramatically onto the bed with a groan.

"Feel better?" Shea laughed softly and joined her, and they lay there, side by side, letting the workday slide off them. After a moment of quiet, Shea said, "I liked your last couple of TikToks."

That surprised her and she turned her head to regard her BFF. "Yeah?"

"Absolutely." Shea wriggled until she was on her side, her head propped in her hand. "I think the new outlook is a good one. I don't know of anybody who's doing that, using that angle."

She took a deep breath and held it for a second or two before letting it out slowly. "It feels right. I don't know how else to explain it. After the Andi thing and the fake girlfriend thing and the Lila thing and especially after the Ellis thing, it feels like the right way to be."

"And how are all those *things* going?" They hadn't really sat down and had an in-depth conversation for what felt like forever.

"Let's see." Cherry sat up and ticked them off on her fingers. "The Andi thing makes me sad. I think I've lost her friendship, but only time will tell on that."

Shea nodded.

"The Lila thing is...I don't know. I'm kind of torn between continuing to be furious at her for the rest of my life and actually getting to know my mom. You know?" She shook her head, not really understanding all the details, but not having the brain power left to roll them around.

"I mean, you're the only one who can decide what path to take."

"Exactly. I think it's time I contact her."

"Look at you, making big girl decisions like a big girl." Seconds ticked by in silence. A full minute. Almost two. Finally, Shea said softly, "And the Ellis thing?"

"Oh, the Ellis thing." The Ellis Thing. Like the title of a rom-com. Was that what they were? If so, was the happy ending nearby? Because she was losing hope. She pushed herself to a sitting position. "She was terrific when I was dealing with the letters."

Shea frowned and sat up as well. "I'm still so sorry I wasn't here for you."

Cherry grasped her arm. "Shea. I've told you a hundred times, you have nothing to apologize for, you weirdo. You were out of town."

"Still." Their gazes held, and Cherry smiled at her, gave her a playful shove. "What are you gonna do now?"

"I'm gonna own it all," Cherry said and didn't realize the truth in the statement until she'd actually said the words out loud. Wow. Okay.

"Yeah?"

"Yeah. I think I need to."

"Making some changes."

"Yes." She met Shea's gaze. "It's about time I did. Ellis…she really got me thinking. Lila. Hell, all of it has. My poor brain is *so tired*."

Shea smiled at her but was quiet for a long time, and her face told Cherry she had lots of thoughts on the subject, but all she did was nod. "Well, I think you're moving in the right direction."

"You do?"

"You're unique, Cherry. Special."

"I am?"

Shea laughed and leaned into her with a shoulder. "Yes, you dumbass. I think you should keep running with what you just started. The unfiltered stuff." She turned to look at her. "It sounds like a Netflix documentary, doesn't it? *Cherry on Top: Unfiltered*."

Cherry's laugh bubbled up then. "If only, right?"

Shea's voice went soft. "If anybody can do it, you can."

"Thanks, Shea."

"For what?"

"For having faith in me. For being my friend. For being you." She leaned her head on Shea's shoulder.

"I've got you, babe. Always. You know that."

And she did.

CHAPTER TWENTY-FOUR

Another week later was too long, but Cherry couldn't bring herself to contact Lila until that much time had passed. There was definite guilt about that, about leaving the poor woman hanging for such a long stretch. And then she reminded herself who she was talking about, and that guilt vanished into thin air. Besides, she'd promised to give herself enough time to absorb all the new information she'd received over the past weeks before diving back in.

It was all completely insane.

So, there she sat, in the Dunkin' again, but this time, she was the one who was way early. Like, *way* early. As in she'd been sitting there for over an hour before it was even *close* to time to meet. She'd watched a good thirty customers come and go. Easily thirty. Maybe more. Amanda wasn't happy that she'd called in sick, but she also couldn't argue it, as Cherry had about nine million sick days because she very rarely took one. Shut up, Amanda.

Her brain hurt. Like, literally hurt. Constant headache. Clearly, she had too much going on, and the organ was revolting, staging a mutiny, maybe trying to leave her skull altogether. Between her job, her rebranding, Ellis—God, Ellis, and this unexpected mess with Lila, her poor head was beyond overloaded. She couldn't sleep. She couldn't eat. As it was, the coffee she'd been sipping felt like it was burning a hole in her stomach, and she was absently wondering if maybe she'd developed an ulcer, when the door opened, and Lila walked in. She glanced at her watch, noticed Cherry, and grinned widely as she crossed to her table.

"It's only thirty minutes before our scheduled meet time," Lila said. "Looks like we both prefer showing up early." Cherry gave her points for not saying anything remotely resembling *like mother, like daughter*. Lila stood there for a moment, just looking at Cherry, before asking, "Can I get you anything?" When Cherry shook her head, Lila held up a finger and said, "I need coffee. Be right back."

This time, instead of not wanting to see her, Cherry studied her. The way she was built, the way she walked, the way she stood. How she leaned ever so slightly over the counter when placing her order. How she turned and caught Cherry looking and gave her a reassuring smile, even though she must've known Cherry was sizing her up.

I walk like her.

The thought shot through Cherry's head as Lila headed toward the table with her coffee. She didn't bounce at all when she walked, just sort of glided along the floor, and Cherry knew she did the same thing. Shea had poked fun at it once or twice. Called her Michelle Kwan because Shea said it looked like she was skating rather than walking.

Lila pulled out the chair and sat. She looked much like she had last time, like a regular person. Somebody's mom. Her hair was fluffy but neat, her dark eyes observant, her outfit simple—jeans and a T-shirt.

"Do you burn easily?" she blurted before she even knew she was thinking the question.

If Lila was surprised, she didn't show it. "Like a lobster." She grinned and held out a leg. "Thus, the jeans in summer."

She nodded slowly, taking that in. And then, suddenly, she had no idea what to say. She'd rehearsed several versions of the speech she'd planned, but strangely, they all flew from her head, and she was left with a big ol' blank where her thoughts used to be.

Lila took the lid off her coffee, blew on it, sipped, and did not seem rushed at all. She didn't hurry Cherry along. She simply smiled gently and waited. After all, Cherry had called this meeting. Lila was obviously waiting for her to take the lead.

Cherry took a big breath, blew it out, and made the decision. "Okay. I'm gonna dive right in then." She reached into the bag on the floor by her feet and pulled out Lila's letters, which she'd rubber-banded into three stacks. She set them on the table, and Lila gave a little gasp. "I just found these recently. After our last meeting. In my dad's stuff. With the exception of the first one, they were all unopened."

Lila's big eyes, a shade of brown so like hers, filled with tears, and she clamped a hand over her mouth as if to keep any wayward sobs in. She took a moment. Cherry saw her swallow twice, then she seemed to pull herself together. She removed her hand, cleared her throat, and said, "You found them."

"Yeah. Dad had hidden them. And I swear to God, I don't know who I should be more pissed off at, you or him."

Lila frowned and looked into her coffee cup. "I get that."

"No. You don't. Forgive me for being a bitch about it, but you absolutely *do not* get it."

"You're right. I'm sorry. And you're not being a bitch, but you have every right to be if you want to. I apologize." No argument. No defense. Just an apology. Okay, that was surprising. Lila took a closer look at the stacks. "You opened them then?"

"I did. Read them all. Was gonna bring you back the cash because I don't really want anything from you, but then decided to hell with that, I earned it."

A nod from Lila. "That's totally fair. It was meant for you anyway. I wouldn't want it back."

Okay. Fine. That was good. Cherry sipped her now very cold coffee and wished she'd taken Lila up on her offer to get her something. At the same time, she felt jittery enough. More caffeine wasn't going to help.

The silence went on for what felt like forever but was probably only a minute or two.

"So," she began, slowly turning the cup between her fingertips. "What do you do in Durham? Do you have a job? Are you married?" She glanced at the diamond on Lila's ring finger. "I assume so. Kids? Well, *other* kids?" Yeah, snarky. It was allowed.

More slow nodding from Lila. Cherry was starting to understand this was a nervous habit of hers. Or maybe something she did while she organized her thoughts. "I do data entry for a medical billing company. I work from home, which means I can work on the road, too. That's how I've been able to be here indefinitely."

That hadn't even occurred to Cherry, and she took it in, the fact that Lila had been away from her home for weeks, judging by how many times she'd been in the diner before actually approaching her. "You've been here a long time."

"Two months, actually." Lila laughed, but there was an edge to it.

"To answer the rest, yes, I am married. I also have a son. Noah. He's nineteen and in college at NC State."

I have a brother. Cherry blinked rapidly as her brain took in this information as well. Wow. "Do they know you're here and why?"

More nodding. "They do. They encouraged it, in fact."

"Really."

"Yes. I've been…struggling lately. We all sat down and talked about it, and they pushed me to come here and try to meet you, try to explain, try to apologize." Lila's voice was quiet, barely a whisper, and her eyes filled.

Cherry swallowed down the sudden lump in her throat, annoyed that Lila's emotion was affecting her. She absently sipped her coffee, then grimaced.

"Look. Cherry. I'm not asking you to forgive me. What I did to you was unforgivable. I'm not asking you for anything. I wasn't even sure I'd get to meet you, and if I did, I wasn't sure it would go beyond you telling me to fuck off and leaving. So this?" She waved a finger between the two of them. "This is so much more than I was even hoping for. And I want to thank you so much for sitting down with me. Twice now. I can never apologize enough to you, but I want you to know that I'm so happy and so grateful to be sitting across from you in this moment. You are more beautiful than I imagined. You're smart and you're creative, and I'm just so grateful."

The lump was back. Bigger. Dammit. She cleared her throat. "How do you know I'm creative?"

"Are you kidding? I've been following Cherry on Top since the beginning. I love it. It's so much fun."

"You—" Cherry sputtered. Actually sputtered. Because what? "You have? It is?"

"How do you think I found you?" Lila smiled then, and for the first time, Cherry was struck by how much they actually really did look alike. A sip from her coffee and then Lila asked, "Can I ask you something, though?"

Cherry nodded, not trusting her voice yet.

"What's the deal with the girlfriend you always referred to but never showed? All mention of her is gone now. Did you guys break up? I mean, I'm not surprised, because I've seen you with that blonde at the diner, and if you don't mind me saying, you two have some off-the-charts chemistry." She arched one eyebrow as she brought her cup to her lips.

OMG, does my mother think I was cheating? It was a ridiculous thought for so many reasons. So ridiculous that she suddenly burst out laughing. When she pulled herself together, she pointed at Lila. "Okay, first of all, I think I just got a taste of your Disapproving Mom face."

Lila had the good sense to look sheepish. "Yeah. Noah calls it the arched brow of doom. Force of habit. Sorry about that."

Cherry felt herself soften. Like, literally, all her muscles relaxed, and she smiled. "It's okay. No need to apologize. So..." She took a deep breath. "I'm gonna tell you the story. The *whole* story." And to her own very unexpected surprise, she unloaded all of it. She talked about Alyssa. About Andi. About making up a girlfriend. And mostly, about Ellis. A lot about Ellis. About their date. About how good it was with her. Even about how Ellis wrote the article. And even how Ellis came over, no questions asked, when Cherry had found the letters. How she'd sat with her the entire time she opened and read each one.

"Yikes, she wrote the article?" Lila's eyes were wide as she asked the question.

"Yeah, that was rough." Cherry sighed. "At the same time, I never should have kept that from her, so despite what it's done to me, to us, I can't really hold her responsible for a mess I helped create. I see that now."

Lila was quiet for a few minutes and seemed to be searching for the next right thing to say. "Where do things stand with her now?"

"Honestly? I'm not quite sure. She was really supportive when I read all the letters. And it was kind of by unspoken agreement that we didn't talk about us at that time, so I guess things were kind of left in her court." A small shrug because she honestly wasn't sure.

"Do you miss her?"

"God, so much. It's ridiculous." She shook her head and stared out the window at the passing traffic. "I haven't even known her that long. How is it possible to miss somebody you've not spent a ton of time with?"

Lila smiled tenderly. "That's the great mystery of love, isn't it? Sometimes, you just find your person." She seemed to stop herself, as if she wanted to say more but thought better of it.

Cherry cleared her throat. "Is...is your husband your person?"

Lila nodded, not elaborating, but the light behind her eyes was clear.

"That's cool," Cherry said, nodding. "I'm glad."

"Yeah?"

"Yeah." They were quiet for a moment before Cherry studied her empty cup and spoke. "Can I ask you something?"

"Anything."

"What do you think I should do?" Wow. Now that was a step. A laugh burst out of her as Lila smiled, confused. "Sorry. I just, I literally just asked my long-lost mother for advice on my love life. It's kinda surreal."

Lila's smile blossomed wider. "You did, didn't you?"

"So much for baby steps, am I right?" She gave a laugh-snort combination that had Lila's eyes going wide. "What?"

"I make that sound when I laugh sometimes, too."

They held each other's gazes for a beat. And Cherry didn't say the words because, yeah, way too soon for that. But she thought them. They were loud in her head.

Maybe this thing with Lila is going to be okay.

"This isn't easy for me to say, so I'm gonna just say it." Cherry cleared her throat as she looked directly at the camera. Her hair was pulled back off her face in a ponytail. Her cheeks were flushed. She visibly swallowed. "I've had some eye-opening realizations lately. They've been painful, to say the least. They've left me confused and sad and unsure of what to do. But I think I've figured it out. If you're a regular follower of mine, then you know I often refer to my sweetie, my honey, my sugarplum who prefers to stay behind the camera instead of showing up in my photos and videos." She took a deep breath and let it out slowly. "Here's the thing, loves. Yes, I posted about her a lot and told you all she was my girlfriend, but…" She hesitated for a beat, swallowed again. "That's not true. It was never true. There is no sweetie, honey, sugarplum. I made her up because I thought that's what you wanted to see. A happy, cheerful lesbian in a stable, enviable relationship. But that's not me. Not right now." She blew out a little breath, just a small puff of air, clearly relieved, then shook her head.

"I'm so sorry. I didn't set out to deceive you, but I won't try to offer up some weak ass excuse. What I did was wrong. And worse, I messed up something *really* good because of it. I had somebody who is nothing short of incredible. And I kept the truth from her. Let me tell you, karma is no joke. She drives a *big ass* bus, and she's got everybody's address." An uncomfortable chuckle. "I am truly, sincerely sorry."

Ellis hit pause on the TikTok video, shocked by what she'd watched, what she'd heard, feeling like she needed to take a breath. She was really doing this, Cherry was. No. Not *doing*. Did. Done. The video was posted several hours ago. She'd really done this. First, she'd talked about how she was going to stop using filters and such. And now she'd admitted to her followers—and anybody else who happened across Cherry on Top—that she'd lied. That she'd deceived them, played them for fools. Surely she was gonna get clobbered. People were notoriously brutal online, especially when they felt like they'd been suckered. Nobody wanted to be made a fool of. Nobody liked that. Especially people who could let you know how pissed off they were by saying mean, hateful things and still stay anonymous. She didn't want to think about what Cherry's comments and DMs were going to look like after this. Colorful wouldn't begin to describe it.

Ellis rubbed her chin with her fingertips as she sat in Michaela's room, feet propped up on her bed, open laptop on the table next to her. It was hard because Cherry had brought all of this on herself by being deceptive. At the same time, Ellis hated the idea of people coming at her with torches and pitchforks. She wanted to shield her, protect her, keep her safe.

Still. After everything. All Ellis wanted was to keep Cherry safe.

What the fuck? She shook her head with a groan, her frustration bubbling to the surface. Cherry was doing the work. It was kind of impressive. She was putting everything on the line by admitting what she'd done. Her brand might never recover. She had to know that, yet she did it anyway.

She glanced at Mikey, on her side today, seemingly looking right at her, but not seeing her at all, she knew. She wished more than anything that they could talk, that she could get her sister's take on what was happening right now.

With a sigh, she restarted the TikTok and continued watching.

"Anyway," Cherry was saying. "I met somebody recently. The

person I messed things up with. Somebody wonderful. Somebody *real*." She stressed that word, Ellis noticed. "That's the key phrase. She's real, and she's inspired me to stop trying to be what I think other people want me to be and just be me. And some of you will hate it, and I apologize in advance for that. But from now on, we're gonna live life. Actual life. Real life. I'm gonna be open and unfiltered and as real as I can be for you. You might hate it, many of you will unfollow me I'm sure, but you also *might* be pleasantly surprised. I hope you'll stick around to find out. Peace." She flashed her signature two-fingers-up peace sign, and the video ended.

Ellis found herself with tears in her eyes, and she blinked in surprise. She hadn't expected this.

What are you gonna do now?

She could almost hear Michaela's voice in her head, asking her that question. Because that was the only question right now, wasn't it?

What was she going to do now?

Chapter Twenty-five

July was not playing around, and being outside was like walking around inside an oven. Ellis was pretty sure she was just going to end up roasting like a red pepper. It was better in the diner, but not by much. The air-conditioning system was probably older than she was, and it did more groaning and straining than an old man trying to get out of a recliner.

Lately, she'd found herself doing something she never thought she'd do—scrolling the socials on a regular basis. Well, not so much scrolling as checking one place. That place being Cherry on Top. Cherry was everywhere: Facebook, TikTok, Tumblr, Instagram, and probably other platforms she didn't know about. She stuck to Instagram, where she could see Cherry's considerable talent with photography, and TikTok, because she could watch entire videos and they made it feel like she was close to her. And since Cherry'd posted about her fake girlfriend and about the something good she'd messed up, she hadn't posted anything new.

Even Ellis knew that was dangerous, the kiss of death for an influencer. It was all about content, and to stay relevant, you had to post. Often. Two weeks with nothing new wasn't doing Cherry's desired career trajectory any favors.

Meanwhile, the comments Cherry had received had been harsh, to say the least. The very least. Yikes. She knew Cherry had thick skin, but brutal, mean, and downright cruel were all good ways to describe the words that some people sent her. Ellis didn't understand it, couldn't imagine saying such horrible things to a stranger. Publicly, where anybody and everybody else could read them.

They hadn't talked since the day with the letters. It was clear Cherry was leaving things in her court, letting her set the pace, letting her do the reaching out, and she really wanted to know how things were going with Lila, if they'd talked or if Cherry had decided against contact. She had so many questions and even picked up her phone more than once, but always set it back down again, second-guessing herself.

She's doing the work, though, isn't she?

She was, and that thought kept reverberating through Ellis's head at random times, like her brain was actually on Cherry's side and was trying to sway her. Cherry was definitely doing all the work, and Ellis thought maybe it was time to let her know she'd seen it. She'd heard it. She appreciated it. It was time to let the poor girl off the hook, as Kendra had said the other day.

The thought brought unexpected tears to her eyes as she sat in her office in the diner, listening to the muffled hustle and bustle of the breakfast rush, and she realized there was only one person she wanted to talk to right then. Just one.

She picked up her phone.

❖

Two weeks of no content was dangerous.

Cherry knew that. She hadn't planned on it, but once the comments started to roll in on her last video—the one where she came clean about her deception—they'd nearly paralyzed her.

She'd expected them. Or, rather, she'd thought she'd expected them. She knew people would be mad. She knew they'd say mean things, that they'd unleash their anger on her. It was nothing she didn't deserve. Besides, she was tough. She always had been. Shitty comments in her feeds had never really fazed her. That was part of the game.

Except they kept coming.

The bulk had shown up immediately. From how much she sucked to what a terrible role model for lesbians everywhere she was. That second one was rough, and that's the one she got most often. How she'd let her people down. She didn't care if some idiot troll of a guy slid into her comment section and talked about all the gross sexual things he'd like to do to her—she expected that, and blocking somebody took no effort at all. Sadly, it came with the territory and was almost normal, alarming as that was. What she hadn't counted on was the Alphabet Mafia smacking her around and saying they always thought she was sus because everything was too perfect and how dare she deceive her people by making shit up, as one person so eloquently put it. Which she wanted to argue over, but it wasn't exactly wrong, was it? She'd made a conscious decision not to reply to any of the comments. She was just going to let her followers get it all out of their systems while she stayed quiet.

She didn't expect to still be getting snarky comments two weeks later, but maybe she should have.

Also, she'd lost a good fifty percent of her followers. A full half. That was sobering.

Ellis wasn't aware of what she'd done—they hadn't talked. Cherry didn't feel it was right to tell her, to make it seem like she'd made some heroic choice. She hadn't. Besides, she didn't do it for Ellis—she did it because it was the right thing to do. Ellis had held up a mirror—a real one, devoid of filters and airbrushing and such—and Cherry hadn't liked the reflection she'd seen. Maybe one day, she'd be able to thank Ellis for that. She definitely should because she felt different. And *that* was another thing she hadn't expected.

She'd taken a sick day from work. There was no way she wanted to deal with Amanda and her pinched face and her demands today. Despite her bank of sick days, she hesitated, but Shea convinced her maybe she should take a couple. Just to clear her head.

Besides, it was time to start again.

"Ready?" Shea, having also taken the day off, appeared in her doorway with a smile and two cups of coffee.

"Yes." She crossed the bedroom and took one of the cups, held it in both hands, and closed her eyes as she inhaled the aroma. "Bless you, my child."

"You'd never know it was a million degrees out by the way you're clutching that mug."

"Well, if somebody in this apartment didn't set the air-conditioning to Arctic Tundra, I wouldn't have to."

Shea snorted a laugh, and they got to work. Fifteen minutes later, she was holding Cherry's phone and videoing her as she sat on her bed.

"Hi, loves. It's been a while, I know," Cherry began, giving a small wave to the camera. "I took a little time off. I needed it. Had to get my head on straight, so to speak." A wink. "But now I'm ready to visit with you again." She lifted her arms as if presenting the room. "This is my bedroom and where I shoot a lot of my videos." She got up and moved around to various points, stopping in one corner. "Here's where I've done my clothing try-ons. And then down this hall…" She left the room and headed toward the bathroom, Shea following her with the camera. "This is where I do the makeup samplings. And that lovely person you see in the mirror behind me is my roommate, Shea." Shea peeked out from behind the camera and gave a little finger wave. "No, not quote-unquote *roommate*." Cherry made the air quotes. "'Cause we're being real and honest now, remember. Shea is my BFF, the most amazing person on the planet, and sorry ladies, she's straight." She looked at Shea. "And gorgeous. And I don't know what I'd do without her. I hope you loves have a BFF as awesome as mine." Their eyes met in the mirror, and she blew a little kiss to Shea. Then they walked some more, Cherry displaying different parts of the apartment. "This is where I live with Shea and our other roommate, Adam, who's at work right now. I don't have a fancy town house or an expensive condo. Our furniture is old and needs to be replaced, but we're all too busy to take care of that." She flopped down on the worn couch. "We eat dinner at this coffee table in front of the TV while we watch *The Bachelor* or *Dateline* or marathons of *The Office* or *Gilmore Girls*. My point being, I'm just a regular lesbian with a regular life, and if you followed me before and you stuck around, I thank you from the bottom of my heart. And if you're new here, welcome to Cherry on Top, real life of a real lesbian. We'll talk again soon. Peace." She flashed a peace sign.

Shea did as she was instructed and waited an extra five seconds before stopping the recording, leaving space to edit. "Nicely done. That was great."

"You think?"

"Definitely." Shea handed the phone back to her. "It's a nice start to what I think is the exact right way to go. It felt like the real you, you know?" She picked up her mug and sipped her coffee, staring over the rim at Cherry for a full ten seconds before saying, "I'm proud of you, Cher."

"Yeah?"

A nod. A smile. Then, "Do you think you'll let her know?"

They both knew who Shea meant by *her*. Cherry inhaled a deep breath and blew it out through pursed lips. "I'm honestly torn."

Shea sat on the chair in the corner and focused her full attention on Cherry. "Tell me why. What are you torn between? Talk to the *most amazing person on the planet*."

"Please. You love that I called you that. Admit it."

"Oh, I totally admit it. And it's true." They laughed together, then became serious again. "Talk to me."

"I don't want her to think I'm making any of these changes just to win her back," Cherry blurted, then wrinkled her nose and groaned. "'Cause I'm not. I mean, she was definitely the catalyst, but this just feels right now. You know?"

"I do. I already told you I'm proud of you, and I am. I just think…" Shea frowned, then lifted one shoulder in a half shrug. "I just think she deserves to see this new you. This *real* you. The you I've known all along. Because she's pretty wonderful."

Her soft words brought tears to Cherry's eyes, and she was about to playfully scold her for that when her phone pinged a text. "Ugh. Probably Amanda trying to give me work on my day off." She grabbed her phone and her heart rate kicked up as she read the message.

From Ellis.

Hey, you. I've been thinking a lot about you lately and I was wondering if we could, you know, really talk. About everything. You up for it?

She must've made a face because Shea sat up straight and said, "What? What is it? Is everything okay?"

"It's Ellis."

"Oh my God, we conjured her!" Shea nearly shouted. "We are *that* good. What did she say?"

"She wants to talk."

"Good. That's good." The expression on Cherry's face must've been concerning because Shea's eyes narrowed. "Isn't it?"

She blinked a few times at the phone in her hand before looking back up at Shea, wide-eyed, she knew.

"Well? You up for it?"

"I really, really am, Shea. I really, really am."

"I kinda thought so." Shea tipped her head to one side and her smile was wide.

"What if she just wants to tell me off again?" It wasn't likely, but it was also a possibility. "I mean, she pretty much blames the whole of social media for what happened to her sister."

"Okay, *tiny* bit of an exaggeration there." Shea held her thumb and forefinger a scant distance apart.

"Yeah, okay," she admitted, her tone begrudging. "But she blames people like me."

"She blames people like you who create goals and lives that are phony and unattainable." When Cherry met her eyes, she added, "That's not you anymore, is it?"

One determined head shake. "It's not."

"Do you miss her?"

"God, yes. More than I can even explain."

"Then talk to the woman."

"Okay. Yeah." She texted one simple word. *Absolutely.*

The gray dots bounced, and the next message surprised her. *What time are you out of work tonight?*

"She wants to know when I get out of work." Slight panic set in, and her heart began to pound in anticipation of what that meant.

Shea voiced it. "She wants to talk, like, now."

A steadying breath. "Probably better that way. Maybe she just needs closure." That thought made her sadder than she even expected.

"Or maybe she doesn't, Little Miss Darkness and Gloom."

With a scoff, Cherry texted back that she was off for the day and was free anytime. Ellis answered quickly. Cherry's head snapped up and met Shea's gaze. "Oh my God, you were right. Now. She wants to meet now. Oh my God."

"That's okay because you're ready for that." Shea's voice was soft, her eyes kind.

A calm settled over her. She inhaled, exhaled slowly. "I am," she said, not even having to think about it.

Their gazes held across the room, and Cherry felt suddenly energized. Suddenly confident. She could feel Shea's love and her own confidence in the moment bolster her, and she sat up a little straighter. She texted Ellis back that she'd love to meet her, and they set up a place by the lake. With a glance down at herself, then a look back up, she asked, "How do I look?"

"Like the coolest, strongest, kindest woman I know."

Again, Cherry felt her eyes well up, and her voice broke as she said, "Thanks, Shea." She ran a finger under her eye. "Also, stop that. You're gonna ruin my makeup."

They stood together, and Shea held her arms open. Cherry walked into them, and they hugged fiercely. When the hug ended, Shea took Cherry's face in both hands and looked her right in the eyes. "You got this?"

Cherry nodded, feeling astonishingly sure of herself. "I got this."

"Yeah, you do. Now go get the girl."

It hadn't gotten any cooler, of course, as it was now midafternoon in the middle of July. The sun was blazing, and the humidity made Ellis feel like she was walking through water, her skin covered in a sheen of perspiration, her hair a frizztastic mess. Maybe she should've asked to meet Cherry someplace *inside*. That would've been smart.

"Now's a good time to think of that," she muttered to herself as she shook her head and walked along the lakeshore. But then the sun gods smiled on her, and she noticed an empty bench in the shade of a large oak tree, set back from the beach area, closer to the playground. Picking up her pace, she hurried to it before anybody else could snag it, and she sighed with relief as she sat down, the temperature noticeably cooler out of the sun. She sent Cherry a quick text letting her know exactly where along the lake she was, then slid her phone away and focused on breathing.

She was nervous.

There was no denying that. No way around it. She smoothed a hand over her hair and tried to focus on the kids that were shrieking with childhood joy on the nearby playground, swinging or sliding or spinning. And then there were the kids running into and out of the water, the gentle waves from the small lake teasing and chasing them as they squealed with delight. She flashed back to when she and Michaela were young, and their parents took them to a cottage in the Thousand Islands for a week one steamy summer. It was a hell of a long drive, but totally worth it. They'd played every single day in the water, having races and daring each other with handstands and flips off the floating raft that was anchored far below. Ah, to have that innocence again, no worries, no dread, no anxiety or stress about what was to come. She exhaled on a sigh.

"Well, that's an ominous sound."

Cherry's voice tickled her from behind, and then she was there in front of her, the sun behind her as she looked down at Ellis through her sunglasses and grinned, and somehow—Ellis couldn't explain it, or even begin to explain it—her world was suddenly righted. Like it had been slightly tilted, crooked, and when Cherry arrived, it straightened out, everything balanced and perfect once again. How the hell did she do that?

Pulling herself together quickly, she gave a small laugh. "I was just remembering what it was like to be that." She pointed at two little girls in matching pink flowered bathing suits—clearly sisters—picking up shells from the edge of the water and showing them to each other.

Cherry sat on the bench next to her. "I always wanted a sister to play with. People say only children are spoiled, but they forget about the lonely part."

"That's sad," Ellis said.

"Eh." Cherry shrugged it off, and they both laughed softly. Then Cherry pushed her sunglasses up onto her head, met her eyes, held her gaze for a beat, and said quietly, "Hi."

"Hey, you. How are you?"

"I'm hanging in there. You?" Cherry looked beautiful, despite the simple denim shorts and black tank top. Her skin was creamy, her lips sparkled with gloss, and she smelled like coconut, so perfectly apropos for the weather. Ellis inhaled quietly, taking in the scent.

"Same. How are things with Lila?" She was careful not to refer to the woman as Cherry's mother until she was told that was okay.

"She's been…honestly, pretty amazing. And I can't even believe I'm saying that." Cherry's shoulders lifted and dropped. "I'm still not sure what to do with it."

"That's fantastic. I'm so glad to hear it." And she was. "And you don't have to do anything at all with it right now. Maybe just breathe, you know?"

"Yeah, that's been my course of action." It was clear by the expression on her face that Cherry wanted to say more, but even though Ellis would've been happy to go down that path with her, it wasn't the path they were there to travel, and they both knew it.

Ellis cleared her throat the same time Cherry turned to face her.

"So—"

"I—"

They stopped. Laughed. Cherry nodded at her. "You first."

Here we go.

"I've been following Cherry on Top."

"You—" Cherry blinked at her, opened her mouth, closed it again. It was kind of adorable and made Ellis smile. "Really?"

"Really."

"But why?"

"Well…" Ellis gazed off at the water, her eyes tracking the little sisters in pink again as she rolled different responses around in her head. Finally, she settled on the best one. The only one. The truth. "I missed you. That's the main reason."

"You did?" Cherry stared at her, clearly surprised.

"Yes, I did. And I decided I wanted to see what kind of content you posted."

"Even though you were mad?"

"Even though I was mad." She glanced down at her hands before saying, "I was shocked when I saw your post where you came clean about the fake girlfriend and everything."

Cherry's nod was subtle. She wet her lips. "Yeah," was all she said as she looked Ellis in the eye.

"I didn't tell you I was looking because I wanted to see what happened. Wow, you got *decimated*."

Cherry's stare broke and her face was half grin, half grimace. She gave a chuckle that sounded nothing but rueful. "Understatement of the year, right there. And I lost half my followers. Also fun." The look she shot Ellis then was sheepish. "My own fault."

Ellis grimaced and tipped her head one way, then the other. Cherry was right, but it didn't make it any easier to know how bad the consequences had been. "Think you'll get them back?"

Seeming to ponder the question, Cherry gazed out at the water for a moment before saying, "I don't know that I'll get old followers back, but I think maybe I might get some new ones."

"Funny, I though the same thing. Especially after watching the one you posted today."

Cherry's head snapped around so fast, Ellis was surprised it didn't make a whipping sound. "You watched *that* one?"

"Yes, ma'am."

Cherry clenched her teeth and made a face, which made Ellis laugh.

"What? It was great. I love this new angle, this new path." She waited until Cherry looked at her. "The real life of a real lesbian." Her air quotes were not sarcastic. At all. "It's unique."

"Shea said the same thing." Cherry swallowed—Ellis saw it. Then she watched her face, watched her clearly debate whether to tell Ellis what was on her mind, and saw exactly when she decided she would. "I think this could be good. I have a lot of ideas."

"Yeah? Like what? Tell me." Ellis turned on the bench, bent one knee and rested it near Cherry's thigh as she faced her, and in that moment, it hit her. Like a two-by-four to the head. She wanted this. She wanted to sit and listen to Cherry talk, listen to Cherry tell her what her ideas were, listen to Cherry give her opinions on life. She couldn't stop smiling.

"Why are you grinning at me like that?"

A laugh burst out of her. "Sorry. I was just enjoying the moment."

Cherry seemed to like that, to hold it and roll it around a little bit before getting back to the subject. "It's the real life of a real lesbian, right? So I want to do recipes. Real recipes, even if they don't work. I want to not only test makeup and clothes, but be honest about it, tell the truth. I want to go places and see how they treat LGBTQ folks. I want to mix drinks and bake cookies and go to Pride and document it all, but truly document it. No filters. No convenient edits."

"I think that's fantastic." And she did. Plus, the excited light in Cherry's eyes was contagious.

"Do you think…" Cherry nibbled at her bottom lip for a moment, as if debating whether to continue. "I think you have a unique angle, given what you and your sister went through. Would you be willing to sort of…help me? Review things before I post them? Let me know if I'm veering offtrack?"

The request took her by surprise, but her brain apparently needed no time to even think about it because it made her answer immediately. "I'd love to."

"Yeah?" Cherry's smile grew.

"Absolutely. Love to."

"I think we would make a good team."

"I think we *do* make a good team." She held out her hand, palm up.

Cherry didn't even hesitate. She laid her palm against Ellis's and intertwined their fingers, and it honestly felt like their hands were made to be linked together, they fit that perfectly. "Thank you," Cherry said softly.

"For what?"

"For showing me there's a better way."

She took the words to heart as they sat quietly, holding hands and watching summer life around the lake, and Ellis knew one thing for certain—nothing had felt so very right in a really long time.

CHAPTER TWENTY-SIX

Cherry was bummed that it was already mid-August because that meant September was just around the corner, and then they would be headed toward fall. She liked fall just fine, but fall meant winter and winter meant cold and she hated to be cold. Couldn't summer stick around for just a bit longer?

She sat in the diner at her usual corner table working on the latest claims she'd received. She only had another half hour before she'd have to head off to her first appointment. Until then, though, she was perfectly happy to nibble on the deliciously warm biscuit in front of her, the one that had been brought to her by the very sexy fill-in waitress with the blond hair and fabulous legs. She drizzled some honey over the butter she'd spread on it and took a bite, watching as Ellis topped off somebody's coffee and then laughed at a joke one of the old gentlemen at the table must've told. When those blue eyes met hers across the diner, everything south of Cherry's stomach tightened pleasantly.

Ellis had that effect.

They'd been moving very slowly and doing a ton of talking. On the phone. Over text. Face-to-face. *Slow and steady wins the race*, she'd said to herself more than once. And at this point, it wasn't even a strategy. It just was. They were learning and growing, and they were doing it together. What more could she ask for?

Ellis approached her table. "Warm that coffee up for you, ma'am?"

"Please," Cherry said, holding up her cup. "And if you call me *ma'am* one more time, we are over."

"Liar," Ellis said with a wink. She glanced around at the remaining customers and, seeming satisfied, sat down next to her. "It's Friday."

"All day."

"Wanna come over for dinner?"

Cherry blinked at her. They'd spent the past month talking and meeting, but they hadn't been to each other's homes again yet. So this felt like a step. A big one. "I very much want to, yes."

Ellis's smile was soft and gorgeous. "Good. I'll cook. You bring wine."

"You're bossy."

"You love it."

She wasn't wrong, and Cherry watched as Ellis stood and walked away, the gentle sway of her hips doing delightful things to Cherry's lower body.

God, was it time for dinner yet?

❖

Dinner had been pretty amazing, if Ellis said so herself. Bolognese wasn't complicated at all, but it tasted like it was, and if the sounds Cherry had made while eating her pasta were any indication, she'd knocked it out of the park.

"Oh my God, I'm so full," Cherry said as they carried glasses of wine to the couch. Nugget lay sprawled on the back of it, and when they sat down, he put one paw on Ellis's shoulder.

"Look at him, owning you," Cherry said, reaching to stroke the cat's soft back.

"He does this every time. He's not big on me picking him up, and he doesn't cuddle because *I* want him to. He cuddles when *he* wants to."

"A cuddler on his own terms."

"Exactly. I admit, I kinda love that about him."

"Me, too."

"But when I sit on the couch, he likes to put a paw on me."

Silence fell for a moment, and then Cherry said softly, "It's really nice to be back here."

"I thought it was time," Ellis said, and that was the truth. "We've done a good job of dancing around each other. Of talking…God, we've talked each other to death, haven't we?" And when she rolled her eyes, Cherry laughed.

"Yes, oh my God, can we be done with talking now?" But it was good-natured and playful, and that was enough for Ellis to ask her next question.

"What do you think we should do instead?"

Cherry's laugh died in her throat. Without saying a word, she took Ellis's wineglass out of her hand and set it on the coffee table next to hers. When she looked back, Cherry's eyes had gone darker, circles of pink had blossomed on her cheeks, and she wet her lips. Her fingers were soft and gentle as she tucked Ellis's hair behind her ear, then leaned in and softly kissed her. Pulling back just enough to speak, she whispered, "I think we should do this," and kissed her again.

In Ellis's head, in all the various versions of the next time she kissed Cherry, she'd gone slow. Almost painfully so. She told herself she wanted to take her time, to ease back in. But all that went right out the window when Cherry's mouth was finally on hers. Zero to sixty, that's what kind of kiss it was. No. Zero to ninety. A hundred. A hundred and fifty. There was no slow. There wasn't even a medium. They blew past both until they were kissing with such energy and fierceness, and the only thing that got their attention was when their teeth banged together.

"Ow," Cherry said with a laugh.

"Sorry." She laughed, too. They were both breathing raggedly, Ellis's hand still in Cherry's hair. "Well," she said. "We're still exceptional at that."

"God, right?" And then Cherry's expression went soft, and she said, very, very quietly, "I missed you, Ellis. I missed you so much."

"I missed you, too, baby." Ellis stood up and held out a hand. Cherry took it without a word, and they headed into the bedroom.

It was different this time, and they did slow down. They slowed way down. Clothing was removed with care, with reverence, as if unwrapping a gift. Ellis took time to look, to take in the shape of Cherry's body, clad only in her yellow panties and matching bra. The expanse of her skin, the tone of it, the shape of her legs, the dip between her breasts as she sat on the edge of Ellis's bed, looking up at her with soft, loving eyes.

Yes. Loving. It was there. She could see it. She could feel it.

She knelt down between Cherry's knees, dipped her hands into her bra, and pulled her breasts up and out until they were free of the cups and right there for Ellis to take into her mouth. One at a time, she did just that, pulling soft, sexy sounds from Cherry that only served to shove her arousal up into the stratosphere. Cherry's fingers were in her hair, her head was thrown back, and when Ellis pulled back enough to look, it was the sexiest thing she'd ever seen.

And that was all she needed to speed back up again because she couldn't wait any longer. She suddenly felt a blinding, aching need like she'd never felt before, and the shift into high gear was instant.

The rest was a blur. A blur of limbs and stroking and pumping and pushing and tongues and hands and cries of ecstasy. They would both be sore tomorrow. There was no doubt about it.

At one point, on her back on the bed, Ellis looked down the length of her own body, and a fresh wave of arousal hit her at the sight of Cherry, kneeling between her thighs and poised to do what she was about to do. As if sensing eyes on her, Cherry glanced up, and the eye contact held. The moment was heavy, weighted. When Cherry spoke, her voice was low and sexy. Gravelly.

"I love you, Ellis."

Ellis didn't wait for more than half a second before saying, "I love you back."

The smile that bloomed on Cherry's beautiful, sexy face was one she'd never forget. And then she dipped her head and her tongue touched her center and every coherent thought flew right out of Ellis's head.

They slept that night like two vines that had grown entwined with each other. Limbs twisted and tangled until Ellis didn't know where she ended and Cherry began. Her last thought before drifting off to sleep was that she was exactly where she was supposed to be.

She'd never felt that way before. Ever. Not once in her entire life.

❖

Cherry woke up slowly, which was unusual for her. But she'd put her body through the wringer the night before—or rather, Ellis had put her body through the wringer the night before—and her muscles were like wet dishrags. In the best of ways.

Eyes still closed, she reached to her left but felt only empty bed, and she sighed. Then she felt tiny feet walking up her thigh, her stomach, and then a weight set down directly on her chest. She opened her eyes slowly to find big feline ones staring at her. Nugget blinked slowly, as if completely unimpressed. She dug her fingers into his soft fur, and his motor started up, gently vibrating through her ribs.

"Good morning to you, too," she said just before her nose was grabbed by the wonderful mix of smells coming from the apartment. "Oh my God, Nugs, are there any better morning smells in the world than coffee and bacon?"

"Good morning," came Ellis's voice from the doorway.

"How is it you look that gorgeous right out of bed?" It was a legitimate question, as Ellis's hair was tousled and still stupidly sexy. She wore plaid sleep shorts in red and black and the same white T-shirt Cherry had borrowed her first night here. The one that left absolutely nothing to the imagination, Ellis's nipples clearly visible and doing things to Cherry's body without her permission.

"You should talk." Ellis crossed the room, cup of steaming coffee in hand.

"Coffee in bed?" Cherry pushed herself to a sitting position, working hard not to dislodge Nugget from his cuddly position. "I may never leave."

Ellis handed the mug over and said, "I'm okay with that." Then she bent and kissed her on the mouth. "Hungry?"

"Mm, yes." Cherry deepened the kiss. Several luxurious moments later, she pulled back, grinned, and said, "Oh, you meant for food."

"I did, but this is better." Ellis kissed her again. "Much, much better."

"I agree."

They were still kissing when Cherry's stomach rumbled. Loudly.

Ellis laughed. "Okay. Breakfast it is."

A few minutes later, they were sitting at Ellis's small, two-person table, eating eggs and bacon and sipping coffee and glancing at each other and grinning just like two people who'd had mind-blowing sex the night before. Cherry couldn't remember the last time she'd felt this relaxed in her own skin.

Finally.

"It's Saturday," Ellis said. "You have plans?"

Cherry shook her head and bit into a strip of bacon. "I do not. Zero plans. I am planless."

"I'd like to take you someplace."

Those blue eyes sparkled, Cherry would swear to God. She'd never seen eyes sparkle until she looked into Ellis's baby blues. "I'd go anywhere with you, you know." And she'd never uttered a truer sentence in her whole life.

Ellis simply smiled back at her.

❖

Ellis was nervous, and she was pretty sure Cherry picked up on it. Neither of them had said much on the drive, but once Ellis took a right and pulled into the parking lot of Hearts and Hands, Cherry understood exactly what was happening. She let out a small gasp and her head snapped around so she gaped at Ellis. At first, Ellis took it as fear, thought she was afraid. But then Cherry spoke.

"You're sure?" Cherry's voice was quiet in the interior of the car, and it was clear that she knew what a big deal this was to her.

"Positive. You're okay with this?"

"With finally meeting your sister? Absolutely. I'm honored."

Those were the perfect words.

They headed inside and Ellis greeted each staff member and chatted with a few.

Once they were alone and walking down the hall, Cherry said, "I love that you know everybody's name, that you pay attention to their lives. That's a special thing, you know."

"You think?"

"Definitely. It means you see them. People like to be seen."

They stopped at Michaela's doorway. Kendra was inside, straightening the blanket and talking away to her patient. When she looked up and saw Ellis, her face lit up. "There she is! Hey there, baby girl. I feel like I haven't seen you in ages." And her arms opened, and she enveloped Ellis before she could speak. They parted and Kendra's gaze fell on Cherry, who'd hung back slightly. "And who do we have here?"

"Kendra, this is Cherry Davis. Cherry, my dear, dear friend Kendra, who also happens to be one of Mikey's caretakers."

Cherry stuck out a hand and Kendra made a *pfft* sound, then opened her arms again. "I'm a hugger." And in the next second, Cherry was wide-eyed but smiling at Ellis over Kendra's shoulder. Once Kendra had released her, she said, "I've heard a lot about you, sweetheart."

"Uh-oh," Cherry said, then laughed.

Kendra waved a hand. "Please. My girl here has been *smitten*."

"Oh, really," Cherry said, drawing out the word and turning a mischievous expression Ellis's way. "Smitten, you say?"

"A smitten kitten. For sure," Kendra said.

"I hate you both right now," Ellis said, but she was laughing.

"*Pfft*. Lies." Another wave of the hand. "Well, I'll let you two visit with Miss Michaela. Let me know if you need anything. It's wonderful to finally meet you, Cherry." And Kendra was gone before either of them could say another word.

Ellis watched her go, then turned to Cherry and grasped her hand. She took a deep breath. "Okay. Well, this is my little sister. Michaela." Michaela was on her back today, her bed tilted slightly so she was propped up a bit. Her blue eyes seemed to stare at the painting on the wall across from her, two horses in a lush green pasture. "Mikey, this is Cherry. The one I told you all about." Ellis smiled, then watched as Cherry let go of her hand and approached the side of the bed.

Cherry laid her hand on Michaela's forearm. "It's really nice to finally meet you, Michaela. I've heard so much about you. Ellis talks about you a lot." She reached behind her, grabbed the front of a plastic chair, and pulled it close. As she took a seat, she said to Ellis, "Can you give me a little time alone with your sister? Is that okay?"

"Oh, um, sure." Ellis blinked in surprise but nodded. "I'll just be out in the hallway." And she scurried out of the room. Once in the hall, she could hear the murmur of Cherry's voice, and a warmth spread through her body from the inside. She turned just as Kendra came out of the room next door.

"What are you doing out here?" Kendra asked, looking concerned.

"Cherry wanted some time alone with Mikey."

Their gazes held and Kendra's smile blossomed slowly. Then she pointed at the room and gave a nod as she started down the hall. "That girl's a keeper."

Ellis laughed at the *I told you so* tone of her voice. But she wasn't wrong. She could see that so clearly now. She inched closer to the doorway of Mikey's room, not wanting to eavesdrop, but also, really,

really wanting to eavesdrop. She strained to hear but finally could make out Cherry's soft voice.

"…And I promise you, I will take the best care of her. I will have her back. I will put her first. You don't have to worry, okay? I've got her. I promise."

Ellis's eyes welled up as she took a few steps away and tried—and failed—to read the notices on the bulletin board through her tears. She swiped at her cheek with the back of her hand and heard Cherry's voice behind her.

"All done." When Ellis turned toward her, Cherry's face shifted to concern. "Oh no. Honey, what's wrong?" She laid her warm palm against Ellis's cheek. "Are you okay?"

Ellis took a moment to collect herself, and she covered Cherry's hand with hers. "I am way more than okay. I am so many things right now. But mostly? I'm just happy. I'm so happy."

"Me, too, sweetheart."

Ellis turned her face and placed a kiss in Cherry's palm. "I usually spend a little time reading to Mikey. You okay with that?"

"Only if you let me read to her, too."

"Deal." She led Cherry by the hand back into Michaela's room. "Are you thirsty?" she asked her as she picked up the book she'd been reading. "There's soda, juice, and water in the fridge in the kitchen we passed on the way in."

"You want me to grab you something?"

She nodded, and as Cherry turned toward the door, she could almost hear her sister's voice in her head.

Being in love looks really good on you, Ellie.

Ellis reached down and squeezed Mikey's arm. "It's the best, little sister. It really is the best."

EPILOGUE

Fifteen months later

"Hello, loves, and welcome to Cherry on Top: Holiday Edition," Cherry said into the camera. "Guess what season it is. That's right!" She held up her green and red striped apron that said *Santa's Little Helper* on it, then dropped the top strap over her head. "Christmas cookie season! And for those of you who don't celebrate Christmas, it's just hell-of-a-lot-of-cookies season." She tied the apron around her waist. "Today, we're coming to you from a new location, my mother's house in North Carolina, because her kitchen is to die for. First, we're going to start with a basic cookie that many, many families make—your basic cutout cookie. And my lovely assistant Ellis is going to help me. Right, honey?"

"Yes," Ellis said as she slid into view.

"What…" Cherry looked at her and reached out to brush the flour streaking her cheek. "Already? We haven't even started yet."

"I had an itch," Ellis said quietly, rubbing at the same spot but only adding more flour. "You can edit that out, right?"

"Absolutely," Cherry told her, and when Ellis looked away, Cherry shook her head at the camera and mouthed *not editing that*, then winked.

Behind the camera, Lila covered her mouth, presumably to keep from laughing out loud.

"Okay, bring that mixer over here, would you, Lovely Assistant?"

Ellis hauled the KitchenAid to the counter and dropped it, not quietly, in front of Cherry. "Sorry," she whispered, with an exaggerated grimace.

"No problem. Now, do you have our ingredients?" Cherry read off the measurements, mixing and adding and stirring until they had a dough, which she rolled out of the bowl. "Okay, here we go. You wanna roll?" she asked Ellis, holding up a rolling pin.

"Hell yeah, I do."

As she watched Ellis roll, have the dough stick to the rolling pin, sprinkle flour—too much flour—then remove some, then blow her hair out of her face, then wipe her flour-covered hand across her forehead and shoot a look of frustration at the camera, she couldn't hold back the grin. Ellis was good TV. She'd edit this together in a series of fast clips, and it would be awesome. She glanced at Lila, who was looking back at her with the same gleam in her eye, and she knew they were on the exact same page.

God, who knew her life would turn out like this?

She slid back into the frame once Ellis had rolled the dough out, and they began cutting out the cookies and placing them on a prepared cookie sheet.

"What do you think, Mom?" she asked when the sheet was full. "Do they look right?"

"They look perfect," Lila said from behind the camera.

"My mom, loves. Behind the scenes, as she prefers, but when we mix some holiday cocktails, she's gonna join me in front of the camera." She lowered her voice. "She's nervous about that, so be gentle."

They would. She knew that. Since the Disaster of Lying Liars Who Lie, as she'd not-so-affectionately dubbed that span of time the previous year, she'd taken a different direction with her socials, and her following had gradually increased. Slowly but surely, she'd built her brand back up. She didn't really get mean comments any longer—well, except from the trolls, and there would always be trolls, unfortunately—because there was nothing to be mean about. Her posts were real. She'd stopped using filters altogether. She was honest with her followers about everything, from makeup to clothing to public places and how they handled LGBTQ clientele. She was open and honest, and there was something about that. She let miscues and dropped items and flubs stand, and that ended up being smart because it was *funny*. Who knew?

Something about being unabashedly *herself* was utterly liberating, and she couldn't believe it took such a crisis to make her see it.

Well. A crisis and a wonderful woman.

And a long-lost mother, apparently.

"Why didn't you tell me I have frosting on my face?" Ellis said later as they were decorating the baked cookies.

"Because green is most definitely your color," she said, swiping a smear of frosting off the side of Ellis's nose. "Also, seriously, how do you get so much stuff on your face?"

"I don't know, but we're editing it out, right?" Ellis was focused on the snowman cookie she was decorating.

"Of course we are," she said, then looked to the camera and shook her head and mouthed, *No way*.

Her followers loved Ellis.

She hadn't made a conscious decision to start including her girlfriend in her posts, but there had been one when they were walking in the woods last spring. Cherry had been taking photos and videos of the gorgeous trees, the just-blooming daffodils busting up through the soil, the green buds on the trees, and there was Ellis. Standing in a spot where the rays of spring sun filtering through the trees looked almost ethereal, making Ellis's blond head glow. She took the shot, and it was too good not to post, so she did, with the caption, *This is Ellis and she's my actual girlfriend. No tricks. No lies. No deceit. I am a lucky woman, loves. #nofilter* The likes had exploded, and from that point on, she would occasionally include Ellis in a video or a photo. She'd talk about her, about them.

And now?

She watched as Ellis used cinnamon dots for buttons on her snowman, the tip of her tongue out and at the corner of her mouth.

"Does the tongue thing help you concentrate?" she asked.

"What tongue thing?" Ellis asked, glancing up.

Cherry mimicked her, and Ellis's eyes went wide.

"Oh my God, am I doing that?"

"Yes, ma'am. It's adorable."

"*Noooooo*, you can edit that out, right?"

"Absolutely," Cherry said, then did her head shake to the camera.

They finished up the cookies, and Cherry took the camera off the tripod, got some shots of them to splice into the video, and then they were done.

"Whew!" Lila said. "That was so much fun! I feel like I'm behind the scenes at a movie shoot."

"Well, thank you so much for letting us use your kitchen. It's so pretty and way better than either of ours." She wasn't kidding either. Lila had a large, gorgeous kitchen with lovely white cabinets and a gray granite countertop. The island made the perfect spot for shooting cooking videos—something Cherry had started doing more of, mostly because she wasn't great at cooking, and she wanted to show others it was okay if you weren't a gourmet chef. You could still learn, and you could still cook successful meals. She'd already had a couple of companies send her products to try.

The back door opened, and suddenly a tall, fair-haired young man came in. Noah. Home from college two days ago for the holidays. Noah. Her brother. She still couldn't get over that sentence. She said it in her head more often than she cared to admit. *My brother, Noah.* It had a nice ring.

"Hey, Ma," he said and crossed to hug Cherry. "How'd the shoot go?"

"Just finished," she said. "Wanna help me edit later?"

"Seriously? That'd be dope." His eyes lit up, and he moved to hug Ellis.

When she shifted her gaze from him to Lila, she noticed Lila's eyes were extra wide. "Mom? You okay?" she asked.

"Are you kidding? This is all I've ever wanted." And then Lila's tears spilled over, and she glanced away, clearly embarrassed, waving a hand in front of her face as if that would make the tears disappear.

"Us making a mess of your kitchen?" Ellis was excellent at lightening the mood with humor. "'Cause we did a damn good job, if I say so myself."

It worked. Lila laughed through her tears, but she made an all-encompassing gesture with one hand. "This. This. My kids together, in my house for the holidays." She looked from one to the next to the next. "My heart is full," she finally said, her voice soft. She laid a hand on her chest and said it again. "My heart is full."

"Aw, now you're gonna make me cry," Ellis said and went around the island to hug Lila. Because Cherry had realized recently that she wasn't the only one who'd been missing a mom. And Lila was more than happy to step into that role for the both of them.

Cherry went around the counter and joined them until they were a wriggling mass of arms and heads and laughter. Over the top of Lila's head, she met the blue of Ellis's eyes, and she smiled, and she knew that Ellis was thinking the same thing she was.

This. Love and warmth and family. She had all three now.

This.

This was the cherry on top.

About the Author

Georgia Beers lives in Upstate New York and has written more than thirty novels of women-loving-women romance. In her off-hours, she can usually be found searching for a scary movie, lifting all the weights, sipping a good Pinot, or trying to keep up with little big man Archie, her mix of many tiny dogs. Find out more at georgiabeers.com.

Books Available From Bold Strokes Books

The Artist by Sheri Lewis Wohl. Detective Casey Wilson and reclusive artist Tula Crane are drawn together in a web of passion, intrigue, and art that might just hold the key to stopping a killer. (978-1-63679-150-0)

Cherry on Top by Georgia Beers. A chance meeting leaves Cherry and Ellis longing for a different life, but when Ellis's search for truth crashes into Cherry's insta-filter world, do they have any hope at all of a happily ever after? (978-1-63679-158-6)

Love and Other Rare Birds by Angie Williams. Ornithologist Dr. Jamie Martin and park ranger Rowan Fleming are searching the Alaskan wilderness for a bird thought to be extinct, and they're about to discover opposites really do attract. (978-1-63679-108-1)

Parallel Paradise by Mayapee Chowdhury. When their love affair is put to the test by the homophobia of their family, community, and culture, Bindi and Rimli will need to fight for a chance at love. (978-1-63679-203-3)

Perfectly Matched by Toni Logan. A beautiful Cupid named Hannah, a runaway arrow, and just seventy-two hours to fix a mishap that could be the best mistake she has ever made. (978-1-63679-120-3)

Slow Burn by Missouri Vaun. A wounded wildland firefighter from California and a struggling artist find solace and love in a small southern town. (978-1-63679-098-5)

The Inconvenient Heiress by Jane Walsh. An unlikely heiress and a spinster evade the Marriage Mart only to discover true love together. (978-1-63679-173-9)

Closed-Door Policy by Erin Zak. Going back to college is never easy, but Caroline Stevens is prepared to work hard and change her life for the better. What she's not prepared for is Dr. Atlanta Morris, her gorgeous new professor. (978-1-63679-181-4)

Homeworld by Gun Brooke. Headed by Captain Holly Crowe, the spaceship Velocity's crew journeys toward their alien ancestors' homeworld, and what they find is completely unexpected—and they're not safe. (978-1-63679-177-7)

Outland by Kristin Keppler & Allisa Bahney. Danielle Clark and Katelyn Turner can't seem to stay away from one another even as the war for the wastelands tests their loyalty to each other and to their people. (978-1-63679-154-8)

Royal Exposé by Jenny Frame. When they're grouped together for a class assignment, Poppy's enthusiasm for life and love may just save Casey's soul, but will she ever forgive Casey for using her to expose royal secrets? (978-1-63679-165-4)

Secret Sanctuary by Nance Sparks. US Deputy Marshal Alex Trenton specializes in protecting those awaiting trial, but when danger threatens the woman she's falling for, Alex is in for the fight of her life. (978-1-63679-148-7)

Stranded Hearts by Kris Bryant, Amanda Radley & Emily Smith. In these novellas from award-winning authors, fate intervenes on behalf of love when characters are unexpectedly stuck together. With too much time and an irresistible attraction, anything could happen. (978-1-63679-182-1)

The Last Lavender Sister by Melissa Brayden. Aster Lavender sells her gourmet doughnuts and keeps a low profile; she never plans on the town's temporary veterinarian swooping in and making her feel like anything but a wallflower. (978-1-63679-130-2)

The Probability of Love by Dena Blake. As Blair and Rachel keep ending up in the same place despite the odds, can a one-night stand turn into forever? Or will the bet Blair never intended to make ruin their happily ever after? (978-1-63679-188-3)

Worth a Fortune by Sam Ledel. After placing a want ad for a personal secretary, a New York heiress is surprised when the woman who got away is the one interested in the position. (978-1-63679-175-3)